MURDER FOR PROFIT

MURDER FOR PROFIT

Veronica Heley

**SEVERN
HOUSE**

First world edition published in Great Britain and the USA in 2022
by Severn House, an imprint of Canongate Books Ltd,
14 High Street, Edinburgh EH1 1TE.

Trade paperback edition first published in Great Britain and the USA in 2023
by Severn House, an imprint of Canongate Books Ltd.

severnhouse.com

British Library Cataloguing-in-Publication Data
A CIP catalogue record for this title is available from the British Library.

ISBN-13: 978-0-7278-5097-3 (cased)
ISBN-13: 978-1-4483-0781-4 (trade paper)
ISBN-13: 978-1-4483-0780-7 (e-book)

This is a work of fiction. Names, characters, places and incidents
are either the product of the author's imagination or are used fictitiously.
Except where actual historical events and characters are being described
for the storyline of this novel, all situations in this publication are
fictitious and any resemblance to actual persons, living or dead,
business establishments, events or locales is purely coincidental.

All Severn House titles are printed on acid-free paper.

Typeset by Palimpsest Book Production Ltd.,
Falkirk, Stirlingshire, Scotland.
Printed and bound in Great Britain by
TJ Books, Padstow, Cornwall.

ONE

The best thing about returning home after a holiday is that you can sleep in your own bed.

Ellie and Thomas had gone to stay with relatives in Canada for a few months while their sprawling Victorian house was being turned into two semi-detached units. The rebuild had taken longer than expected, but at long last they had been able to return and pick up the threads of their life again.

That was the good bit.

The downside? They'd arrived on a Sunday morning; not only was the house in chaos but they were greeted with the news that the sky had fallen in, Henny Penny style. Apparently something was seriously amiss at Ellie's housing charity, and she must attend to it immediately if not sooner!

Ellie had never thought of herself as a businesswoman, so had assembled a group of trustees to run a project to buy rundown houses, rebuild and develop them where necessary and rent them out at affordable rates. The charity had attracted a very large inheritance, which in turn had enabled them to take on their biggest and most ambitious project to date. And this was now at risk?

Jet-lagged to the eyeballs, Ellie couldn't work out what time of day it was, never mind deal with business affairs.

Not for the first time, Ellie was grateful to their young friends Susan and Rafael, who had moved into the rebuilt semi next door some time ago with their brood. Not only did Rafael fetch Ellie and Thomas from the airport, but Susan had filled Ellie's freezer with home-cooked dishes so that she didn't have the bother of shopping and cooking for the time being.

Susan and Rafael were fostering Ellie's two grandchildren since their mother had disappeared into the blue, and they came round for a short visit, plus their own little imp, who was now fourteen months and into everything. Ellie had heard that there'd been tantrums from her three-year-old granddaughter and anxiety issues from the boy, but Rafael had developed into a fond if strict father figure while Susan's big heart had provided the children with the loving home they'd so desperately needed. They didn't stay long, as neither Ellie nor Thomas felt up to coping with them as yet.

Thomas almost lost his temper, trying to reconnect Ellie's computer in her new study, and Ellie wept when she found her best teapot – which had been her mother's – had been broken and left in pieces in the cupboard.

Oh, dear! In their absence, the house had been redecorated from top to bottom but some of the furniture was in the wrong place. The grandmother clock in the hall was sulking because it needed another piece of cardboard under its front right-hand corner to stand straight and oh, the kitchen! Chaos ruled! Not one spoon or pan was in its accustomed place. Ellie couldn't even find the tin in which she kept her favourite brand of teabags. A new carton of them sat on the dresser, but where was the tin?

Worse still was what had happened to her beloved garden and conservatory.

Ellie was a great gardener who liked nothing better than to spend time with her plants, aiming to have colour all the year round from snowdrops and winter jasmine in January to holly and viburnum in December.

Surrounded by high brick walls and partially shaded by mature trees, her back garden had been a haven from the world, with a well-tended lawn which stretched across the back of the house and flowers in a deep herbaceous border beyond. Between house and lawn there was a patio on which, if she had the time – which she rarely did – she would have sat and taken her ease.

And now? Disaster!

The wall and the trees remained, but it looked as if someone had run a tractor over the beds and the lawn was rutted and patchy with moss. It wasn't just the builders who'd laid waste to what had been there.

There was still some bright colour to be seen but it was the bright hues of children's playground equipment and not that of flowering plants. It was all very well saying that it was her very own grandchildren who had done the damage, but there wasn't one yard of the garden unaffected.

Almost, Ellie regretted her decision to turn the big house into two, three-bedroomed units with space to move into the attics if required.

Because of the links between the two families, the project had made perfect sense at the time.

Rafael was an astute, half-Italian businessman who had recently been asked to join the board of trustees for the charity which Ellie had founded, and his red-headed wife, Susan, seemed able to cope with anything . . . even the advent of yet another baby.

On the third day Ellie announced that she might soon be able to cope with small doses of reality. Thomas, a semi-retired minister, received a phone call from an old friend asking him to visit and Ellie encouraged him to go. Did Thomas feel up to it? Not really, but he went, anyway.

After he'd gone, Ellie had dragged an aged but capacious ottoman from the entrails of the hall cupboard and manoeuvred it into the sitting room. The children's toys had always been kept in that, and Ellie needed to be prepared for their next incursion.

That was when the phone really started ringing.

She was told she'd been given a couple of days' peace and quiet and now really must attend to business.

The future of the charity she'd founded was at stake!

Ellie tried to clear her mind. All she could think of was that something must have gone wrong with the development at the Ladywood site, the latest and biggest project that the charity had ever taken on. They had invested so much time and money in it that it would be a tragedy if they had to pull out at the last minute.

But no, apparently it wasn't that. So what was it?

It seemed that her trustees were at war with one another. She was requested to hang, draw and quarter the wrongdoers . . . although who the wrongdoers might be varied according to whoever was speaking.

Ellie was told that she could deal with the garden some other time. It was desperately important that she have a meeting of the trustees that day.

Ellie told herself that business came before pleasure. If only she didn't feel so woolly. She'd heard jet-lag called 'brain fog'. It was a good description.

Dependable Stewart, general manager of the charity, had been the most temperate in his language. 'Ellie, hate to worry you so soon, but the charity's in deep trouble.'

'Something's gone wrong at the Ladywood site?'

'No, not at all. What made you think that? No, it's the agency. We need to get together asap. Perhaps not everyone. Just you and me and Kate, the original team. As for Rafael, well, I know he's something of a favourite of yours, and perhaps you'll want him to come, too, but I must warn you, he's not thinking straight about this. Kate says he should resign and . . .'

Then clever Kate, whose financial brain had steered the charity through rough waters to its present respected position, phoned. 'We can't sidestep this, Ellie. It affects our future. It's clear what we ought to do, but Rafael . . . I really think he ought to resign and give us some space to come to terms with . . .'

What had young Rafael been up to? Perhaps due to his Italian ancestry, he was generally considered to be a trifle on the tricksy side, but he'd been a real asset to the charity precisely for his ability to think outside the box.

Perhaps he would never be considered a hundred per cent respectable, but he was clever and – which is more than might have been expected of him – he seemed happy to take on his part in bringing up Ellie's grandchildren.

When Rafael had collected Ellie and Thomas from the airport, he'd not even hinted that bad news was in the offing. He told them that Susan had left a casserole in the oven for them to eat that evening, and that she had filled the freezer for them. He'd apologized in advance for the mess in the garden, which he said Susan was planning to deal with.

He hadn't said anything about trouble at the mill and yet it seemed that Kate and Stewart blamed him for whatever it was that had gone wrong at the charity and thought he should resign.

Which was ridiculous, wasn't it?

Ellie didn't understand the problem. Some online hate mail had been circulating which might affect the work of the charity?

Really? Annoying, yes. Serious? No.

So why did Kate want Rafael to resign?

Ellie dithered. She had half an hour till the trustees would descend on her. She liked to put flowers in the sitting room but there were none in the garden at the moment. They could do with flowers, but they couldn't do without chairs to sit on.

One: for her, as chair of the meeting.

Two: for their finance director, Kate, who would need space to lay out her laptop and papers.

Three: for Stewart, the charity's general manager, who would bring common sense and an iPad to the table.

The last chair would be for Rafael, the man who Kate and Stewart said had caused the trouble which was tearing the charity apart.

Ellie looked at the clock. Time to make proper coffee for the meeting . . . though from what she'd heard, a dose of aspirin all round might be more appropriate.

Was her hostess trolley still sitting in the corner of the kitchen? Were there any biscuits in the tin? Biscuits heavily covered with chocolate would probably calm them down better than aspirin. If only she could locate where the biscuit tin might have been put? It should be . . . ah, it was. And filled to the brim.

Susan was wonderful!

Ellie approached the coffee machine with trepidation. Rafael had given it to them as a coming-home present. Thomas had fallen in love with it and used it already but it frightened Ellie silly. It was so very . . . robotic? It looked as if it would switch itself on and start cleaning the carpet at the word of command.

Using the new machine would show Rafael she was on his side.

On his side? Don't be ridiculous!

Ellie told herself she was taking the situation far too seriously. But still, there was time for an arrow prayer.

Dear Lord, you know I'm no financial brain. I haven't a clue who's in the right in this matter. You know we founded the

charity to help those in need. Please clear the muddle in my
mind so that I make the right decisions.

Ellie scolded herself into action, finding a jug for the milk
and a basin for the sugar; laying out mugs and biscuits on the
trolley.

She told herself she'd done the right thing when she'd
proposed Rafael as a trustee for the charity. His background
had been perfect for their purposes. He'd inherited a rundown
block of flats, done most of the renovations himself and now
ran the place as a business. His experience of such work had
made him a most suitable candidate to join the charity. Although
that ought not to matter, he was also a young man of considerable charm; tall, dark and handsome.

It was true that he'd had a reputation for cutting corners in
his younger days, but he'd promised never to go down that road
again when he'd persuaded his red-headed Susan to marry him.

And he was doing a great job bringing up the two children
who'd been abandoned by Ellie's daughter Diana.

Oh, Diana! How could you just walk away from your
children! Yes, your husband had just died in tragic circum-
stances, and the man you'd been meeting on the side had not
been prepared to divorce his wife and marry you . . . but surely
you could have worked something out so that you could keep
the babes with you?

Ellie told herself that she would NOT get aerated about that
today! What's done was done, and the children were a lot better
off with Rafael and Susan than being taken into care.

The fearsome coffee machine produced a brew which smelled
both rich and strong.

The doorbell rang. Two sharp rings.

That would be Kate, stick thin, always in a hurry, always on
time. Financial affairs always in order.

Ellie hastened to let her in.

Kate gave Ellie a hug. 'Lovely to see you back. How are you?
It's been far too long. We must get together some time soon.'

Predictably, Kate's smartphone rang at that point, and she
powered her way into the sitting room, high heels clacking
over the parquet floor. 'Yes, yes. I said I'd get back to you
this afternoon and I will . . .' She put her laptop down, shed

her jacket and took a seat while continuing to talk on the phone.

Ellie was halfway back to the kitchen when the doorbell rang again. One long ring. Stewart.

She let him in and was lifted up off her feet to get a hug and a kiss. She could feel his love surround her. He was a big, quiet man, who didn't give his affection to everyone. He'd been almost destroyed by his first marriage to Diana who'd left him when their son was very young. Fortunately his second foray into matrimony had been more successful and he and his second wife had made a good job of bringing up his son and their own twin daughters together. 'Dear Ellie. So good to have you back.'

Ellie reached up to touch his cheek. 'Dear Stewart. Good to see you again. The family are all right?'

'They send their love.' He went on into the sitting room while Ellie went to fetch the coffee . . . only to be brought back to the hall by someone tapping on the glass door into the conservatory.

Rafael, wearing a stone face and carrying a large bouquet of flowers, which he presented to her. 'With apologies for the garden. Susan sends her love and says she's making a chicken and mushroom pie for this evening if you'd like some?'

She let him in. 'Of course. Good of her.'

Rafael's black eyes were flat, without emotion. No hugs or kisses.

Something is wrong but he doesn't want to talk about it?

She said, 'I'll put these in water and bring in the coffee.'

'It smells good. Let me take the trolley through for you.'

The others hadn't thought of helping her. Elle patted his shoulder. His mouth quivered, and then stilled.

Yes, something is very wrong.

She put the flowers in a large vase and took them into the sitting room while Rafael came behind with the trolley.

Small talk. How's the family? What happened to the lawn here? Your youngest must be at school now? How's your boy finding his first year at university?

Coffee and biscuits. Everyone being very polite.

Someone pounded on the door into the conservatory, and everyone jumped.

Ellie went to open the door. There was no one there.

Something brushed past her knee and stormed into the sitting room. Fifi, Rafael and Susan's fourteen-month-old daughter. She approached the first pair of men's trousers and commanded, 'Up!'

Stewart, who was used to the ways of children, laughed and lifted her up on to his lap.

Fifi wasn't the name she'd been christened with, but it was a nickname that had stuck. She was definitely Rafael's child; dark of hair and eye, and as bright as they come. She surveyed the table and its occupants.

Rafael got to his feet. 'Sorry, everyone. She's supposed to be having her morning sleep. I'll tell Susan she's escaped and take her back.'

Stewart settled Fifi into the crook of his arm. 'She's all right here for a while.'

Even Kate's tight expression relaxed. 'Those eyelashes!'

Ellie thought, *Fifi knows her father is stressed about this meeting. She's understood he's being court-martialled and she's come to stand at his side.*

Rafael spoke on his phone, calming his wife who'd just missed the child.

Fifi twisted round to consider the man on whose lap she was sitting.

For heaven's sake! She's judging him!

Stewart jiggled the child and laughed.

Fifi responded with a wide smile and a bounce on his knee. Stewart had passed muster. Next, Fifi twisted round to give Kate the once-over.

Kate treated Fifi as if she were an equal. They stared at one another until Kate dropped her eyes, giving an embarrassed laugh. 'How old is this child?'

'An old soul,' said Rafael. He lifted his arms towards Fifi and she plunged into them, sure he'd catch her safely. Which he did.

Kate said to Stewart, 'I feel we've passed some kind of test.'

Ellie said, 'Shall I get her some frothy milk in a cup for her? Or a biscuit, perhaps?'

'Biccy,' said Fifi, who never wasted words. She took a biscuit

Murder for Profit 9

and turned her eyes on Ellie, who held her breath. The child had only just been born when Ellie and Thomas had left for Canada. Yes, she'd visited Ellie the other day, but that would hardly have registered with such a small child. Would it? Did Fifi approve of Ellie?

Fifi smiled at Ellie, a gap-toothed grin full of charm. Ellie felt like applauding.

Kate stirred. 'Shall we start?'

Ellie recognized her cue and sighed. For a long time she'd thought the members of the board tolerated her as chair because the money had arrived through her contacts, her house offered a quiet meeting room and she provided biscuits with her coffee. But over the years she had learned that although she seldom understood exactly how the finances worked, and often failed to follow Stewart's projections of how long it would take to make this or that building habitable, by the application of basic common sense she could help them get through the agenda quickly.

So now she said, 'I understand that a problem has arisen and that you're all very worried about it. I'm not clear about what's happened. Do you think you could each one of you tell me what you know? Quite simply, in words that even Fifi can understand.'

There was a general relaxation of tension and a couple of smiles. Fifi fixed her eyes on Kate, who was fidgeting with the papers, so Ellie indicated Kate should start the ball rolling.

An upright line appeared between Kate's eyebrows. She concentrated. 'As you all know, shortly before you went to Canada the charity received a large sum of money which almost doubled our resources. It enabled us to acquire more properties which in turn led us to increase our workforce in order to deal with the extra work involved.

'At this point we reached the parting of the ways with the old-established firm of estate agents we've been using for some years. They'd recently been taken over by an international company whose clients were multi-millionaires, and their sights were set on supplying rich people with accommodation which included quarters for live-in servants, swimming pools and cinemas. They were no longer interested in affordable properties for the people our charity was set up to serve, such as those who were struggling to get on to the property list or to upsize from one-bedroomed flats as their families increased. The parting with our old estate agents was therefore mutually agreeable.

'Rafael suggested that we explore a relationship with a local estate agency who would be in a better position to find and vet potential clients for us. Various local firms were suggested, which we whittled down to two. Rafael strongly recommended one and we came to a trial arrangement with an old-established firm called Walker & Price.'

Kate looked across the table to Ellie. 'You were still in Canada at that time, but we did consult you about it, and you did agree.'

Ellie nodded. 'I thought the move was only sensible.'

'At first,' said Kate, 'it looked good to us, too. Then, most unfortunately, something happened at one of the houses we'd recently renovated and let through Walker & Price. There was a wild party and a student fell to his death from the top storey into the garden. Everyone agreed that it was an accident, but negative comments began to circulate on social media about it.'

Ellie was puzzled. 'Why?'

Kate leaned back in her chair. 'The hate stuff is not directly aimed at the charity but at Walker & Price, the estate agents, who are accused of renting out a property which they knew was unsafe, and of bribery and corruption.'

Ellie gaped.

Rafael continued to be stone-faced. Fifi leaned back against her father and looked up into his face, concerned for him.

Stewart rubbed his chin. 'I've checked and everything our builders have done has been passed and signed off in the usual way. The agency says they didn't take bribes to let the house and I believe them. But the thing is, you can't fight social media. It's hydra-headed. You chop off one head, and another pops up.

'Walker & Price are in shock. Every day they get another accusation of malpractice thrown at them. They insist they've always done everything by the book and I believe them, but their name is now mud and we can't give them any more of our properties to let just *because* their name is now mud. We've a couple of flats and a semi-detached house out by the airport which have been refurbished and are now ready to be re-let. But, we haven't dared give the details to Walker & Price, which means that we're losing money every day that they stand vacant.'

Rafael turned his head away to gaze out of the window.

Kate looked at Rafael, and then looked away. 'Rafael thinks it's a campaign to destroy Walker & Price. I suppose it might be, though I've never heard of anything bad about them before. But we simply can't afford to be associated with them any longer. Stewart agrees with me; Rafael doesn't.'

Stewart said, 'I've had our solicitors look at our contract with them and there's a clause saying we have to give Walker & Price six months' notice. I'm all in favour of doing that. Personally I think they'll have to close down long before that.'

Rafael spoke up at last. Very quietly. 'Yes, Walker & Price are an older couple. They have never been accused of corruption in all the years they've been in the Avenue. They've no idea what's hit them. They don't understand it, and they don't know what to do about it. I believe they're innocent and we should back them up.'

Fifi put up her hand and wiggled her fingers. Rafael took her hand in his and held on to it.

Daughter sees Father's in trouble. Daughter comforts Father. Father is comforted.

Stewart wiped his forehead. 'Even if they're innocent – and surely there's no smoke without a fire – what can we do? The charity exists to provide affordable housing, not to get involved in a media war. And there's something else you might like to take into consideration. I had a phone call this morning from Streetwise . . .'

Everyone but Ellie knew the name. She looked at Stewart for enlightenment.

Stewart nodded. 'They're the other estate agents we considered. They commiserated with us about our problem and suggested they might be able to help us out on any property we can't now shift through Walker & Price. They say we could

tell Walker & Price that we want a pause on their contract for
a while, just till they can clear their name.'

Ellie didn't know what to think.

Dear Lord, tell me what to do.

She said, 'Where's the proof that Walker and Whatsit have
done anything wrong? I mean, the odd letter of complaint can
usually be dealt with quickly enough.'

'There's too much of it. Twitter, local community groups,
they've all got stuff on it. I did think at first that it might be
just one or two aggrieved customers but no . . . there's dozens
of complaints. I'm beginning to accept that it's true, and they've
messed up big time. The allegation that someone at Walker &
Price took a bribe is on there every day.'

Kate said, 'The partners seem genuinely shocked, but I agree
with Stewart that their position is untenable. The only thing to
do is to disentangle ourselves from them as quickly as possible,
and make other arrangements.'

Ellie turned to Rafael. 'What is your thinking?'

He gave a tiny shrug. 'I've looked at the online posts. Some
of it is verging on the hysterical. The same accusations keep
being repeated. From the general style and content, I think that
two separate people started a campaign and later on others
joined in on the basis that there's no smoke without a fire.
There's not a single fact. It's all "everyone knows . . ." and
"someone told me . . ." So, I ask myself what's behind it?'

Kate threw her hands in the air. 'The same old, same old.
Rafael, there is no conspiracy. Just because you've taken against
Streetwise Estate Agency . . .!' She turned to Ellie. 'Rafael
thinks they started the muck-throwing.'

Rafael coloured, slightly. 'I didn't say that. What I did say
was that I get bad vibes when I go near them.'

Stewart said, 'Rubbish! "Bad vibes", indeed!'

Kate screwed up her face. 'Actually, to be fair . . . I'm not
ruling bad vibes out completely. A couple of times in the past
I've had an uneasy feeling about a client's accounts and both
times there was good reason for me to suspect bad practice.'

This was the difference between Stewart and Kate. Stewart
had very little imagination but a good work ethic. Kate's ability
to sense problems made her far more than a jobbing financial

consultant. Rafael thought outside the box. It made them a formidable trio so long as they respected one another's positions . . . which at the moment they did not.

Ellie asked Kate, 'Do you have any reservations yourself about these new people? What's their name: Streetwise?'

Kate twiddled a pen, thinking about it. Ellie reflected that that was another thing about Kate. She could look at both sides of an argument. In the end she said, 'The worst I can say about them is that their style is not mine; they are somewhat brash, but then, lots of people appreciate that. "Thrusting! Forward thinking!" That sort of thing. They're a newish firm, all glass premises, expensive advertising, bright young men and women offering the sun, moon and the stars to prospective clients. Walker & Price are quieter, a smaller outfit, and the partners are older and more experienced. I think it's fair to say the two concerns are aiming at clients in different age groups.'

Stewart said, 'We're wasting time. Ellie, you've heard what we think. The vote is two to one that we shed Walker & Price, sign with Streetwise and get the charity back on the road.'

Ellie dithered.

Rafael said, 'I vote to delay until—'

Kate was impatient. 'The charity is losing money every day we have properties standing empty.'

Rafael said, 'In that case I can only tender my—'

'No!' Ellie stopped him. His resignation wouldn't help. 'Let me think for a minute.'

Dear Lord, help! What Stewart and Kae say is only reasonable. Rafael is being difficult, but I have a horrid feeling he's right.

Something brushed against Ellie's legs and she jumped.

Her ginger cat, Midge, which had taken up its residence elsewhere while Ellie and Thomas had been away, leapt on to her lap and pushed his head against her in a gesture of affection. Apparently he hadn't forgotten Ellie.

'Gracious!' said Stewart. 'What a start that cat gave me. Which reminds me; I'm not superstitious . . .'

People who say that, usually are.

'But two deaths in the house Walker & Price let to the students is one too many. I'd like us to get rid of it. People will say it's jinxed. First that woman with the cats, and now the student . . .'

'What?' said Ellie. 'Woman with the cats? Hang on a minute. Where is this house that we're talking about? It isn't the one I found for the charity, is it?'

TWO

Wednesday mid-morning

S tewart consulted his laptop. 'You've pointed us in the direction of several houses, haven't you? This one . . . Ah, yes. You did refer it to us, saying it might be suitable for conversion into three flats. It doesn't say how you came to know about it. I seem to remember it was something to do with cats.'

Ellie said, 'The owner . . . Now, what was her name? Got it. Mrs Pullin. She died and left some money to Thomas so I popped in to see her niece . . . Yes, it was a niece, I think. The police thought at first that the woman had cut herself and bled to death while preparing food for her cats, though it turned out there'd been an altercation with her cleaner who'd sort of accidentally stabbed her.'

Their faces! She could see them thinking, *What on earth is she talking about?*

Ellie said, 'Um, well. The long and short of it was that Mrs Pullin bled to death, her cats were rehomed and her cleaner met a sticky end under a bus. The house had been neglected, the heirs couldn't afford to do it up and were looking at a sale price far less than its real value if only it had been maintained properly.'

Stewart and Kate referred to their tablet and laptop, checking the facts. Both nodded.

'Wet rot, out-of-date plumbing and wiring,' said Kate.

Ellie said, 'I seem to remember suggesting we turn it into three flats. Did that happen? You mentioned a student's death?'

Rafael said, 'It was my idea to turn it into student

accommodation. Making it into three flats would have meant building a three-storey extension at the back to supply kitchen and bathrooms on each floor. On the ground floor we already had a loo and we squeezed a shower room in as well. We made the sitting room and kitchen at the back into communal areas, turned the dining room at the front into a bedsit. First floor became three bedsits, with a refitted bathroom. The attic floor was converted into two bedrooms plus a shower room and loo, and we put in a fire escape as well. The cost was far less and the conversion took no time at all which meant we could let it out much more quickly than if we had had to build out at the back to make it into self-contained flats.'

Stewart tapped his laptop. 'Mrs Pullin's heirs were happy with the sale to us. Walker & Price already had their contacts with the university, who were pleased to learn of more accommodation for students. One of the students signed the lease and sublet to the rest. He paid in advance and collected from the others. Job straightforward and well done.'

Kate said, 'That is, until one of them fell out of the top window. And now we're all in trouble. Was the conversion safe? Are we liable for damages for the death of the lad who died? The students have left and are trying to get out of the remainder of the lease. Walker & Price are flapping around like headless chickens. We need to settle this matter straight away or we'll be dragged into any court proceedings that someone might try to start.'

Stewart was sombre. 'People forget quickly, but I don't think we can try to re-let to another group of students. I suggest we ditch Walker & Price and get rid of the house for whatever we can get for it. Or maybe revert to our original plan to turn the house into three flats?'

Ellie sat back in her chair, considering the matter. 'I don't understand what's going on here. Presumably the student's death was accidental. That's very sad but the charity wasn't at fault, were they? I mean, proper safeguards were in place?'

Stewart nodded. 'Of course. He'd taken too much to drink, went out on to the balcony to show off, slipped and fell.'

'Then why have the remaining students left? Why are Walker & Price being targeted?'

Stewart shrugged. 'Someone with a grudge against them? Someone who blames them for getting gazumped when they tried to buy a property through them? Nothing to do with us.'

Ellie said, 'What does Mrs Thing think? The woman next door? In her eighties, bright as a button. I seem to remember she had post-graduate students living in her house, too. Or are they lodgers?'

The others looked puzzled.

Stewart said, in the tones of one trying to be patient with an elderly woman who was losing it, 'Mrs Thing?'

'Begins with a J,' said Ellie. 'Not Jones. I met her, once. Jermyn. That's it. Have you spoken to her?'

Kate looked at her watch. She was always in a hurry. 'Ellie, I don't understand why you think this woman might know anything about—'

'You haven't spoken to her? Oh dear. You see, the wall between her kitchen and next door is very thin. That's how Mrs Jermyn knew Mrs Pullin was in trouble and why it was Mrs Jermyn who called the police. Her cleaner knew who went in and out of Mrs Pullin's house and that's how they found out what had happened. I seem to remember suggesting that we put in some insulation on that wall when we did the renovations.'

Stewart said, 'I have no idea.' He and Kate exchanged the very slightest of glances. Neither of them could understand what Ellie was on about.

Kate said, 'Ellie, I don't see that what a neighbour might have seen or heard could make any difference to the situation we find ourselves in.'

Ellie tipped the cat off her lap and got to her feet. 'Possibly not. But I'm not at all clear in my mind as to what is going on here. I suggest we adjourn this meeting for a few days. Till next Monday morning, perhaps? At the same time?

'Rafael, you'd better take Fifi back for her morning sleep; Kate, could you send me an email with all the relevant information on it? How we converted the house, how much it cost, that sort of thing. Stewart, could you do the same with regard to the coroner's inquest and the charity's contract with Walker & Price – and give me a note of what the rival estate agents suggest?'

Kate wasn't happy. 'Yes, but Ellie; the sooner we disentangle ourselves from Walker & Price—'

Ellie wasn't listening. She stacked used coffee cups on to the trolley, saying, 'See you Monday, then? Now, Stewart, students can be good tenants or bad. In what condition have they left the house?'

'I haven't sent anyone round yet. We are busy, you know, and yes, someone's booked to go there at the end of the week.'

'I think I might pop round there this afternoon, see if Mrs Jermyn has any light to throw on the subject. Can someone hold the door open for me to take the trolley out? Thank you, Rafael. I'll drop in to see Susan later if I may.'

Which was one way to close a meeting which wasn't going anywhere.

The house rented by the students was just as Ellie remembered it; semi-detached, red-brick, with a small front garden bounded by a neglected privet hedge.

Ellie made a mental note to get someone to deal with the hedge. People who rented property often neglected front hedges and had to be reminded. She would ask Stewart to attend to it. Now the house was empty and about to be rented out again, it was more important than ever to keep the place looking spruce.

A tiled path led to the front porch which was also tiled. Lots of period features. The blinds at the front window had been drawn, adding to the slightly neglected look which the over-grown hedge had given.

There was no estate agency board outside. Why not? Ah, because the lease with the students was still valid. How were the students coping? Accommodation hereabouts was limited and they would have found it difficult to get anything else so far on in the academic year. Then again, could Ellie take it for granted that the conversion had been done properly? If safety rules had been neglected, where did that leave the charity? Answer: out of pocket.

The house next door – Mrs Jermyn's – looked spick and span and the hedge had been neatly trimmed.

Ellie pressed the intercom beside Mrs Jermyn's front door.

All was quiet. A rumble of distant traffic. A builder working down the road threw something heavy into a skip. An aeroplane crossed the sky, making for Heathrow Airport.

'Yes?' A tinny voice.

'Ellie Quicke, from the charity which owns the house next door. We met last year.'

The door opened. 'I remember your voice.' And there was little Mrs Jermyn, as bobbish as before but smaller than Ellie remembered. She was now using a walker and there was something about her eyes . . . they'd been very bright before but now . . . cataracts?

Mrs Jermyn said, 'You've come about the new death.'

'Accident, wasn't it?' said Ellie, hoping against hope that it was.

Silence.

Ellie shivered. Not an accident, then?

Mrs Jermyn grinned. 'How would I know, being an ancient, forgetful, old woman who walks with difficulty and whose faculties are dimmed by age? I remember you, though. You sorted out what happened when that woman with the cats died and you got some people to buy the place and get the builders in. Someone said you'd gone adventuring. America, was it? Come in, come in. I was just about to have a cuppa . . . down here . . . mind that bike. I tell him to take it through to the garden shed, and he says he will but he doesn't. Only, he brings me fresh croissants from the bakery every day so I can't say too much, can I?'

The hall was wide enough to make it easy enough to pass by not only the bicycle but also a folded-up wheelchair.

Ellie followed Mrs Jermyn into a sunny kitchen at back of the house.

A radio burbled softly to itself on the shelf and something in the oven smelled delicious. A chicken casserole?

The kitchen units hadn't been changed for years but every-thing was spotless and welcoming. Outside, the back garden was full of flowers growing up through vegetables, cottage style. And, oh! Didn't it just remind Ellie of the mess in her garden back home! Which is where she ought to be this minute, instead of chasing around after an estate agent's mess-up.

Mrs Jermyn switched a kettle on. Her hands went roving for a couple of mugs, which she found and clattered together on the work surface.

She's almost blind?

Ellie said, 'Can I help?'

A snort. 'If I needed help, I'd ask for it. Sit down and tell me where you've been.'

Ellie sat. 'Canada. Visiting family. Yes, I've been away for months. Just back. Heard some tarradiddle about next door. The charity that let the house doesn't know whether they're on their head or their heels. I thought you might shed some light.'

'Ah.' Mugs of tea plonked down on the table. Biscuit tin taken down from shelf. Radio switched off. 'You're thinking it was murder?'

'What? No! At least, goodness me, I hope not. Surely not. What makes you think that? Have the police been round asking questions?'

'They did. They asked my lodgers, who said they hadn't seen anything, heard anything, didn't know anything. Well, they wouldn't, would they? PhDs, both of them, working on projects that I can't understand a word they say about them, but kind to an old lady and paying their rent on time through Direct Debit. But would they notice anything going on next door? No, of course not.'

Ellie narrowed her eyes. 'You're different.'

A snort. 'When the police came, it was I who let them in. They asked if my son or daughter was around. They called me "Granny" and didn't look any further than the top of my head. I said I hadn't seen anything, which was true. I asked which of them it was that had copped it and they cut me off. I might as well have been invisible. I was that cross! Then I thought that if they didn't want to know what I thought of that lot next door, then I'd keep it to myself.'

'But you'll tell me?'

'I might. And I might not. It shook me up a bit. I began to doubt myself. After all, what did I really *know*?'

Ellie waited. Mrs Jermyn *was* old, and her eyesight was *not* good, but there was nothing wrong with her mind. Ellie said, 'It seems to me that you're doing all right.'

Mrs Jermyn relaxed. 'I thought I might have to go into a home when I broke my hip and my eyesight started to fade. It would have killed me, but I couldn't see any way out. But my two lodgers wouldn't hear of it. Suits them to stay on, that goes without saying. But kindness is something different. They have a floor each and moved my bedroom downstairs. We put in extra loos and shower rooms. They did all the decorating themselves.

'They organize weekly deliveries of this and that from the shops and they take me out in the car – one of them's got a car, the other's got that dratted bicycle that clutters up the hallway – and we get on fine. They call me Granny. They bully me to take my pills, and I scold them as if they were my grandchildren, which is what I never had, my husband and I not being blessed with offspring. No, they look after me well enough, and I won't be carried out of here until I'm in a box. One of them's getting married next year and his wife's moving in here. It's her as does the garden for me.'

Ellie said, 'You've got it made. Good for you.'

'Then my cleaner, she's been with me for years, but now she comes every day, prepares an evening meal for me, and does their laundry. The boys see to all that for me. They're not noisy, and they know not to interrupt when it's *Strictly Come Dancing* or *Call the Midwife* on the telly. They're old enough to know how to behave, see.'

Ellie considered what had not been said. 'Not like the lot next door?'

'I can't talk about them, can I? I wouldn't recognize them if I saw them in the street, which is not very likely anyway, as I don't go out by myself much nowadays. The police said as I wasn't to worry my poor head about it. So I don't.'

Mrs Jermyn peered at the table, located her mug and drank from it.

Ellie sipped her tea, too. It was good. She helped herself to a biscuit. Chocolate. 'You suspect foul play but you don't think anyone will believe you if you say so?'

'I tried to tell that dratted social worker that they wished on me about it, she only came twice, I couldn't be putting up with her mealy mouth and the way she kept raising her voice when she spoke to me as if I were deaf, which I am not. She made it plain that a nearly blind old woman is not a credible witness.'

'I believe you are still totally on the ball,' said Ellie.

'Do you, now?' A wistful note in her voice.

A kettle whistled. Not Mrs Jermyn's. Nearby.

On the other side of the party wall! What? In a house that was supposed to be empty!

Ellie had asked that the charity put some insulation on that wall, but they hadn't done so, had they?

Ellie swivelled to look at the wall, and then cut her eyes back to Mrs Jermyn. 'The students are still here?'

Mrs Jermyn grinned. 'So you heard their kettle, too? Did you? I was beginning to think I was going doolally. Right. Now, shall we go and sit in the garden while the sun's out?' She hobbled out of the back door, managing her walker with ease.

Five-foot-high fencing gave the illusion of being in an enclosed space. Private. Mrs Jermyn's garden was long and thin. There was a wide path leading down to an arbour at the end, with deep beds on either side, filled with flowers and vegetables. At the end, another fence divided this garden from another belonging to a house in the next road. You could just see the top windows of the buildings across the gardens in the next road, but no more.

Next door to the left was the students' house. Ellie couldn't see much for a bushy creeper – summer jasmine? – which was climbing up and over the fence.

There were a couple of chairs outside on the patio. Mrs Jermyn felt for the back of her chair and sat on it. Ellie sat on its companion.

Now why has she brought me out here?

Mrs Jermyn sighed with pleasure. 'A G & T on a summer's evening in the garden is what I fancy when there's nothing I want on the radio. Sometimes my boys join me but they find the midges too much for them, though they've never touched me. Odd, that. Maybe I'm pickled in G & Ts.'

Ellie felt drowsy. She was still suffering from jet lag. She leaned back in her chair and closed her eyes. The sun was beautifully warm. She might have to move soon or she'd get burned.

Someone started up on a drum kit nearby. It shocked Ellie into sitting upright. Across the garden? In one of the back rooms of the houses in the opposite road?

'Drat the boy. He's left his window open again. At number thirty-eight. He's at college. Media studies, if you'll believe. Wants to be in a pop group. My cleaner works for his mum. She says you should see the state of his room.'

A child screeched, more in play than anger. In a garden to their right? Another child whined, 'It wasn't my fault!' A youngish woman's voice called to the children to come in for their lunch.

Mrs Jermyn said, 'That's Mrs Mills, two doors up. Two kids and another on the way. Her husband's an electrician – fixed up my kitchen a treat. We've got this neighbourhood gossip thingy, what do they call it? WhatsApp. This road and the next. Anyone wants something, or there's a scam going around, or a cat missing, they post the news.'

Mrs Jermyn could manage a smartphone? Could she really post items and receive news that way? No, I don't think so.

'Fiddly things, smartphones. I can't manage them but my neighbour that's three doors up drops by once a week for a cuppa and a gossip, so I keep up with what's going on. We used to sing in the local choir together, years back. Her eyesight's still all right but she's waiting for a knee replacement.'

Water gushed down a pipe nearby. To the left. The students' house.

Mrs Jermyn said, 'Their kitchen's the same as mine with a bit taken out of it for a shower room. They've made the downstairs kitchen and dining room into a communal area and they use that all the time. All the downpipes are on the outside of the building and you can hear whenever they run a tap, use the washing machine or the dishwasher. I know what they've got because they used the same plumber as me, been around for ever, everyone knows him. He told me they bought the same shower trays as I did but their loos have got those square seats which he says he's never seen a bottom that fits it. We had a good laugh about that.'

Ellie got it. Mrs Jermyn might be old and her sight might be failing but she still had all her marbles. She had contacts.

She knew who was doing what, to whom, why and when. She'd brought Ellie out into the garden to prove that she had grounds for suspecting . . . whatever it was she did suspect.

It left a metallic taste in Ellie's mouth. 'So, you think it was murder?'

'No. Maybe. It's just that one of them, well, he didn't fit in and I found out later that it was him that copped it. Liked the sound of his own voice, had to be nagged to do his share about the house and mostly managed to get out of doing it. A voice with an edge to it. It was his party, there were lots of gate-crashers, which I can tell you the others wouldn't have liked, and then he fell. It gives me a creepy feeling, and that's all I'm going to say about it.'

Ellie digested that in silence. 'The one that died didn't fit in?'

'The others are older, nice manners, would run an errand for me now and then and would chat over the fence. When my aerial fell off and my boys were away, the older one with the soft voice got it replaced overnight. Most of them, they'd laugh and chat in the garden of an evening and have a barbecue now and then, no bother. Always popped a bite to me over the fence as a treat. But the moment *he* came around there'd be a change in their voices, going sharp like.

'He lived up at the top, had music blasting out till all hours till the others shouted at him to shut it. I had to get earplugs. They had the council round a couple of times because the people round here, especially if they've got young children, well, they couldn't get them to sleep. The other students were considerate but that one was so full of himself he thought he could do anything he liked and get away with it.'

'And you could hear all that because you sit outside here in the evenings with a drink.'

'Voices carry. They have a roster for cleaning the communal rooms on the ground floor and you should have heard him grumble about it. To be fair, there's one girl chivvies the others to keep the place clean and tidy, and I suppose that's the same with all young people, not wanting to keep the place tidy, though a couple of them are old enough to know better. I have a lot of time for that girl. Nice alto voice, good diction. Middle class, hint of a Welsh burr. State school, not private, judging by her accent.'

'Name?'

'Patsy. Short for Patricia, I suppose. She keeps the garden, likes to sit in it of an evening. Passes the time of day with me sometimes.'

'There were both men and women next door?'

'Two girls, four men. They're better than some. I have a friend let her basement to a couple of students and wished she hadn't. The dirt! The toilets! The clutter! She said you could see the floor in only one of the rooms. But at least the lot next door kept the place decent, not like the ones my friend let to, who never remembered to take the rubbish out, and left their windows open on hot days and forgot to close them when it rains.'

'Right, so most of the students next door were a cut above the usual. Were you sitting out here when the loud boy fell?'

'No, that was too late for me. It was one of the last warm nights we'd had. Patsy had warned me they were having a party so I put my earplugs in and went off to sleep, thinking someone would call the police if it got out of hand – which of course it did, though I didn't know that till the next day.'

'There were gatecrashers, you say?'

'I could hear them banging up and down the stairs before I put my earplugs in. It sounded like fifty but I suppose it was more like twenty. You're going to get in touch with the students now, aren't you?'

'I don't know. I might. Tell me more about them.'

Someone inside the house shouted out, 'Hello! Gran, are you ready?'

Mrs Jermyn jumped in her seat. Did she blush? She called out, 'Go away! I told you I don't want them messing about with me, and that's it!'

A tall, dark man wearing a Sikh turban appeared in the doorway of the house. 'Come on, Gran. It's taken me for ever to get you this appointment, and you did promise you'd go if I took you.' He must be one of Mrs Jermyn's lodgers. Thirties, handsome, intelligent, soft-voiced but no pushover.

When he saw Ellie, he frowned. 'Mrs . . .?'

Ellie got to her feet. 'Ellie Quicke. I met Mrs Jermyn last year but have been away for some months. I was passing and called in to see her, and we were just sitting here, having a nice catch-up . . .' Her voice trailed away. 'I didn't realize she was supposed to be going out.'

He was ultra polite. 'Good of you, but we really must be going. The eye hospital, you know. She's ducked out of two appointments so far.'

'I don't want to go! They put drops in my eyes and I can't see anything for hours!' Mrs Jermyn sounded like a small child. Her lower lip had come out, and she swished her legs to and fro. A small child about to have a tantrum.

He smiled. A glimpse of perfect teeth. 'Come on, Gran. Here's your jacket, and your handbag's in the hall. I've got your medical card and the car's outside. It's good of your friend to drop in. I'm sure she can come back another day.'

Ellie looked around for her own handbag. 'Yes, of course. They can do such a lot to help people with cataracts nowadays.' Had she left her bag in the kitchen? Probably.

'I have to go to the loo,' said Mrs Jermyn, reaching for her walker and getting up speed as she passed the man into the house.

Ellie wondered if Mrs Jermyn was going to lock herself into the loo to avoid going, but the man said, with a hint of a smile, 'We took the lock off that door ages ago.' He turned to guide Ellie into the house, saying, 'It was good of you to call. She loves having the occasional visitor. What happened next door upset her a lot. For days she wouldn't even open the door to the postman.' A shake of the head, another smile.

He found Ellie's handbag and handed it to her. Ellie understood she was being hustled away. She said, 'Mrs Jermyn told me you're very good to her.'

'We look after our own, especially when they become forgetful.' The slightest inclination of his head and Ellie was out of the front door.

The message was clear. Mrs Jermyn was no longer quite 'with it'. Not to be trusted, and her lodgers were going to look after her. Good for them. And perhaps they were right to be so protective of an elderly lady who was losing her sight.

Ellie looked up at the students' house. Nothing had changed. It looked empty. Yet she had heard water running and a kettle

boiling on the other side of the party wall. Hadn't she? She
went up the tiled path and into the porch to knock on the door.

Nothing. Silent as the grave.

The house felt empty. Watchful, but empty.

Mrs Jermyn was trundled down the path in her wheelchair,
inserted into a well-polished car and driven away.

Ellie looked around, but there were no helpful neighbours
loitering nearby who might be able to confirm or deny Mrs
Jermyn's suspicions . . . which might well be nothing but that.
An elderly lady's nervous imaginings.

There were the usual rubbish bins by the hedge. Their contents
would be collected once a week. Next door's bins would be
empty at the moment, as the students had all left. Wouldn't
they? Of course they would.

Ellie lifted the lid of the first bin, marked 'Recycling'. It was
pretty full, with a slew of papers; junk mail and newspapers; a
large number of empty wine and beer bottles, ditto carefully
washed jam jars.

Ah. Well, the collections were alternate weeks, weren't they?
Recycling one week, rubbish the next. So the rubbish bin would
be empty . . .

Only, it wasn't. It was full to the brim: pizza boxes, plastic
containers, plastic bags.

Nearby stood the smaller box which would contain food
waste. That ought to be empty if no one was living in the house,
but it was half full; tea bags, half a loaf of mouldy bread,
eggshells, green leaves, some rotten tomatoes . . . And that was
just the top layer.

Ellie slammed the lid down.

She had a vision of a student going round the house, picking
up refuse and dumping it in the bins. Clearing up after the
others had left. Patsy. Possible Welsh background. Good for
Patsy.

Was it she who had boiled the kettle when Ellie was in the
kitchen with Mrs Jermyn? And if so, what did it mean?

Ellie gave up and decided to go home. She was tired and
there was just too much to think about.

She thought how good it would be to go home and have a
sandwich quietly, by herself, in her own chair with Midge the

cat on her lap. In the afternoon she would have a cuppa and a gossip in the garden with Susan next door and not worry about anything except which programme she and Thomas might like to watch on the telly that evening. And definitely not worry about missing students and forgetful neighbours and did he jump or was he pushed . . .

Now, why did she think he was pushed?

No, NO, NO!

She didn't know where to find Patsy anyway. Or did she?

THREE

Wednesday afternoon

Tea in the garden with Susan. And baby Fifi, of course. Although Fifi wasn't so much of a baby nowadays, but a quicksilver mite with enough energy to power a dynamo and an iron will. And charm.

Susan was looking heavy-eyed. Ellie tried to remember if Susan were eight or nine months pregnant. Whichever it was, Susan was looking good, if tired. She wore dungarees over a T-shirt, her hair was a mass of burnished copper curls, and her complexion was peaches and cream. Redheads keep out of the sun; they don't tan, they burn.

The sun shone intermittently, bees hummed and Susan and Ellie caught up on what had been happening these last few months. Ellie talked about how much Thomas had loved being with his daughter and her family, though it had been difficult at times, being guests in someone else's house.

Susan referred to what they'd been doing to their house, adding a blind here and a porch there. She admitted she wasn't sure to be pleased or not that they hadn't seen hide nor hair of Ellie's ambitious daughter, Diana. Perhaps she'd gone abroad?

Ellie shook her head. 'I've heard nothing from her. Not even a text message.'

Susan said she'd been worried that little Evan and Jenny

would be missing their parents, but they hardly ever mentioned Diana and seemed to be settling down in their new quarters with only the occasional tantrum from Jenny.

Ellie had run out of excuses for her daughter, so just nodded and said Susan and Rafael seemed to be doing a great job.

Susan apologized for the state of the garden. She said she was trying to find a landscape gardener who'd do something about it but had been let down by two people who'd said they'd come and then didn't. Susan said she'd pay, of course.

'No, no!' said Ellie. But thought it was a reasonable suggestion.

They neither of them brought up the subject of dividing the garden into two. Ellie wasn't sure she wanted to do it. Susan probably didn't.

Fifi foraged for daisies on the roughed-up area that had once been a lawn, and Ellie sighed with content. How delightful it was to be served tea and a brownie by someone else, and not have to move for a while. Susan wouldn't have to fetch little Evan from school and his sister Jenny from nursery for a while.

So Ellie recounted the saga of Mrs Jermyn's suspicions and the problem posed by full rubbish bins in a supposedly un-occupied house. She tried to pretend that was just to pass the time. A good story to tell.

Susan wasn't having it. She said, 'I know Rafael's really worried about what's happened. He's used Walker & Price for some time now. He rings them up or emails them whenever one of his flats becomes vacant. He was thinking at some point of handing the maintenance over to them as well.'

Ellie got it. Rafael hadn't been entirely open about his contacts with Walker & Price at the meeting. He should have said he'd used them himself. Perhaps he knew something about them which he ought to have told Stewart and Kate?

Susan added, 'Rafael says Walker & Price seem to be a nice pair. Reliable. A bit fussy, but that's not a bad thing if you're dealing with maintenance.'

Ellie recalled that Susan had once been a student herself; that is, until she graduated and married Rafael. Before her marriage she'd rented the attic floor which had once covered the whole of the top of Ellie's big house and that's how she'd become such a great friend . . . and cook.

Susan would know how student housing worked.

Ellie asked, 'How do students find somewhere to live?'

'First year, they're usually in purpose-built accommodation. After that, it varies. I was recommended to you, thankfully. Most students find others who want to join up and rent a house or a big flat together for a year. However many there are of you, you all sign the lease and agree to pay a proportion of the utilities. The agency deducts a fee for collecting the rent and passes the balance on to the owner. The students work out between them who gets the best rooms; some will pay a bit more for a better room.

'Then there's a down payment against damages which you pay in at the start of the lease and that's held by the agency until you leave and they have had a walk through and noted what damage, if any, has been done to the property and how much they should deduct to cover the cost of repairs. Usually the students nominate one person who's responsible for paying the utilities, and he or she in turn collects from the others.'

Ellie followed it thus far. 'So Walker & Price would have the names of all the students who were living in that house? Perhaps I should pop in and introduce myself. I'd like to meet the girl Patsy, who seems to have been the one to keep the place neat and tidy. I was told the students had all left and were trying to get out of the remainder of their lease, but someone is still living there.'

'The leases are usually pretty watertight. I doubt if they can wriggle out of them. Besides, accommodation for students is in pretty short supply. Where would they go if they left that house in the middle of term?'

Ellie had thought that herself. She counted on her fingers. 'How long is it until the end of the university term?'

'A month? Less? I don't know what other accommodation they could find at this time of year. And the cost! They'd have to pay much more for a short let.'

'Which is why they're trying to get out of paying what they owe? There's some chitchat going round which suggests there's been corruption on the part of the agency. This is straining the relationship with the charity, which owns the property and did all the work on it. Stewart has checked and all our paperwork is in order. I suppose someone, without knowing the facts, might think the lad wouldn't have fallen from the top floor into the garden if the window had been secure, or the frame rotten.'

'Even if it had been found to be rotten when the charity bought the place, the builder has put all that right, hasn't he?'

'Agreed. It's all airy fairy, but annoying.'

At this point, Fifi brought a somewhat mangled toy animal over to her mother, climbed on to her knee, and made herself comfortable. Susan stretched out in her chair and closed her eyes.

Ellie thought Susan looked worn out. No wonder, with three children to look after, and one more to come. Was Rafael helping her as much as he should? Um, maybe not.

Ellie said, 'I have to get a couple of things from the shops. Shall I pick up little Evan from school for you? What time? About three?'

'Bless you,' murmured Susan. 'One of the other mums is having Jenny for tea today so I can have a little nap . . . not sleeping all that well . . . Rafael's worried about something . . . and . . .'

Out she went, clonk! Deep breathing, and all.

Fifi fastened her eyes on Ellie, looked right through her and beyond . . . and also fell asleep.

Ellie stole away. She needed some more toothpaste and yes, there were a couple of other things she could get at the shops before she picked up Evan. She must make a list. Did Evan need a pushchair to get him home? No, he'd have a scooter, wouldn't he? All the children seemed to have one from the time they could talk nowadays. Presumably they were left in a secure place at school till the end of the day. Perhaps she could take a look at Walker & Price on the way.

Wednesday afternoon, continued

First, the shopping. This and that from here and there. She didn't meet anyone she knew, which was unusual but did mean she could get her errands done quickly.

She got to the end of the shops and checked her list. All done. Next, the estate agency.

But what was this? A group of people was standing around the shop front of Walker & Price. Why?

The shop still had its original frontage of one big window and a glazed door beside it. It had an old-fashioned appearance, supposed to present a reassuring picture of stability and trustworthiness. But the big window was not what it had been.

Ellie inserted herself into the group just as . . .

Aaargh!

Everyone drew back as a huge piece of the window broke away and tinkled its way to the ground where it shattered into a million fragments. Now there was a hole in the window large enough for a man to walk through.

Cracks radiated in all directions from what was left of the glass. Even as they watched – and took another step back – some of the cracks grew outwards but fortunately no more of the window broke away.

'Careful! Stand back! The workmen are coming, but . . .' An elderly man in a suit and tie appeared from inside the shop. Very distressed. Trembling, in fact. He looked at the damage and fished in his pocket for a handkerchief.

He was followed out by a middle-aged woman who was also wearing a dark suit and was also shocked to the core. Walker & Price?

A young man with athletic build brought a couple of chairs out of the shop and placed them at a distance around the shop window to prevent onlookers getting too close. He disappeared again. Sensible young man. Walker & Price were dithering, but the young man had seen what needed to be done and had done it.

The woman wrung her hands. Her voice wobbled as she said, 'It'll be all right. The builders are on their way. We're still open. It's just . . .' Her voice faded and she dived back into the shop, saying, 'As if we hadn't enough to worry—'

An elderly onlooker with a small white dog on a lead remarked to his neighbour, 'It's a lot worse than it was this morning when I came up to fetch the papers. Just a hole in the middle then. It's the cracks that do it. They spread and then bits fall out. They weren't open then. Just as well, or someone might have been badly hurt.'

The middle-aged woman at his side had a shopping trolley. 'Who dunnit?'

He shrugged. 'Someone at the newsagents said it was a lad on a motorbike. Threw a brick at the window and scarpered. What is the world coming to, I ask myself? They talking of putting cameras in the Avenue. The sooner the better, if you ask me.'

The young man came out of the shop with another couple of mismatched chairs. He was wearing thick leather gloves. A sensible precaution. He placed those alongside the others to prevent people getting any closer.

The man with the dog tugged on his lead. 'Come on, Fritz. Too much excitement's not good for you.' Actually, the dog looked bored. His owner trundled off with his dog walking reluctantly behind.

Ellie took the temperature of the onlookers. They were not displeased to see the damage. They stood well back and indulged themselves in watching someone else suffer.

'Serve 'em right,' said someone, softly, at Ellie's elbow. An elderly woman, leaning on a walker. It was someone Ellie knew by sight. 'It's not surprising, with what this lot have been up to.' She wasn't shouting, but she was loud enough to be heard for all that. One or two others nodded. They agreed.

Ellie said, 'What do they say? I've been away for a while, see.'

A shrug. 'All sorts. They're bad news.'

'Irresponsible,' the middle-aged woman with the trolley agreed. 'Not doing their job properly. That lad shouldn't have fallen from that window . . .'

Heads were shaken.

Ah, so this went back to the death at the students' house, did it?

Ellie edged into the front row of watchers. She noted with interest that there wasn't much glass on the pavement. Most of it had landed inside.

The woman with the shopping trolley said, 'I blame the

builders, leaving their skips in the road, full of rubbish and that. Anyone could help themselves to bricks. Everywhere you go, they're pulling down this and building up that. And the noise! And the dust! There's one skip that's been left in our road two doors from me, night and day, thud, thud, throwing things into the skip, and my hedge is white with dust.'

Another said, 'They'll have to board that window over till they can get the glass replaced. That'll cost.' This was said with some satisfaction.

Ellie could now see into the shop. Just inside the glass there had been a set of shelves which held pictures of houses and flats to let. Ellie remembered that Walker & Price were supposed to be managing a number of lettings. Within arms' length there was a desk which now sported a brick and some fragments of glass. It was indeed fortunate the shop hadn't been open when the brick had been thrown at the frontage, or someone sitting at that desk might have been badly injured.

The young man with the athletic build came out on to the pavement with a broom and set to, sweeping broken glass to one side.

Mr Walker – or Mr Price? – shot out of the shop, saying to the younger man, 'Stop! No, leave it! The police said they'd be coming. They have to see it. The builders can deal with it. They'll be properly equipped . . .' And he dived back into the shop, shooing the younger man before him.

Mrs Price – or was it Mrs Walker? – was on the phone inside the shop in a voice that rose higher and higher, complaining about the builder not turning up as soon as he'd promised. She was holding it together but she was definitely losing it. In shock.

As there seemed to be no more action, the little group began to disperse. An Asian-looking girl pushing a sleeping baby in a buggy looked at her watch and said she must hurry or she'd be late to pick up her little boy from school.

Ellie said, 'Oh, dear. Yes. I'm picking up my grandson for the first time. I do hope Susan let the school know it'll be me not her to collect him.'

They walked briskly along, side by side. The Asian-looking girl said, 'I haven't seen you at the school gates before?'

'We went to Canada to see relatives and stayed far longer

than we intended. My grandson was at nursery when I left, and now he's at proper school. We saw him and his sister yesterday for the first time for months, and my, hasn't he grown! I wonder if he's in the same class as your son?'

'My little one is shy. I hope he will make friends soon. He is not used to . . .' She hesitated, looking worried. 'We were very quiet, before. My husband was away a lot on business and then we came here and Lin . . . he finds it all very noisy.' She tried to smile. Didn't make it.

Ellie concluded that Lin was perhaps not settling into school as well as he might. His mother was clearly concerned for him.

Ellie liked the look of the girl. She said, 'My name is Ellie, and I live up the hill at the other end of the shops.'

'My name is Lily, and my son is Lin. The baby is Lou. We're renting at the moment but looking to buy.'

They arrived at the school gates just as the children began to rush out past a teacher, who was shouting at them not to run. Naturally, the children took no notice.

'Granny!' Evan saw her before she'd spotted him ploughing his way through the throng. Fair-haired, blue-eyed, solid of build, he was towing a small, fragile-looking Asian boy along behind him. 'Granny! This is Lin and he's come from the other side of the world and he's brill at sums and can read and write better than me, but he got picked on and he looks like Fifi so I stopped the boy who was trying to take his satchel and sat on him so can we have an ice cream on the way home?'

All in one breath and while struggling out of his satchel and handing it to Ellie to carry.

The boy Lin was also carrying a satchel. It looked almost as big as he was. He dived into his mother's arms and whispered something to her. He was neat in all his movements and yes, intelligence shone from his dark eyes.

Lily listened to her son, and then looked embarrassed. 'Another day, Lin. We have to ring his mother first and ask permission.'

'Ask him what?' said Evan, looking into the baby buggy. 'Your baby looks like Fifi, too! Granny, Lin can come home with me, can't he? I want to show him how we play cricket in the garden.'

Ellie and Lily said, 'Not today.' As one. And smiled at one another.

Lily said, 'We must ask Evan's mother.'

Evan said, 'Mummy's gone away and Susan won't mind.'

Lily looked a question she was too polite to put into words.

Ellie tried to explain. 'It's a bit complicated. Evan and his sister Jenny are my grandchildren but their mother can't care for them at the moment and their father died, so they're being fostered by my neighbour Susan, who is wonderful with them.' They started to walk back home.

Evan still had enough energy to dart from one side of Ellie to be with Lin, and then back again. He said, 'Susan's a brill cook, and Jenny's mad about computers. She'll like to see your tablet, Lin, because it's better than hers, and Fifi's . . . well, Fifi's like you, only different.'

Lily said, 'Is Fifi from Hong Kong, too?'

'No,' said Ellie. 'Fifi's father is half Italian, and it shows. She's only fourteen months but older than you or me, if you know what I mean.'

Lily nodded. They had reached the wrecked window of Walker & Price. A workman was there at long last, measuring up. A van had been driven up on to the pavement and a second man was easing out some plywood sheets to cover the damage.

They walked on, with Evan running ahead with Lin, shouting, 'Race you to the corner.'

Lily said, 'Someone doesn't like them much. Last week it was a rude word painted on the window.'

'What word?'

'Murderer. I saw it. I'd taken Lin to school and then popped into the bakery, which is always open early, same as the news-agent. I saw it through the window. I couldn't believe my eyes. I couldn't see what the word was from there but I saw it when I crossed over. It happened so fast.'

Ellie was intrigued. 'Did you tell the police?'

'I couldn't stop. Lou was fretting. Other people saw it, too.

By the time I came back to fetch Lin from school, they'd cleaned the window. No big deal.'

'What did you actually see?'

'Someone parked their bike outside the shop, went to the window, sprayed the word on it, got back on his bike and was off. It was all over by the time I'd paid for the bread.'

'Did you get the registration number?'

Lily shook her head. 'Too far away. The bike was black with no colour on it, and the driver was wearing black and a helmet and black gloves.'

Ellie said, 'There are a lot of boys around on bikes nowadays, delivering pizzas and acting as couriers. One of those, you think?'

'Maybe. The Polish girl in the bakery who served me, she's no fool. She said, "Look at that!" She said the driver seemed very young. I think that yes, the person was very young, very slim. Not tall. I think it might have been a girl but it all happened so quickly . . . I can't really say.'

'You think it might have been the same person who threw a brick at the window today? Did you see that, too?'

'No, I was not so early today because I didn't need bread. I didn't see anything. I asked my husband why someone would write wrote a bad word on a shop window and he said estate agents are all thieves. We had a bad experience when trying to buy a place here, you see.'

'With Walker & Price?'

'No, with another one. We went to two others. They kept showing us flats which were far above our price, and when I said so, they were . . .' She blushed a little. 'They were not nice. They said we shouldn't have gone to them if we hadn't the money. Then they found this flat for us, a new build, so good, just right, and we were going to buy it but a neighbour told us not to because it had this cladding on it which is not fireproof but the agents hadn't told us, which we think they should have done. So we looked online and found something that will do for the time being.'

It transpired that Lily's husband was a consultant now working at a local Ealing hospital, that Lily herself had been a radiologist but given up work to look after her little family.

They exchanged telephone numbers and separated, going in

different directions at the end of the road. Evan whined, wanting Lin to go home with him, but he was soon cheered by the thought of the nice big tea which Susan would have waiting for him.

Thursday morning

Ellie stood outside Walker & Price. The big window had been boarded over and a handwritten notice stated that the firm was open for business as usual. The pavement had been swept clean, but there was a glint of glass from tiny fragments which had lodged between the paving stones on the pavement.

Ellie opened the door and went in. The room seemed dark, although ceiling lights were on. One wall was covered in a huge map of the area; helpful and easy on the eye, as were several thriving plants in large containers. The general impression was business-like in an understated way.

The desk which had stood immediately inside the window had been moved further into the room. There were two more desks at the back with chairs for customers beside them. A computer on each desk was displaying a screen saver. None of the desks were occupied. A phone was ringing somewhere, but no one was attending to it.

A huddle of people at the back of the room resolved itself into Messrs Walker & Price coming forward to meet Ellie, while the junior member of the team faded into the background.

'Good morning. How can I help you?' The man managed a smile which was supposed to be welcoming, but which advertised that he was a bundle of nerves.

The woman turned away, blew her nose and seated herself at a desk away from the window.

Ellie said, 'Mr Walker? Mr Price? I'm Mrs Quicke, chair of the—'

'Yes, yes. Of course we know who you are. Mrs Quicke, founder of the charity, a public benefactor. I imagine you've come to ask what we're doing about the student house, which is . . . What a tragedy! Everything is in order. The students have left. It's all paid up. Don't know what the fuss is about. Dr . . . what's his name? Hallett. That's it. Dr Hallett. He saw to all that.'

Doctor? Oh dear, the man *had* got his facts wrong. He was in Cloud Cuckoo Land, not thinking of the students' house at all. The agency was clearly doomed to extinction. She might as well leave now.

He pulled out a chair for her at the desk furthest from the window. 'Would you take a seat? And some coffee, perhaps? We must apologize for the . . .' He waved a hand at the shuttered window. 'Vandalism. The police are . . . Yes, they're on the ball. Of course they are.'

He wasn't actually shaking, but there was a decided hint that he, like the glass in the front window, had been hit by something hard and that cracks might well develop and leave him in pieces.

She hesitated, then seated herself, glancing at her watch. Five minutes more and she'd be gone.

He seated himself opposite her and attempted nonchalance. 'I suppose you've heard about . . . Pure spite, not a word of truth . . . We would never, dear lady, never! I started this business with my cousin twenty years ago. Properly accredited. We have always prided ourselves on . . . We can assure you that . . .'

Ellie cut him off. 'How bad is it?'

He gaped. And was silent. He'd given up, rolled over, presented his neck to the executioner.

Ellie was patient. 'I've been away for a while. My fellow trustees have told me something of what's been going on in my absence and are divided as to what action we should take. I thought it would be good to meet you, and see what you had to say. If it's just a question of one disgruntled customer, perhaps . . .'

A phone on one of the other desks rang. No one picked it up.

He said, 'I wish it were just one customer. That would be simple. Everyone can make a mistake but this is . . . It's too much. I'm sorry, I . . .' He eased himself up out of his chair with the movements of a very old man, shambled off to the back of the shop, and disappeared.

The woman – Price or Walker? – came forward. 'I'm sorry. I must apologize. This business has hit him hard.'

It had shaken her, too. There were lines on her face which had deepened since Ellie had seen her the day before. She was younger than her partner, perhaps only in her fifties? And not yet completely defeated. She wore a simple gold wedding ring on her left hand and a gold brooch in the shape of a house on her lapel.

The phone continued to ring.

The woman picked up a pencil. 'They'll leave a message. They always do. Sometimes they're nasty. Nuisance calls. Often, it's cancellations. Viewings which had been arranged have been cancelled. Excuses as to why contracts can't be honoured. People looking for an opportunity to get out of paying their rent. It's . . . difficult.' The pencil snapped in her hand. She looked at it. She let it fall from her hand. She, too, was near breaking point.

Ellie said, 'I think a cup of tea is in order, don't you? Shall I make it?'

'What . . .?'

Ellie got up. 'The tea-making things will be at the back somewhere? Where's your young man?'

'Er . . . Gone out somewhere. Showing someone . . . we have to keep going, but if they've heard then they'll probably . . .'

'First things first,' said Ellie. 'Tea or coffee? A pastry of some kind, perhaps? Or chocolate?'

There was no sign of Mr Walker-cum-Price. Ellie located a tiny kitchenette, a loo, and a door to a yard at the back. The older man was standing outside in the open air, looking up at the sky.

Ellie spoke to him, but he didn't seem to hear her.

She made three mugs of strong coffee – there was no milk – took one out to the man, who hadn't moved. She said, 'Do you have sugar in your coffee?'

He didn't react. She put the mug down and went back inside. She took the two remaining mugs back to the woman, who was still sitting where she had been, looking down at the remains of her pencil.

'Cheers,' said Ellie, and then was annoyed with herself for saying something so inappropriate.

The woman looked at her, empty-eyed. 'Why are you bothering? Isn't it clear that we're finished?'

In truth, Ellie had not formed an opinion yet as to whether Walker & Price had done their job for the charity properly or not. She was canny enough to know that old-fashioned practices do often go to the wall when new blood arrives on the scene. Walker & Price had, perhaps, rested on their laurels; their frontage hadn't been updated for years, their computers were not the latest and the mugs in which she'd made tea, were stained with tannin. Now she came to look carefully, she could see that the carpet could do with a good hoovering, too.

Perhaps it was time for W & P to retire?

Something rattled into the letterbox, and Mrs W – or was she Mrs P? – jumped a mile, spilling some of her mug of coffee.

Ellie turned to look.

The woman cried out, 'Don't! Don't touch! It's not the postman. He doesn't come till midday.'

FOUR

Thursday morning, continued

Ellie spotted a packet that had been posted through the letterbox. It looked inoffensive.

The woman had her hand to her throat, her eyes on the packet. She made no move to collect it. From where she sat, with the window boarded over, it wouldn't have been possible for her to see who had posted the packet through the door, but she wasn't making any move to pick it up.

Ellie got it. 'You've been having anonymous letters? How distressing.'

The woman cleared her throat. 'Not just letters. Doodahs from dogs. A stinking fish. I'm sorry you had to see . . . I'm sorry, I'm sorry, I'm sorry!' She was near to cracking up.

'What do the police say?'

'They say they're looking into it. They imply that there's no smoke without a fire and ask if we're sure we've been behaving ourselves. They think it's hilarious.'

Ellie said, 'Aren't you going to see what's in the package?'

The woman shook her head. 'Better drop it straight into the rubbish bin.'

Ellie got up, thought about fingerprints, decided that if the police weren't interested, it wouldn't matter what she did and picked the package up. Brown paper, wrapped round something light. A cardboard box? Secured with Sellotape. No stamp, no address.

Ellie undid the paper to reveal a small round plastic tub, the sort which is sold with perishable food in it. It had been washed clean and there was no label. Inside . . .

Ellie dropped the tub.

The lid came off, and something large and hairy scuttled out and crouched there, wondering what to do next. A very large spider.

The woman screamed.

So did Ellie.

The man blundered back into the room, assessed the situation, snatched the tub from Ellie, shovelled the spider back into the tub and disappeared through the back door into the yard.

Ellie reflected that men have their uses.

'What a fright that gave me.' The woman tried to laugh. 'I hate spiders.'

Ellie said, 'My heart's racing.' She tried to laugh, as well.

With trembling hands, the woman picked up her mug and slowly, with care, sipped the coffee.

Ellie admired the woman's control.

They drank in silence. Ellie waited for some energy to return. A shower of rain hit the front of the shop and drummed against the boards. A door slammed at the back of the shop so presumably the man had let the spider loose in the yard and returned.

The woman dropped the remains of the pencil into the wastepaper basket. She ran her fingers back through her hair – an expensive cut, well done. She straightened her jacket. She wasn't yet able to think constructively but she was getting there.

The phone on her desk rang. She looked at the display. She

said, 'Number withheld. Another nuisance call. They'll leave a message if it's important.'

It continued to ring. Ellie's nerve broke. She reached across to pick the receiver up. 'Walker & Price. How may I help you?'

Someone laughed. A real cackle. And said, 'Naughty, naughty! Incy Wincy Spider . . .' Then cut the connection.

Ellie replaced the phone, and it rang again.

The same thing happened. Cackle, cackle. 'Naughty . . .'

In tones of weary despair, the woman said, 'It'll be on speed dial. We get a nasty message, every day different, and it's repeated every ten minutes. It keeps that particular phone out of circulation. We've tried to trace the number. We've told the police. They say someone's using burner phones and they can't do anything.'

Ellie said, 'Tell me about—'

'What's the use?'

Ellie had been going to ask when this persecution – for that's what it was – had started, but changed her mind. It would be better to speak of something which had no relation to the present problem, until the woman had regained her self-control. So Ellie said, 'Tell me how you came to start in this business? Do you and your partner each have a different area of expertise or do you both do everything?'

The strategy worked, for this was something the woman could talk about. 'My cousin – that's Mr Walker . . .' She gestured to the back of the room where the man had returned and seated himself at another desk. Staring into space. So if he were Mr Walker, then she must be Mrs Price? 'He trained as a surveyor, like his father before him, and I trained as a secretary and bookkeeper because that's what women of our generation did. Then I took all the exams and joined him in this business. We've always got along well, never any trouble. All those years.'

'So you're both qualified, but he did most of the managing of properties and you do most of the office work? What about the young man?'

'We had another woman who worked with us for many years, keeping the office open, taking phone queries, looking after us beautifully. We didn't realize exactly how much she contributed till she retired last year. Since then we've had several youngsters who want to get experience in this work and some have worked out and some haven't. Archie's the latest. He's the best we've had so far. He won't do the washing up or hoovering, but he's good with clients. I don't suppose he'll stay, though. Who wants to be associated with a failing business?'

'I know you've been here for many, many years. You have an excellent reputation. One of our trustees says—'

'Rafael? A sharp brain, that one. We've known him some time as we've been handling the rental of his block of flats. When this trouble started he came round and spent some time with us, checking to see if we had by some mischance misrepresented ourselves. He was very nice about it. He said we'd done everything by the book and he would recommend that the charity continue to use us.' A little colour came back into Mrs Price's face. She'd liked Rafael, hadn't she?

So why hadn't Rafael mentioned that he'd been to look at the agency's books?

Ellie said, 'So you're still handling the rental of his flats?'

'Yes, of course.'

So what was Rafael busying himself with now, if he'd shed the work he used to do there?

Ellies guessed, 'You're acting for him in the acquisition or management of another building?'

A professional smile. 'I couldn't possibly say.'

Which meant that she probably was. Ellie recalled that Susan had said Rafael was worried about something. What on earth was going on here? Mrs Price wouldn't talk for professional reasons. Ellie respected her for it. In fact, Ellie was inclined to think that Rafael was right in backing Walker & Price.

The problem remained that something was very wrong in the state of Denmark. Someone had it in for the agency, orchestrating a campaign in social media, on the phone and with inappropriate gifts in order to drive them out of business. But who and why?

Mrs Price provided some sort of answer. 'I don't think we can carry on here much longer. We'd had an enquiry as to whether we'd be prepared to sell before all this happened. My cousin wants to retire. He was planning to move to the south coast. I had intended to carry on for a couple more years, but I can't do everything. And now . . . the agency who wants to buy us out has dropped the price because of what's been happening. Sorry, you don't need to hear this.'

'I can see the attraction of getting out and leaving it to someone else to deal with the nastiness you've been experiencing. I suppose you might be interested if they offered you a partnership and a reasonable price?'

'Rightly or wrongly, my cousin won't have anything to do with them. He feels that they're not the sort who . . . oh, well. You know?' She folded her lips. She was not going to slander anyone, but her meaning was clear.

Which was a pity, really.

The phone, which had been silent for several minutes, started up again. This time Mrs Price looked to see if she recognized the number, and picked up the receiver. 'Yes, and a very good morning to you, too. Now, you wanted a second viewing of the property above the shops here. Did we fix a date? Yes? I have it in my diary for . . .'

Ellie picked up a Walker & Price card from the desk and made ready to depart.

Mrs Price switched her eyes to Ellie. She nodded and smiled. Perhaps this conversation would end in satisfactory mode?

As Ellie made for the door, she had to edge past the boards which had been displaying photographs of properties to let in the window. The flying glass had damaged some of the photos but the boards themselves could probably be restored to their original position when the window had been replaced.

And there it was. Bold as brass.

The only nine-storey block of flats which had been built in this area for some years past. The cladding looked all right, but Ellie knew what had happened when similar cladding had aided the conflagration of the Grenfell high-rise block of flats in the not-too-distant past. She was aware of the investigations into that tragedy, and of the stalemate it had produced. Everyone was clear that the cladding of such high-rise buildings must be replaced not only in London, but all over the country. Only, the developers wanted to pass the cost of replacement on to the leaseholders, who were unable to afford the cost . . . and indeed, why should they? Meanwhile the flats had become unsaleable.

Ellie recalled the girl from Hong Kong saying they'd been warned off buying a flat in a local high-rise.

Oh. Dear.

Ellie knew of only one such building in the immediate vicinity and yes, it looked like the one in the photograph which had been in Walker & Price's window.

The sticker across it read, 'For Sale or Rent'.

It should have read 'Unsaleable' or 'Do not Touch'.

Ellie looked back at Mrs Price, only to see that she was absorbed in her phone conversation.

Ellie guessed . . . No, she knew, she just knew, what it was that Rafael was up to. He was going to buy that block of flats and replace the cladding. It would cost a mint, far more than he had at his disposal. He would have to raise a fortune to do this. When he'd finished – if he finished – he would be in possession of a very valuable property. Instead of the flats being labelled as unsaleable, they would fetch double their normal prices simply because the defective cladding had been replaced.

It would be a gamble, yes. But Rafael was a gambler by nature. Yes, he did have a cool head, but in this case . . .

Ellie allowed herself to explore possibilities as she walked back along the Avenue. Rafael would have to put up his own low-rise block of flats, which he'd inherited and transformed, as collateral for a loan. The interest on a bank loan would be staggeringly high. He had no other assets. He and Susan were renting the house next door to Ellie's.

Ellie paused, checking traffic before she crossed the road.

No, surely he wouldn't be so stupid! Would he?

Yes, oh yes! He was far-sighted, he'd have done the maths, he'd probably had surveys done already, and approached builders about the cost of replacing the cladding. Maybe he'd even got as far as enquiring about permits to close the pathway outside the flats while the work was being done.

He hadn't told Susan. He was going to put their future in jeopardy, but he hadn't told his wife.

Oh, he liked to live life on the edge, didn't he!

Ellie discovered that she was very angry with Rafael. How dare he put his family's future at risk! He ought to be made to put his own block of flats into Susan's name so that she would be safe whatever happened.

Ellie stepped into the road and stepped back quickly as an SUV swished past. Was it going to rain again, and she without an umbrella?

She told herself to simmer down. She'd built up a nightmare of a situation which might only exist in her imagination. Surely Rafael wouldn't be so stupid!

Yes, he would.

No, he wouldn't.

She'd know if he had as soon as she saw him again.

And then . . . oh yes, it hit her what he ought to have done . . .

A bus screeched to a halt not a foot from where she stood in the road.

Someone shouted at her. A man darted into the traffic, seized her arm and hustled her back to the pavement, scolding her as he went. The bus driver slowly drove away, his passengers peering out of the windows to look at this stupid woman who clearly had a death wish.

Ellie gasped. 'Sorry! Sorry! Not paying attention.'

'You ought to be locked up!' The man continued to hold her arm.

A middle-aged woman said, 'Come and sit down for a bit, right?'

Ellie found she was shaking. There was a low wall fronting a semi-detached house nearby. She sat on that, trying to smile, telling everyone she was quite all right, and apologizing over and over again for giving them – and herself – such a fright. Thanking the man who had obviously saved her life.

The man drifted away, growling to himself about stupid women.

The middle-aged woman said, 'There, there! You want someone to see you home?' She produced a smartphone. 'Who shall I ring for you? A neighbour? You shouldn't be on your own.'

Ellie's heartbeat slowed down, and she began to work out what to do. 'Could you call me a taxi? There's no one at home today but there's someone next door who'd look after me.'

'Taxi it is. You should get your doctor to give you the once over. My neighbour did the same thing, walked into the traffic. It was the beginning of Alzheimer's and she's in a home now, poor dear, not knowing what day of the week it is.' She dialled, gave instructions and said, 'I'll sit with you till he comes.'

Ellie thanked the woman, got into the taxi when it arrived and trundled home. Instead of going into her house, however, she rang the bell at Susan and Rafael's front door. They'd only recently had a porch put on, which was a great improvement and handy today with the intermittent spells of rain that were sweeping across the country.

No one came to the door. The house felt quiet.

Ellie tried to look through the window into the kitchen, but the louvres of a blind prevented her from seeing inside.

Susan must be out fetching the little girl from playgroup, or shopping or . . . Well, anyway. She wasn't at home and neither was Rafael.

Ellie used her key to let herself into her own home and was enveloped instantly by the feeling of her life being still in a muddle.

Midge, the cat, liked to sit on the shelf where they dumped any mail that came through the door, but he didn't like the mail being left in a place where he wanted to sit. So, today's mail was on the floor. The grandmother clock was still silent. Through the glass door at the back of the hall she could see the empty shelves of her conservatory, which had always looked so welcoming when full of flowers.

There was so much to do and she hadn't the energy to deal with any of it, inside or outside the house.

But here came her much-loved husband Thomas, emerging from his den with Fifi in his arms.

Ellie dropped her handbag and held out her arms to him. He was big enough and strong enough to hold not only her but also the toddler. She said, 'I'm home,' which felt like the right thing to say while at the same time being ridiculously stupid.

Fifi reached out one hand to Ellie, while holding tightly to her toy Gonk with the other.

'She's teething, poor mite,' said Thomas. 'Susan had to collect Jenny from nursery and take her to a dentist's appointment, so she asked if I could look after Fifi. We've been entertaining one another but are ready for our nap, now. So what have you been up to? Let's sit down next door and you can tell me all about it.'

They sat side by side on the big settee while Fifi, still resting in the crook of Thomas' left arm, hummed herself to sleep.

Now Ellie had something else to worry about. Neither she nor Thomas were in the first flush of youth. They were delighted to have more contact with their grandchildren – and with little Fifi – but they were no longer as spry as they had been. Increasing stiffness limited what they could do to babysit. Lifting youngsters into highchairs and on and off potties was no longer easy. What was to be done about that?

Ellie made herself comfortable in the shelter of Thomas' right arm, and poured out all her worries, including all topics from the clock to worrying about Susan, letting it all hang out, higgledy-piggledy; what she'd seen; what she suspected and what she'd been told but might not be true.

Midge the cat joined them to sit on the arm of the settee next to Thomas. Ellie mopped herself up. 'Of course, it might all be my imagination.'

Still Thomas said nothing. She was conscious of his strength. She realized he was consulting Him above. Oh dear, how trivial were her own little problems.

She said, 'I'm not imagining that Walker & Price are under attack; they are. And the idea that Rafael might possibly be thinking of trying to buy that white elephant is probably just that; a wild idea with no basis of facts but . . . oh, I don't know. Tell me I'm going soft in the head.'

He spoke at last. 'You see through the masks people wear to what they are thinking. I'm fond of Rafael and so are you, which doesn't prevent us seeing that at the moment he's not looking after Susan as well as he might. You're right; he's a risk-taker and enjoys a challenge. I'm perfectly ready to agree that he might have seen a gap in the market that would make him a fortune if he can get proper financing for it, but he can't possibly do it alone. He needs a backer. Does he have one? Surely he wouldn't think of going it alone? Mm. He's not a bad lad, but he needs a quiet word in his ear from time to time.'

'Am I to do it, or will you?'

A longer pause for thought. 'I don't think that is my job here. He respects your opinion. It's you who have a clear view of the situation. It's you who've been in touch with Walker & Price, and you who runs the charity. I think my job is to find some help for Susan.'

'So you think I should tackle Rafael? I suppose I'd better do so. Oh dear. I'm not looking forward to that. And what about Walker & Price? I liked them and thought they had a very professional outlook. Yes, they do seem to have got a bit muddled about this and that; saying a doctor had organized the let for the student house, and there seems to have been a misunderstanding about the rent, but . . . Do I back them or not? What if the media talk is true and the student died because of some mistake on our builder's part? Doesn't that put a different slant on things? The coroner seems to have been satisfied, but people are saying there's no smoke without a fire. Remember that Walker & Price had the word "murderer" painted on their premises. Could there possibly be some truth in that?'

Thomas said, 'You could always ask Lesley what she thinks and take it from there.'

Now Lesley Millard was not only Susan's aunt, who had recommended the girl as a tenant for the attic floor in the big house in the old days, but also a detective inspector in the local police force.

Ellie relaxed. 'Yes, of course that's what I must do. If the police are satisfied, then we can forget about that death. The talk will soon die down. But what seems to be escalating rather than dying down, is the horrible things that have been happening to Walker & Price. The police don't seem to be taking them seriously.'

'But you are. You're thinking that someone you've heard of might be behind these attacks.'

'I know it's absurd and I'm jumping to conclusions but Mrs Price did say they'd had an offer to buy their agency, but the people concerned have dropped the proposed price because of what's been happening. And I thought, maybe that offer came from someone who'd actually caused the problem in the first place. I have no proof that it's the same agency that's after the charity's business, but I did think the Streetwise agency could do with being looked at. Is that such a ridiculous idea? And yet . . . No, surely not. Wouldn't they be disbarred or something if they're found to be behaving that badly?'

Thomas said, 'Define "behaving badly". If you're referring to the online hate mail and phone calls, well, they could be done by people who have absolutely no connection with either of the estate agencies concerned. Some people who use the media seem to exist in a state of envy. Their lives are dull and without excitement, so they jump on bandwagons started by someone else. They get a thrill from it, not least because they know they can rarely be traced, so they can say anything they like with impunity. They are trying to bring in laws to prevent this happening, but at the moment these people who post filth are mostly free from prosecution.'

Ellie shivered. What it must be like to live like that, eaten up with hate?

Thomas said, 'You experienced one lot today. The phone calls are set up to repeat a pre-recorded message. They don't need to have met the person to bombard them with hate mail. The perpetrators might be someone who'd never dream of committing a crime in person. They could be a failed student, a disgruntled client or an old lady with nothing better to do.'

'And the paint on the window? The brick through the glass? The spider posted through the door?'

'No, that's different. Be careful, Ellie. Once people start throwing things in person as apart from making anonymous phone calls, they progress from bricks to brickbats.'

'Well, they don't know about me. Yet.'

Ellie told herself she ought to be getting up and doing

something but found it hard to do so. It was so comfortable sitting there, with Thomas' arm around her. She relaxed. She said, trying to laugh, 'Look at me! We come back from a lovely long holiday, to find a house which is all topsy-turvy, a ruined garden, a domestic crisis threatening next door, children needing to be babysat and me interfering in other people's businesses instead of looking after you.'

He said, 'My arms were empty before I met you. I am content.'

Thursday lunchtime

Jenny bounced in through the empty conservatory with Susan at her heels. Jenny was a happy bunny because she'd been given the all-clear at the dentist.

Susan had brought duplicate keys to her house, saying it was ridiculous standing on ceremony as everyone was already going from one house to the other via the garden. And would they like a steak and kidney pudding for supper? Of course they would.

Time to get moving again.

Fifi became Thomas' shadow because he was doing such interesting things. She 'helped' him fiddle around with pieces of card to put under the front of the clock in the hall until it condescended to work again. She learned to open the door of the clock to see the pendulum swing to and fro. She clapped her hands with joy when it chimed the hour.

Ellie sorted things in the kitchen. She looked at the mail – all junk – and put it back on the shelf to be dealt with later. At which point Midge jumped up and pushed it off again. Ellie put the whole boiling lot in the bin without looking at it again.

Fifi and Jenny, protesting, were taken home for lunch, but within minutes Ellie and Thomas could hear Jenny having a tantrum about something. Her screams of protest could clearly be heard as she rampaged to and fro, in and out of the garden, stamping on everything in sight. Jenny was the child most like her absent mother Diana, who had also tried to get her own way by making herself unpleasant.

Ellie sighed; Jenny was a difficult child, needing a firm hand. Susan was doing a very good job of making the child understand that screaming blue murder got you nowhere . . . but, as Thomas remarked, it must be taking its toll on Susan's patience. And where was Rafael? Nowhere to be seen.

Thomas shut the windows at the back of the house to block out the sound of Jenny screeching. They had a scratch lunch in the kitchen after which, worn out by the day's excitements, Thomas retired to deal with emails on his computer, while Ellie took a nap.

Thursday afternoon

Ellie cut short her rest and stirred herself to go next door and return Susan's dishes from the meal they had eaten the night before.

She found that Jenny had recovered sufficiently from her tantrum to play happily on her tablet behind the television set. Susan looked tired. She said that Jenny had discovered she could get Susan's complete attention by refusing to use the toilet until bribed to do so. Susan said she knew it was wrong to give in to the child, and that it was shocking to realize that a three-year-old could defeat her, but there it was . . . Susan had come to the conclusion that there were times when it was easiest to give in.

But, Susan said, she wasn't too tired to miss out on a good chat with Ellie, and would she like a cup of good coffee?

Ellie accepted, seeing that Susan wanted to talk. Evan was at school and Fifi was happily building towers of bricks and knocking them down again, closely watched by Midge, the cat.

Susan let herself down on to the settee beside Ellie and sighed.

Ellie noted that Susan was heavy-eyed, and getting slow in all her movements. She asked, 'How are you feeling now?'

'Fine. A bit tired, naturally. The last scan showed that all was well and it is going to be a boy.'

'You need help. Is Rafael organizing something for you?'

Susan lifted her hands and let them drop. 'We did have someone to help with the children before you came back, but she's doing her school exams at the moment. Rafael says that I'm a warrior and he's full of admiration for the way I'm coping; so what can I say? I've tried to explain what pregnancy does to you, but he won't listen. Honestly, I could clock him over the head with a frying pan sometimes.

'The thing is that when he's got a project in mind, he can't think about anything else. First he had the flats to make habitable. Then he schemed to marry me and have a baby. Then there was this house to divide into two. And now . . . I'm not sure what it is that he's up to, but he refuses to talk about it. He says I don't need to bother my head about business affairs. Have you any idea what he's thinking about?'

'I'm guessing,' said Ellie. 'I'll have a word with him. I suppose he's like that because that's the way he was brought up. He's reverting to Italian papa type, expecting the little wife to be responsible for everything at home while he acts as hunter-gatherer.'

Susan eased her back. 'You're right. His mother was happy to be the little wifey who stays at home, cooks delicious meals, brings up the children and believes it when she's told she doesn't need to bother her head with politics. His father still thinks that's how it should be. At least Rafael's not quite as bad as that.'

Ellie smiled. 'He told me he takes after his rascally old uncle, who was always sailing too close to the wind but who did accept that times change.'

Susan grinned. 'He sounded fun. And he did leave Rafael his block of flats, which has been the foundation of everything he's done since.'

Ellie said, 'Rafael has a special something. He has an ability to think outside the box. That's why I thought he'd be so good working for the charity, and he's been a real asset there.'

Susan yawned and didn't try to hide it. 'He says I'm not to worry, which of course makes me worry all the more.' She looked at the clock and struggled to her feet saying it was time for her to put Jenny and Fifi in the double pushchair and fetch Evan from school.

Ellie was horrified at the thought of Susan having to push the two children around and volunteered to stay and babysit Fifi while Susan took Jenny alone.

Jenny, predictably, said she didn't want to go. Susan remarked that they'd be passing the ice cream van on their way, and if someone was a really good girl, she might perhaps have one. Jenny then got into the pushchair of her own accord and off they went to collect Evan.

Fifi abandoned her bricks to bring one of her action books over to the settee for Ellie to read to her. She was an agile little imp and managed to climb up – with a helping hand from Ellie – and settle down at Ellie's side. Both of them enjoyed the books which had appropriate actions and sounds to use in the stories.

From one second to the other, Fifi fell asleep. She was so active she needed frequent naps to keep her strength up.

Ellie thought of lifting her up and carrying her out to the hall so that she could lay her down in her buggy. That would be the right thing to do. The only problem was that she didn't think her back would stand for it. Fifi was by no means overweight, but at Ellie's age she knew what she could and could not do without hurting herself.

Ellie decided to let Fifi lie where she was in the corner of the settee. She fetched a blanket from the buggy to lay over the child and lay back down beside her. She let her eyes wander round the room. This had once been Thomas' study and library but had been transformed by Susan into a comfortable space in which the whole family lived. Nowadays the room was not only decorated with children's toys, but there was a variety of Victorian watercolour seascapes on the walls, several side lamps placed on shelves high enough so that small children couldn't interfere with them and a large television.

Now that she was alone, Ellie realized she was nervous about talking to Rafael. She tried to pray but the lines of communication seemed blocked, probably by her own anxiety. She tried not to think about anything. Especially about her stupidity at stepping in front of a bus . . .

She started awake. What was that? Fifi hadn't stirred, but yes, someone had turned a key in the front door.

Rafael dropped a bag in the hall and came through, soft-footed, expecting to see Susan. He stopped short when he found Ellie stretched out on the settee with Fifi asleep beside her.

Ellie said, 'I ought to put you over my knee, young man. Overreached yourself, haven't you?'

FIVE

Ellie could see Rafael wasn't sure how to react – with a smile or a scowl. He decided she was joking. 'What are you talking about? Where's Susan?'

'Taking Jenny along to fetch Evan from school. She looks tired. What are you doing about it? And what about the problems at Walker & Price? Nasty minds at work there, don't you think? Then there's this business of a block of flats for sale. Cladding. Takeovers. Money to be made by someone who thinks outside the box. But there's a big risk attached, isn't there? And someone I know is attracted by danger.'

'You mean me?' he said, smiling but wary. 'You think I'm dipping my toe into deep waters? I can swim pretty well. I won't drown.'

Ellie struggled to sit upright. 'Under normal circumstances, I think I might agree with you. Buying an unsaleable block of flats and replacing the cladding would be expensive but would double or treble the value of the property. It sounds like a proposition which any bank might accept. But not when the agency concerned is being targeted as inefficient or worse.'

His smile vanished. 'You've only been back two days and you've put your finger on a possible problem. How do you do it?'

'Thinking outside the box,' said Ellie. 'Or rather, trying to follow the corkscrew bends in your brain. Rafael, this is not like you. You've missed a trick. You should have brought this proposition to the charity, who might well have backed you when you'd explained the sums to them. Why didn't you? Was it because you'd have to admit you're already working closely with Walker & Price on the letting of your block of flats?'

Rafael flung himself down into an armchair and tried to pretend this discussion was not important. 'I did think of it.

The proposition in itself is sound. I agree that Kate and Stewart would have been horrified at the cost at first, but yes, I think she'd have come round pretty quickly, and that she'd then persuade Stewart to agree.'

'So why didn't you?'

He shifted uncomfortably in his seat. 'I was going to do so, until all this trouble started with Walker & Price. I've signed up with them to act for me in the matter of the flats and I can't get out of that. I don't want to. They've done good by me right up to the point that these rumours started and now . . .' He shrugged. 'They're pariahs. Can't sell anything.'

'Is there any substance behind the rumours? You've looked into them, haven't you?'

'About the lad killing himself? That's when the online hate mail started. Of course there's nothing in it. It wasn't a result of corruption by the agency or bad practice from the builders. The students had a party, there was a mock fight and some stupid git took too much to drink and fell off the balcony. It happens.'

'Why did he fall off the balcony? Was it unsafe? Did you go and examine it? Did you attend the inquest? Are the police satisfied that the death was accidental?'

He moved uneasily. 'I didn't personally visit the site, no. I checked what alterations our builders had made to turn the house into student accommodation, which did include putting in a loft conversion. The work was done and passed health and safety regulations. The agency let to a student at the usual rates. The charity is in the clear.'

'Someone doesn't think so.'

He grimaced. 'I know. I could understand it in a way if the hate mail was directed at the charity, but it isn't. They – whoever *they* are – are targeting Walker & Price, and they had nothing whatever to do with the rebuild. They didn't even have a sight of the property till it had all been properly signed off. All they did was to arrange for some student to view the property, draw up the lease, get it signed and collect the rent. They cannot be held responsible for the student's death; that was a combination of alcohol and stupidity. The coroner tactfully softened the blow to the family by bringing in a verdict of accidental death. That is what it was. The agency is blameless.'

Ellie said, 'I visited Walker & Price this morning. A nasty packet containing a huge spider was popped through the letterbox while I was there followed by repetitive, taunting phone calls. The agency had the word "murderer" painted on their window last week and now the front window itself has been smashed. The partners are getting abusive phone calls. They're on the brink of giving up and selling out but are afraid they won't get a decent price for the business. The police are not taking the matter seriously. And neither, it seems, are you.'

Rafael bit off a hasty word. He didn't like being criticized, even by default, did he? And, knowing him, he was sneakily aware that he'd tried not to see how big a problem this could all become.

Ellie said, 'I will back your presentation to the charity about buying the flats and replacing the cladding on two conditions. One is that you make over at least some of the flats you inherited to Susan—'

'What? But if I do that—!'

'You won't be able to raise the finance yourself but would have to rely on the charity to back you. Yes, I know. But if you go ahead by yourself and miscalculate, if the deal goes sour, then Susan will be up the creek without a paddle. She's looking after three children under the age of six at the moment and finding her second pregnancy hard going. One child is at school, another at nursery, and the third barely out of nappies. How much help are you giving her?'

'I do what I can. I pay the bills.'

'And if there comes a time when you can't?'

He got up and took a turn around the room. He looked down at Fifi, who was still asleep. He reached out to touch her cheek and withdrew, deciding it was best not to wake her when they were in the middle of this argument. He threw back his shoulders. Ellie understood that she'd dented his pride by insinuating that he was a poor provider. She could see him think, how dare she!

He didn't like it. Oh, no. For two pins he'd . . . No, she could see he'd decided it wasn't worth quarrelling with Ellie. He shook his head. His eyes switched from left to right.

Well, yes. There was a risk factor. He'd not wanted to think about the possibility of failure, which would leave Susan and the babes in penury.

No, that wouldn't happen. He wouldn't allow it.

Ellie's suggestion was a vote of no confidence in him!

Well, it was also an offer to help. And maybe it wouldn't be a bad idea to look into the problem. He said, 'And your second condition was . . .?'

'You help me work out what happened to the student who died. Exactly how did he happen to fall from the balcony? Did the charity skimp on the rebuild? If so, we may be liable for millions of pounds of damages. As a corollary, I want to know why Walker & Price are under attack.'

'The police—'

'Yes, I'm going to speak to Lesley Millard about the matter, and I think that we should pay a visit to the house where the lad died and find out what his friends are saying about it.'

'The students left. The house is empty.'

'No, it isn't. Someone's living there. Both dustbins are full.'

He hit his forehead. 'The dustbins! Who but you would think of looking at the dustbins!'

Friday morning

There was a certain procedure to be followed when visiting one of the charity's properties. Entry to vacant premises was simple; no notice had to be given. Both the charity and Walker & Price had a set of keys which would be available for maintenance purposes. You signed a key out, and let yourself in. Easy.

When the property was occupied, notice had to be given to the occupants of an intending visit, a key was picked up and in you went. Also easy.

In this case the managing agents had been informed that the house was empty, and therefore no notice was required to be given of a forthcoming visit. However, Ellie was sure someone was there. She'd heard them. Perhaps it was squatters? In that case, legal action would have to be taken to evict them.

If it were one or more of the students who had returned, then the situation was less clear.

Ellie told Rafael to risk it, so he took her round by the charity's offices to get their key and they omitted the formality of giving notice of their arrival.

Rafael's preferred mode of transport was a humongous beast of a motorbike. Ellie refused to go anywhere near it, so he had to take out the sedate family saloon which he disliked, and which Susan feared driving. In this case, he had no option; Ellie was *not* riding on the back of a motorbike.

They parked outside the student house. It still looked deserted.

Rafael surveyed the frontage and shrugged. Ellie went straight to the dustbins. The food container had been emptied as had the recycling bin. The ordinary rubbish bin was still full.

Rafael said, 'I give in. Someone is still living here.' He rang the bell. Nothing happened. He rang it again. He used the doorknocker.

He used the key to let them into the hall and closed the front door behind them.

Ellie observed that the layout of the house was the same as for Mrs Jermyn's next door but the opposite way round. They were standing in a wide corridor with a tiled floor. Ahead were stairs leading up to the first floor and there were a number of doors leading off the hall.

They opened doors as they went along. None were locked. The first gave on to a large bedsitter, which had been stripped bare. A faint trace of an expensive aftershave? The blinds had been lowered over the windows and the place was in semi-darkness.

At the end of the corridor a door opened on to a bright and comfortable sitting room with lots of squashy seating round a couple of low coffee tables. The blinds were up, a window was partly open and the place smelled sweet. A free newspaper with today's date on it was on the table, together with a bowl of fruit. Someone was definitely living here.

There were two doors under the stairs, giving on to a shower room and a loo. Both were clean and bright with use.

Then there was the kitchen. Here was more evidence of daily living. The dishwasher door was open and it was half-full of dirty crockery. A couple of mugs had been used and left on the table, and a trail of cornflakes led to a packet on the side. There

were some fearsome-looking knives in a block of wood and a
damp dishcloth had been used and hung up to dry.

A faint aroma of good coffee.

Ellie opened the fridge, which was running. Milk, salad stuffs,
marge, perishable sliced meats, cheese, yoghurt and fruit.

Someone came down the stairs: plonk, plonk, plonk.

'Who are you and what are you doing here?' A strapping
girl with a mass of dark hair and fire in her eyes. An MA student
in her mid-twenties? Welsh background? Probably. Flushed
with anger, or scared? She was carrying a load of bedlinen,
which she dumped in the washing machine. She glowed with
health and cleanliness and smelled of a good soap.

Rafael held up the front door key. 'We're from the charity
that owns the house. We were told the house was empty, that
the students had all left.' He was laying on the charm and it
wasn't working.

'Yes, we did leave after Brandon's death, but we're returning
one by one. We worked out we'd still have to pay for our
accommodation here until the end of the lease, though we are
hoping to get some kind of rebate. The thing is, we can't get
to lectures unless we're living locally and we can't afford to
pay for different accommodation. If you thought the house was
empty and were aiming to rent it out again—?'

'I'm sorry,' said Ellie. 'We were told that everyone had left.
I'm Ellie Quicke, by the way, and this is Rafael, and we're both
trustees of the charity. I went to see Mrs Jermyn next door and
she said—'

'How is she?' The girl's attitude softened. 'I'm worried about
her. Her eyes, you know. Or perhaps you don't know, but she
wouldn't go to the hospital and—'

'One of her lodgers took her yesterday.' Ellie pulled out a
stool at the central island, and hefted herself on to it. 'You're
Patsy, are you? She said you were the student who tried to keep
order.'

Patsy looked as if she were torn between telling Ellie and
Rafael to get out and making them welcome. She inspected
Ellie and saw through the housewifely exterior. She looked at
Rafael. She registered that he was a bright lad but that Ellie

was the one in charge. She turned back to Ellie, saying, 'I'm glad Mrs Jermyn's all right. She's such a dear. Would you like a cuppa?'

'Love one,' said Rafael, smiling sunnily at Patsy, who ignored him to turn the tap on.

Weeesh!

Ellie remembered the sound of the tap here running from when she was sitting in the kitchen on the other side of the wall. Mrs Jermyn's account of things was looking better and better. She said, 'Yes, I'd love a cuppa. It's a problem, students leaving before the lease is up. I believe it's best to sort this sort of thing out over a cuppa, rather than going to court and wasting everyone's money on solicitors and such.'

Patsy frowned. 'Frankly, we haven't known what to do. It's been a worry. After the tragedy Jocelyn said he'd sort it but he hasn't. Oh, Jocelyn's the one who found us this house. Jocelyn Hallett. Two of us were having problems in the last place we were at; leaking roof and black mould, ugh! We were desperate to find somewhere else so we were delighted when he said he'd taken a house for a year and needed at least two more people to share with.

'That's Mona and me – we're both history buffs – and Terry, he's IT. Then Jocelyn found Imran who's also IT in some weird by-way and he found Brandon, or rather, Brandon was wished upon him by his family, you know? This house doesn't cost nearly as much as most of the other student accommodation round here and we were really glad to get it.'

She grinned. 'Jocelyn didn't lose by it, either. He knew what he was doing when he picked us.'

Rafael was interested, 'How did he do that?'

'Well, me because I can cook and look after the garden and he enjoys both . . . Which reminds me, I must cut that front hedge. It's a disgrace. Then he took Mona because she's my friend and because he likes girls with a bit of spice. He thought she might be amusing to take out now and then; which she is, of course. He picked Terry and Imran because they like a good argument. We reckoned those two should go in for politics but they're only interested in IT. You should hear them when they get going, with Jocelyn changing sides every other minute, just for fun, till we threw cushions at him. We had some good times, so much laughter.'

Her smile vanished. 'All except Brandon, poor thing. Jocelyn had to take Brandon to oblige his family, A bit of a black sheep, you know? He looked like Jocelyn in some ways but he hadn't his brains nor his kindness. Also, Brandon told us this and that about Jocelyn which wasn't true and . . . No, let's skip that. We soon realized Brandon was lying. He wasn't here that much, anyway. He had a snooker cue in his hands more often than a book. He never really fitted in but there, we mustn't speak ill of, you know?'

Ellie probed. 'You were a happy household except for Brandon?'

'We were. I only wish it had lasted to the end of the academic year. We're all of us strapped for cash, you see; except for Jocelyn, of course. Don't get me wrong, he's great company. Talk about diplomacy! We never had a cross word that he couldn't counter with a laugh, or an arm round your shoulders.'

She shook her head, shaking away a fond memory. 'Anyway, he said he would talk to the agents and arrange to let us off the rent for the rest of the year. We thought they might indeed let us off some of it, but then we thought that wasn't realistic and we ought to pay something. Maybe half? Jocelyn texted that he'd sorted it but he hasn't come back even to collect what the rest of us owed for the last month or for this, or for the utilities. It's unsatisfactory because we don't know exactly where we stand.'

Ellie said, 'I'll see what I can do.'

Patsy said, 'Thanks. The day after it happened – Brandon dying, I mean – Mona and I went to stay with her parents. It's some distance and it was a bit of a bind, cycling to and from uni every day. Also, I have a job tutoring a couple of bright children nearby a couple of times a week and I don't want to lose it.'

There hadn't been a bike in the hall, but Ellie could see a shed in the back garden. Patsy liked everything in its proper place and would keep her bike there.

She said, 'I come from Abergavenny, see, and it's too far

for me to be able to commute and then my dad said – and Mona's dad agreed – that they didn't think we'd be let off the rest of the rent. Then, sharing a small room at Mona's, and trying to study and everyone being around all the time, well, we weren't getting any work done. So we decided to come back and see what we could sort out with regard to the rent.'

Ellie said, 'Where's Mona today?'

A quick upwards lift of the head. 'Upstairs, working. You want to see her, too? I'll give her a call.' She went to yell up the stairwell, and then returned to the kitchen. 'We're going to air Jocelyn's room today. Mona's thinking of moving into it because it's the biggest. And Imran's coming back tonight, I think. It'll be good to see him again.'

Ellie guessed, 'Jocelyn had the best room on the ground floor because he was the one who organized the let? You say he has money to spare?'

Patsy nodded. She made and poured tea, giving an extra-large mug to Rafael and a fine bone china one to Ellie. She said, 'Yes, Jocelyn is older than the rest of us. Slumming, really. He did his PhD at Harvard and had been offered a couple of jobs in his line, and don't ask me what they were because it's all above my head. He's some sort of aerospace communications expert, you see.

Jocelyn Hallett, PhD. Entitled to be called 'doctor'.

'Jocelyn was all set to go back to America a year ago when his mother found she had cancer and begged him to return to this country. He agreed, provided he didn't have to live at home. He got himself a year's research on some weird project or other and visited her every week. Then she got worse and he was going in every day and . . . I don't know what he's doing now. He's too soft for his own good.'

Patsy bit her lip. 'Sorry, shouldn't have said that. He's a really kind man, you know.' A slight smile. 'He likes to act the part of playboy, enjoying one last year of student life before settling down to earning a living. But then Brandon died, phew! Did his parents scream blue murder! His mother and aunt were in pieces, and that was it. Called home for good. Understandable, I suppose. He was the first to leave. I was so

angry with him at the time, but I suppose I understand . . .' She
shook her head at herself.

Ellie wondered if Patsy had missed him more than a little?

Patsy tried to smile. 'I sometimes wonder if we'll ever see
him again. It's a nuisance because we need to sort out the
finances. Mona and I have texted him a few times and he's
replied saying he's dealing with it, but we haven't paid him for
our share of the rent and utilities for the last couple of months
and that's not right. We've tried ringing the agents but either
they don't answer the phone or, if they do, they say the bills
have all been paid, which we presume means Jocelyn's out of
pocket and we can't have that. Can you get it sorted?'

Ellie said, 'I'll see what can be done. So Mona came back
with you, thinking to move into Jocelyn's room. Which room
was she in before?'

'One of the rooms at the top but she doesn't like it up there
now and I don't blame her.' Patsy shuddered. 'Gives you the
creeps. When she came back, she moved into the back room
on the first floor, the one which used to be Terry's. It was
reasonably easy to get clean, and it was good having her next
to me. But it's true that the ground floor room is the best.'

'Was it her room that the party was in?'

'She was up top, yes. But next door. That was Brandon's
room. He's the one who died. Ugh.' She hugged herself and
shivered.

Ellie hinted, 'Things got a bit wild?'

'Brandon's birthday.' She looked away and down.

Ellie had the odd thought that Patsy was going to lie? Or
perhaps be careful with the truth?

The girl said in a neutral, non-judgmental voice, 'Brandon
had a wide circle of friends and those friends brought in more
friends. You know how it is: they hear there's a party on somewhere and they gatecrash. The music's too loud, everyone drinks
too much, it's surprising there aren't more accidents.'

Ellie guessed that Patsy hadn't liked Brandon much.

Patsy said, 'It still upsets me to think about it.' Her complexion
and general air of good health stated that she herself was not
a heavy drinker.

Ellie said, 'How come the lad fell?'

'The big windows at the back were open on to the balcony. Brandon was standing out there with a couple of his mates. There was a lot of shouting and pushing and . . . there are iron railings around the balcony and you wouldn't think anyone could fall over, but he did. Someone may have pushed him, not meaning anything, and he went over backwards. I don't know.'

'Bu it was an accident?'

'Yes, of course. At the inquest they said he'd imbibed some recreational drugs. The police asked us about that, but we'd none of us ever touched them. We offered to take a test to prove it.'

She almost smiled at the memory of it. 'Terry said, straight-faced and without a smile, that he was all in favour of experimentation but knew his girlfriend wouldn't allow it. The police searched the house but found nothing. For the sake of his family, the coroner played down that angle.'

Ellie thought, *Of course! Patsy would have gone through the house with a toothcomb before the police arrived to make sure nothing incriminating could be found.*

There was a clatter of footsteps and a small blonde woman bounced into the room. Bright eyes, considerable intelligence. 'Hiya. I'm Mona. You've come to sort out the rent?' She glanced at Ellie, then homed in on Rafael and gave him the sort of smile which Ellie categorized as 'Come hither!'

Rafael smirked. He liked the look of her, too, didn't he?

Patsy ignored all this. She used a tissue and said, 'If you don't mind, now Mona's here, I'll leave you to it.' She disappeared back up the stairs.

Mona took a step nearer to Rafael. She was using a somewhat pungent soap. Or was it hairspray? She said, 'You're going to help us out? We really can't afford to find another place, you see. You do see, don't you?' And she gave him a pretty, upwards-glancing, sidelong glance. 'Ooh, I still get goosebumps when I think about poor Brandon dying like that.'

The little flirt. With brains.

Rafael grinned back. 'Of course.' He looked across at Ellie with a glint of amusement in his smile. He'd liked the look of Mona, and he didn't object to a little flirtation to liven up the day.

Ellie caught on. Women thought Rafael tasty, and he was susceptible. Oh well, no harm done.

Mona opened her large blue eyes even wider. 'What happens to debts if someone dies?'

Ellie was soothing. 'We'll talk to the charity and see what can be worked out. Now, my dear, do you think you could show us round the house? We need to know what condition it's been left in, before we do anything about it. And as we go, you can tell us who lived in which room and perhaps a bit about them, too?'

Mona nodded brightly and led the way back down the corridor. She opened the door to the big front room, grimaced, and went to the windows to open the blinds. A large, bright and normally airy room. It must indeed be the best room in the house. Like all student accommodation it was furnished with the basics: bed, desk and chair, shelving and cupboard space.

It looked very bare. There wasn't so much as a newspaper or a used mug left behind; nothing to show what the occupant had been like.

Correction: the man who had been here had cleared everything of his away. A careful man. Even the wastepaper basket had been cleaned out. Or had Patsy done that?

Ellie said, 'What was Jocelyn like?'

'Nice. Older than the rest of us. Brain like ice. He and Patsy trounced us all when we went through a phase of playing bridge one night a week. It's not like him to promise to do something about the rent and not carry it through, but out of sight, out of mind. Is it just me, or can I still smell his aftershave?'

She tugged on a sash window in vain. Rafael reached over her, unlocked the catch and slid it down three inches until it was prevented by a thief-proof latch from moving any further.

Ellie opened the built-in cupboard to find it empty. She said, 'Jocelyn's an alpha male, accustomed to getting his own way in everything?'

'With women, you mean? Brandon tried to say Jocelyn was only interested in boys, but that wasn't true. We think Brandon was jealous of Jocelyn. They looked a bit alike but they weren't, really, not at all. I mean, Jocelyn's always got an expensive-looking girlfriend on the go but he's not serious about them. I went out with him occasionally. Patsy wouldn't but I couldn't see why not. He's a good laugh, treats you well. I've got a boyfriend, anyway. He's at Manchester uni, plays rugby. Patsy told him she'd got a steady boyfriend back in Wales, too. We made sure Jocelyn knew about them and he never pushed it.'

She produced the ghost of a smile, echoed by Ellie. Yes, that's how women nowadays set out the rules of the mating game.

Mona looked around. 'It is the best room in the house and if we're allowed to stay and can't get anyone else to share the cost then I'm definitely going to move in here. I did ask Patsy if she'd like it but she says every time she turns round she expects to see or hear him. We all went to him with our problems, you know, him being that bit older and further along in life, but I suppose he was bound to move on and forget all about us.'

Mona led the way out of the room and back down to the communal room with windows looking on to the garden. 'We all used this, some of us more than others. We usually watch telly on our computers, but it's good to meet up and chat at the end of the day. Sometimes we'd each cook just for ourselves, sometimes Patsy would cook for all of us. Good times. Seen enough?'

Ellie nodded.

Up the stairs they went. When the students were all there, they'd presumably locked their doors to preserve their privacy, but now there were only two of them around and they felt they could trust one another, so they'd left their doors open.

Light flooded the landing from a skylight in the roof far above.

Mona gestured to a couple of closed doors. 'That's Patsy's room, overlooking the road. This one at the back' – she opened another door – 'used to be Terry's, but I took it when we came back. It wasn't too bad, easy to clean up. I put the rest of his stuff upstairs in the room I had before . . . Terry comes back now and then to fetch something and to have a bit of peace and quiet for a few hours. I reckon he'll move back in here some time, if we can get the rent sorted out.'

Terry's room showed no signs of male occupancy. Mona had

spread herself, dressing-gown half off its hanger on the back of the door, paperwork on the desk, bed not made. But it smelled clean and there was no dust on the surface of the desk.

Ellie said, 'What is Terry like?'

'He's a nerd, hardly knows what day of the week it is. Regularly breaks things because he doesn't look where he's going – crockery, plates. We never let him wash up or go anywhere near the dishwasher. Always losing his glasses and his keys. He's all right really; just not quite with it. He was over at his girlfriend's place most of the time, even before Brandon died. She *manages* him, if you know what I mean. They've known one another since they were in kindergarten and plan to marry when he lands a job in some high-flying establishment or other. They make a point of telling people they're going to remain pure until they get married. I'm sure they'll be very happy together.'

A slightly acid tone, thought Ellie, but Mona was probably right. Terry and his girlfriend had a low-key, endurable relationship built on old-fashioned values.

Ellie said, 'Terry was at the party?'

'Oh yes. Three-line whip. Brandon's birthday. Terry came for a short time, without his girlfriend. She doesn't approve of strong drink. Yes, I'm sure I saw him, early on. Drinking Coca Cola and pretending to dance. I think he left early, when we got invaded by the joy-boys; Brandon's friends, I mean. They'd come for free beer. I suppose Terry went round to his girlfriend for their usual nightly chat. He came back just after Brandon fell and the ambulance men arrived, not that they could do anything. Terry was in shock. We all were.'

'Terry left here after Brandon died, too?'

'Went to his girlfriend's. Or rather, she came to collect him, packed up a few things while he was still dithering. I'll give you her address, if you like. He said he was going to sleep in their communal room on a sofa. You can believe that or not as you choose.'

Mona turned to the stairs to the attic rooms, and went up them slowly, with deliberation. The set of her shoulders indicated that she was doing this under duress and wanted to be sure that Rafael knew it.

The landing was full of light from the skylight. Doors were open on to the rooms, and the afternoon sun was doing its best but . . .

The place felt airless. It wasn't smelly, precisely. Or was it? Something sweetish?

Mona stopped short; her face drained of colour. 'I'm sorry. I find it hard, coming up here. I mean, it was never very nice for some reason, but it was never this bad. My room looked on to the road . . .' She threw open the door and gestured for them to look.

A room with the usual basic furniture, with several boxes lying around. They'd be Terry's? Yes. A pair of old trainers had been left on the floor; a mug half full of cold coffee stood on the desk with a riffle of abandoned paperwork. There were shadows cast by built-in furniture but nothing unusual to see.

Patsy closed that door and gestured to another. 'The big room at the back of the house, that was Brandon's. That's where the party was held. You can go in if you like, but if you don't mind, I'll . . .' She set off back down the stairs.

Rafael didn't seem affected by the smell. He raised an eyebrow at Ellie and opened the door into what had been Brandon's room.

Ellie found she was praying, 'Lord Jesus, protect me.'

She followed him into the room which was much larger than the others. It was a big loft conversion, occupying the whole width of the house. French windows, floor to ceiling, overlooked the garden. There was the usual basic student furniture, marred by some stains on what had been a new carpet. Nothing personal left to see. Presumably Brandon's parents had taken his things? Or Patsy had packed up his belongings for them?

Sun streamed in through the unshaded window, but it didn't have much warmth in it.

Well, of course it didn't. The weather had turned cool, hadn't it?

The French windows opened on to a balcony from which a cast iron staircase circled its way round and round and down to the ground. A key still hung in the handle of the door. There was a wrought-iron balustrade outside, waist-high, to prevent anyone carelessly stepping off into thin air. Rafael unlocked the window and threw it open.

Ellie told herself to be brave. Holding tightly on to the railing, she leaned over to look down to the garden. And got vertigo.

She was going to fall!

SIX

Friday morning, continued

B reathing hard, Ellie forced herself to shuffle back to the window.

Rafael was inspecting locks and catches. 'Looks sound enough. Shouldn't have been a problem. You can smell it though, can't you? Even now?'

Ellie didn't reply. She was feeling rather shaken. She hadn't realized she didn't like heights. Hadn't thought it a problem.

Rafael closed the window and locked it again. 'Ugh. Cannabis. Never liked the smell. Fortunately never been tempted.'

Cannabis. Marijuana. Mary Jane. And other names. Nasty stuff. So that was why Mona – and Ellie as well – hadn't liked the smell of the place? It was a relief to know that she wasn't descending into dementia, imagining that the place was, well, haunted. No, of course it wasn't haunted. That was ridiculous. All in her imagination.

Rafael said, 'Seen enough?'

Ellie forced herself to concentrate. She was still feeling a bit wobbly. 'Four plus one makes five. There were six students, weren't there?' She led the way down the stairs, treading carefully and holding on to the banister.

Mona was on the first-floor landing, standing outside one of the closed doors. 'Do you need to see Patsy's room?'

'No,' said Ellie, 'but if you could show us where the sixth student slept?'

'Imran. Also IT but not the same type as Terry.' She opened

the door into a small room opposite hers. It occupied the width of the hall and had a window overlooking the street.

'Imran's quiet, keeps to himself. He paid the least because this is the smallest of the rooms. He'd tried studying at home and found it impossible. Multi-generational living isn't the easiest place for a student and if he's having to pay the rent still, he might as well use the room. He's coming back tonight or tomorrow morning, as soon as he can get someone to give him a lift with his stuff.'

This was another room with the usual bedsit furniture in it. Very clean. Very bare.

Mona said, to Rafael rather than Ellie, 'I put the vacuum cleaner round it the day after we came back. I did think at one time that I might like to move into it because it's cheaper than the others, but as we don't know how much we still have to pay and Imran's coming back . . .' She shrugged.

Rafael understood. 'But you think it's OK to move into Jocelyn's room on the ground floor?'

Mona caught a tress of hair in her fingers, and wound it round and round, her eyes fixed on Rafael. She said, 'I might as well, but only if we can fix the rent so we don't have to pay any more. Can you do that for us?'

Ellie was getting annoyed. The other two were talking to one another as if there were nobody else present. She could feel the sexual tension rise between them.

Mona knew exactly what she was doing. She was attracted to Rafael and didn't mind showing it. If only Susan were here!

Ellie gave a little cough to remind them that they were not alone. 'Well, Mona, I think we've seen enough for the moment. Would you give me all the contact details for the others? Phone numbers, home addresses or where they can be found at the moment? I expect I could get them from the agency, but it would be quicker if you did it.'

Mona dimpled. She disengaged herself from eye contact with Rafael, led the way down to the communal sitting room, found a pad and a pen, located the details on her smartphone and wrote them down.

'And yours? How can we contact you?' Mona said this, looking at Rafael and not Ellie.

He wrote down a name and address on a clean sheet and
passed it to Mona.

Mona said, 'Oh dear, I forgot to give you my mobile number.'

The girl added her own private phone number to her list and
handed it to Rafael. He smiled and nodded and said, 'I'm sure
we'll meet again.' And pressed her hand.

Mona managed to blush. Clever girl!

Ellie was not amused. She walked out and stood by the car,
waiting for Rafael to follow her. Which he did, after a pause.
A pause sufficiently long to have allowed for a kiss and a
promise?

Rafael was smiling as he ushered Ellie into the passenger
seat and took his place behind the wheel. The car filled with
the scent of a light but teasing perfume. He checked his jaw
in the mirror, rubbed at a red smudge and only then started
the engine.

So Mona had kissed him?

He said, 'You're upset about something?' He went on smiling.

'You can tell? What would you have said to Susan if you'd
seen her behaving like that?'

'Like what?' He half laughed.

'Flirting. Mona signalled she liked the look of you. You
signalled back that you liked the look of her, too. She upped
the game by ignoring me and devoting herself to you. You
responded in the same way. She let you understand that she
found it laughable that Terry and his girlfriend wanted to wait
for marriage before having sex, which was telling you that she
personally wouldn't be bothered by such niceties. She gave you
her smartphone number and either you kissed her or she kissed
you as soon as my back was turned.'

A shrug. 'An amusing interlude. Nothing serious. We both
enjoyed ourselves.'

'And you gave her your own telephone number.'

'I know better than that. I gave her an old number, years out
of date. She might try it, I suppose, but it would get her nowhere.'

'That girl was taking your signals at face value, and you
know it.'

Another shrug. No smile now. He was getting riled. He jerked
to a stop at the traffic lights. 'It meant nothing.'

'Perhaps it meant something to her.'

'Forgive me,' he said ironically, 'but perhaps you are a little, shall we say, out of date? Nowadays—'

'Susan will chew your balls off.' Ellie didn't usually use such terms, but if ever there was a moment for crude speech, this was it.

The lights changed and he started off with another jerk. 'How would she hear of it? You won't tattle. She wouldn't believe you, anyway.'

'She'll know the moment you enter the house. I can smell Mona's scent on you from here.'

'She kissed me. Women do.' Through his teeth.

'In a moment you'll say it was all her fault.'

Silence. He drove a little faster than he usually did. He was angry. Very. But also beginning to understand that he was in deep trouble. He wasn't ready yet to admit it, but Ellie had made him aware that he had a problem.

He slowed down and turned into a side road, which would not lead home. He said, 'If she smells Mona on me, then I'll just have to admit it, and laugh it off.'

'And promise not to do it again? You think she'll accept that like an old-fashioned, nicely brought up wifey ought to do? You think she'll tell herself that this is what men do, that's the way they were brought up, and if I don't make a fuss he'll always come back to me because I cook well and take care of his children?'

'I admit there might be a bit of a slanging match—'

Ellie laughed. 'And then some. Do you want to start hiding kitchen knives? This is Susan we're talking about here.'

'She married me, knowing what I'm like.' Sulkily.

'You pursued her, knowing what she was like. Susan is feisty. Incredibly attractive. Capable of earning a very good living. She took a chance on marrying you. You promised her you'd be faithful and not bend the rules.'

'I can't change.'

'Yes, you can. Or at least, you can give out a different set of signals. Wear a wedding ring.'

He drew a deep breath and held it. 'A wedding ring is a sign of captivity.'

'For Susan, but not for you?'

Silence.

Ellie felt dreadful. She'd stepped out of her comfort zone and what had happened? She'd made matters worse. She loved Rafael and she loved Susan and she could see they were heading into choppy waters because Susan would *not* put up with Rafael flirting with all and sundry.

Ellie needed to blow her nose. She got out her pack of tissues and used one.

Rafael was sitting with his head averted. Even the back of his neck was red.

She ought not to have scolded him. She really ought to have known better. She was entirely in the wrong. Well, he was in the wrong, too.

She remembered her wise husband Thomas talking about resolving quarrels. He'd said that, if the most sensible and adult of the two apologized for their share in the row, the other would quickly follow.

Maybe that would work, because she had had no right to haul him over the coals like that. She said, in a tiny voice, 'I'm sorry. That was very wrong of me.'

He said, through clenched teeth, 'Yes, it was.' He lifted his hand to start the engine, and then let it drop.

More silence.

She blew her nose again. 'It's because I do care about you.'

'Really?'

'Yes.'

'Have you got a tissue? I've got something in my eye.'

She handed over a tissue. He blew his nose and wiped his eyes. He started the car, drove sedately round the corner, back on to the main road and from there, home. He parked the car in the drive as usual and came round to help Ellie out.

She tested one foot, which had gone to sleep. Stamped on it. It responded. Were they going to part like this? He'd got his key out and was putting it in his front door. Did he intend her to walk off without a word?

He said, 'Well, are you coming in, then?'

Was this his way of saying he forgave her interference? Or did he want a buffer between himself and Susan?

Ellie followed him in. Susan came to the door into the living room, looking tired.

Thomas hove into sight, looking slightly the worse for wear, with Fifi asleep against his shoulder. Thomas said, 'What a good time we've had! But the best thing about being a grandparent is that you can hand the children back when you've had enough.'

Susan took Fifi from Thomas, and then froze. She sniffed the air. Her expression changed. Mona's scent was still sending out messages.

Ellie had thought Susan would throw a tantrum, but she didn't. Instead, she went marble white and said, 'Rafael . . .!'

Rafael threw up his hands. 'Guilty, m'lud. The girl threw herself at me, and yes, I was tempted to kiss her back, but I didn't. Ellie was there. She can tell you. It was one of the students, needed a comforting shoulder to cry on. Honestly, it meant nothing.'

Susan got it! Oh yes, she got it, all right, and she didn't like it one little bit.

She ignored Rafael to speak direct to Ellie. 'Thomas has been great. He's been looking after Fifi for me while I had a little nap. He even offered to fetch Jenny from nursery, but now that Rafael's back, he can do it.'

Rafael hadn't bargained for that. 'Oh, but—'

Susan continued, 'Rafael, don't forget to hitch Jenny's scooter on to the back of Fifi's pushchair so she can ride it on the way back.'

Rafael objected. 'Oh, come on, now!'

Thomas transferred Fifi to Rafael, turned Ellie about and shepherded her out of the front door. Ellie would have hung back but he urged her over to their own front door, and used his key to let them in. He said, 'I gather a storm has been brewing. She was almost in tears when I wandered over this morning. Been up several times in the night. She's exhausted. I don't think Rafael is pulling his weight. And what was all that about him and a girl?'

'Rafael was flirting with one of the students at the house where the lad died. Admittedly the girl led the way, but he was happy to follow. He dismisses this encounter as unimportant.

He says it meant nothing to him and it probably didn't. I don't think it meant much to the girl, either, but she did kiss him, and I think he kissed her back and Susan cottoned on straight away. I warned Rafael. We had words. I probably made matters worse.'

'Lunchtime. Something simple, I think. I'll do it. How about one of those baked potatoes that you do in the microwave?' He led the way to the kitchen and opened the freezer cabinet.

Ellie noted his office diary was open on the table. She sat down, rather heavily. All this anger was bad for her blood pressure. 'You're supposed to be retired. You've only been back two minutes and I see you've got your diary out already.'

He extracted a couple of potatoes and put them in the microwave. 'With butter or would you like some grated cheese with yours? Yes? As for taking on some more work, aren't you supposed to be retired, too? Shouldn't you be thinking of nothing more serious than a crossword, or what ready-cooked meal you might microwave for supper? We're both workaholics. Or rather, we can neither of us refuse a plea for help. The only problem is to decide which is the most important thing for us to tackle next.'

'Surely you have enough on your plate? Settling back in here. Picking up with old friends. Helping me sort out the garden.'

'Someone else is in charge of my old parish. Yes, I have had a couple of offers of work which I said I'd think about, and someone needs a locum this weekend for the early morning service but I have a feeling that what's landed on your doorstep is more important. Tell me all about it. Was the charity in any way at fault for the boy's death?'

So she talked.

He was a good listener. He grated cheese, put together a green salad, and laid the table for lunch. The baked potatoes were fluffy, white and tasty. Yum.

She finished by scraping the last of the potato up, saying, 'It's all tied up with Rafael and his goings-on. At least, I think it is. How did you get on, looking after Fifi?'

'She's a little monkey, bright as they come. Scrambling all over the place. Trying to climb trees. Needs watching twenty-four seven. She's teething, hence the broken nights for Susan. I'm worried about Susan. She's overtired, can't relax even though I made her sit down while I took Fifi out into the garden. Fifi's too young for the kind of nursery which Jenny goes to, but we could perhaps find a playgroup she could attend? It would give her the stimulation and socializing she needs. I did mention it but Susan's too tired to look into the matter.'

She nodded. 'We ought to help more with Evan and Jenny, but we're not really up to climbing trees and playing leapfrog any longer. We'll have to think of something different.'

He cleared the table and loaded the dishwasher. 'You are a wonderful woman, and I love you. Now, we are both agreed, aren't we, that Rafael is heading for trouble and that part of the problem lies with the student's death? So I'd like to help. What would you like me to do?'

She gestured to his diary. 'You said you'd had a couple of jobs offered to you.'

'Sure. I've been asked to arrange the rotas for the services locally, who preaches where on what day and so on. I've also been asked to write an article for the local church magazine on "My Visit to Canada". Boring, boring. So, I am at your disposal. I've preached about the seven deadly sins many a time and heard many a confession on them. I can see that Rafael is displaying the sin of pride. What about those who are slandering the estate agent? Are they bearing false witness? And what about the lad who fell to his death? Was it drink or drugs that caused him to fall?'

Ellie said, without thinking, 'No, it was murder.' She started. 'I hadn't meant to say that. It can't have been murder. I mean, why should anyone want to kill the boy? I did smell cannabis which might have led to some relaxation of normal rules of behaviour . . . but on the other hand, there was a lot of drinking and dancing going on, so . . . Oh, I don't know enough about the drug to know how it affects people. Patsy said there was a lot of drink taken, and a mock fight led to some pushing and pulling, which ended in the lad going overboard. It might have been manslaughter, I suppose, but . . . where's the motive?'

'Sounds more like accident to me.'

Ellie shivered. 'I know. I keep telling myself that. But there's a nasty atmosphere about the top of the house where Brandon lived, which tells me that something's not right. Mona felt it, too.'

She thought about her visit to the top floor and her reaction. 'I'm not imagining things. I did smell cannabis and it is fresh. Mona took Terry's room when she came back and put his bits and pieces into the room at the top which she'd had before. She told me Terry comes back every now and then for a bit of peace and quiet.

'Terry's a cool card. When the police asked about the cannabis upstairs, he said he was all in favour of experimentation but that his girlfriend wouldn't like it if he tried anything. I reckon he found Brandon's stash and is trying it out now and then. Upstairs. By himself. With no one else nearby. And that's why the top floor still smells of cannabis. Mm. I expect Patsy will tumble to it soon and have it out with him. Thomas, you're much better at finding things out on the internet than I am, and I must admit I'm curious about one or two things I was told.'

Ellie slapped the table. 'Now, where's that list of students who deserted the scene of the crime . . .? Bother. Mona wrote it out and Rafael took it. I'm an idiot for letting him.'

They contemplated the idea of speaking to Rafael about it that afternoon and decided against it. Thomas said, 'We can get it from the estate agents. Now, would you like me to find out what Walker & Price's reputation is in the community? Um, who do I know who might have used them? Mrs . . . no, she retired and went to live with her daughter on the south coast somewhere.'

He started leafing through the list of addresses at the back of his diary. 'I visited this couple when they moved into a house near the park. Perhaps . . .'

Ellie yawned. She could perhaps allow herself a little lie-down, just for an hour? Before doing anything else? Except . . . she reached for the phone and dialled the private number for Detective Inspector Lesley Millard, who was not only Susan's aunt, but also an old friend.

'I am unable to take the call. Please leave a message . . .'

Of course. 'Lesley, it's Ellie here. When you've a minute? It may be nothing, but the charity may be getting dragged into the matter of that student falling out of a window at one of our properties. Also, I'd like to check with someone about what's happening at Walker & Price. Again, it's charity business. Now we're back, you must come round for supper one evening. It would be lovely to see you again.'

Ellie switched off and yawned again. She'd done all she could for the time being.

Thomas was still on the phone, chatting away, laughing at some funny story he was being told. He took the phone away from his ear long enough to say, 'You look tired. Go up and have forty winks. I'll wake you with a cuppa at four.'

She didn't like being shoved into the OAP category, but she was still suffering from jet lag and had to admit that, under certain circumstances, and not to be indulging herself in every day, getting on in life had its compensations. So up she went, remembering to take her own smartphone with her. Not that she'd ever get used to all the things it could do, but there, it would be worse having to try to get off the bed and get to a landline if it rang while she was snoozing.

Which is what it did. Peremptorily. Half an hour after she'd laid down on her bed. She heard her smartphone ring.

She groped for it, and at the second try managed to make contact.

Lesley Millard. 'Ellie, what do you know about Walker & Price?' Her tone was sharp.

'Er, not much. I went there . . . when was it . . .? Er, Wednesday afternoon? No, Thursday. I think it was Thursday. I was horrified by what's happening there, but I don't suppose you've had anything to do with it. I mean, it's not murder. Hate mail and vandalism. Not your usual line of work. But I was wondering—'

'You were there on Thursday? What time? Did you see both partners? Wait a minute. What's the time? Are you at home? I'll pop over. Half an hour, right?'

Ellie managed to sit upright. 'What? Why? Has something happened?'

'Mr Walker was found dead this morning. So what do you know about that?'

Ellie gaped.

Lesley clicked off her phone.

Thomas came into the room, with a mug of tea. 'Someone on the phone?'

'Lesley. Mr Walker's been found dead. I saw him and his partner yesterday morning and he was perfectly all right, then. No, he wasn't all right. He was in pieces, didn't know if he were coming or going, but . . . Lesley's coming round. If she's involved . . . does that mean he was murdered?'

'You've got murder on the brain. He was an elderly man, wasn't he? I've been asking around. Nobody had a word to say against him or his partner. They dealt fairly and didn't try to rip off their customers. I think the bulk of their business was management of properties rather than buying and selling. They had a good reputation at that, too. A bit old-fashioned, relied on being part of the community. They've recently taken on a youngster who did Twitter and all that for them but their clientele doesn't go much for social media, although they acknowledge it's necessary to keep up with the times.'

Ellie said, 'Yes.' She was in shock. She held the mug of tea in both hands. She told herself that elderly men do keel over and expire. She told herself that his death was bound to be due to natural causes.

She shivered. 'He was fragile. That agency was his life's work. He was respected, you say. His poor cousin! That's his partner, Mrs Price. She was holding the business together, while he'd more or less given up. What will she do now?'

'Sell up, I suppose,' said Thomas. 'Didn't you say they'd had an offer?'

Ellie sighed. 'I suppose that's what will happen. Where does that leave the charity? Are we tied to the new lot when they take over?' She shook her head. 'Kate and Stewart will know what to do.'

The front doorbell rang. Lesley?

'I'll go,' said Thomas. 'She'll need a cuppa.' Thomas believed that tea and a shoulder to cry on solved most problems.

Ellie thought he was probably right about that.

Down they went to let Lesley in and to migrate to the kitchen where Thomas put the kettle on, found the biscuit tin and left them to it while he made a phone call in his study.

Detective Inspector Millard was in her late thirties by now. She'd married unwisely, lived to regret it and was in the process of divorcing her sports-mad husband. Having walked out of the flat they'd bought together, she was now renting one of the units in Rafael's apartment block.

Lesley had walked around like a zombie while she'd been worrying about the state of her marriage, but was bouncing back very well. In fact, she was now zizzing with energy.

'What do you know, Ellie? When did you go there, and what happened? You don't mind if I record your testimony, do you?'

Ellie drew in a sharp breath. 'So it was murder! I can't believe it, but you wouldn't be wanting to record my testimony if he'd died of natural causes . . . would you?'

SEVEN

Friday afternoon

Lesley wasn't wasting time or words. 'I can't answer that. Come on, Ellie. When did you last see Mr Walker?'

'Thursday. I think. It was Wednesday, wasn't it, that I collected Evan from school and on the way I saw that the window had been broken at Walker & Price? A mother who was also collecting her child from school told me that she'd seen someone graffitiing the window the week before, but of course Thomas and I weren't even in this country then.'

'Who was she? Why didn't she report it? Name, please.'

'Oh dear. I can't remember. She did tell me. Lee? No, Lily. She was from Hong Kong. She gave me her details and I gave them to Susan because the children had taken a shine to one another and they're going to have one another for tea. Lily didn't report the graffiti to the police when it happened – and I don't even know which day it was, but I suppose it might have been Wednesday. You'd have to check that with her.

'The position was that Lily was in the bakery and saw someone drawing up on a motorbike outside Walker & Price.

Lily said the person was all in black and the bike was black, too. He or she – yes, it might have been a she – got off the bike, sprayed a word on the window, got back on the bike before anyone realized what was happening and drove off. I did ask Lily if she'd got the registration number but she said it was too far away and happened so quickly. I believe Walker & Price reported the incident and the online hate mail and phone calls they'd been receiving but they didn't think the police were doing much about it.'

Lesley looked grim. 'It didn't become my case till this morning. So you didn't see anything yourself?'

'I called on Walker & Price on Thursday morning in connection with the letting of a house belonging to the charity. Now that's another matter. Did you deal with the case of the student who died when he fell off a balcony? If it wasn't you, do you know who did?'

Lesley's shoulders twitched. 'That? No, that wasn't my case, though I heard about it. Statements were taken from everyone at the party and there was an autopsy. Too much drink and drugs, some pushing and shoving. He fell. No one confessed to supplying drugs and none were found on the premises. Verdict: accident. No one to blame. Case closed.'

She twitched her shoulders again and looked away from Ellie. 'My boss is on some committee or other with the leader of the council. Not that I sense corruption in any way. Not at all. There is absolutely no evidence to suggest that the young man's unfortunate death should have been dealt with in any other way. The coroner was quite clear about that.'

Ellie blinked. She tried to work out what Lesley was not saying. 'You heard that someone on the council has been making sure the verdict was accidental death? You mean that it might otherwise have been treated as manslaughter?'

'No, no. Absolutely nothing like that. One of the councillors had ties to the lad's family. He knew that the victim's family was in pieces. He merely observed that it would help the lad's mother to recover if she were assured there was nothing untoward about her son's death. The councillor concerned was one of those quiet men who do a lot of good in the community and are generally held in respect. But the fact of the matter is that there was nothing whatever to indicate foul play.'

Lesley is referring to the Hallett family. Remember what Patsy said, Brandon died, and Jocelyn was called home to deal with distraught relatives.

Lesley had got the point across, hadn't she? The Halletts, rightly or wrongly, had exercised their influence to bury the case.

Ellie said, 'I smelled cannabis on the top floor, even all this time afterwards. Did you not find out who brought the drugs in?'

'We couldn't track down all the partygoers. You know how it is on these occasions. Someone posts online that there's a party at such and such an address and all sorts turn up. No one knows how many but probably a couple of dozen, if not more. There was no guest list, and everyone except the students fled the place before the police arrived. True; one of the party-goers might have brought cannabis to the party and given it to Brandon, but we couldn't find anyone who admitted to having done so. We searched the premises and nothing was found.'

You didn't find anything because the remaining students scoured the premises to ensure the place was clean.

Lesley said, 'There was a stupid tussle and he fell. Best leave the matter alone. If someone starts asking questions now, then the authorities might be looking into the safety issue. Was that balustrade not high enough? A case might be made out that the charity had not done their work properly and prosecution might follow.'

Ellie got it, in spades. 'You are trying to tell me that if anyone is stupid enough to ask questions now the spotlight would be turned on the charity, who might then be accused of negligence.'

Lesley nodded. 'No one wants that, do they?'

Ellie said, 'I could scream. The council signed off on the work done at the house, and I saw for myself that the balustrade was high enough to prevent all but the determined from climbing over it.'

'Yes. But, once the papers get hold of the possibility of poor maintenance, there could be a long and damaging investigation. I'm told that the lad's mother is not well off. There's no father in sight. So she might well think she could make some money by suing the charity.'

Ellie bit her lip. 'And Brandon's death is swept under the carpet?'

Lesley shrugged. 'All done and dusted. Now, when did you last see Mr Walker?'

'Thursday morning. A possible conflict of interests had arisen. Rafael is a trustee of the charity, and in a separate matter had contracted Walker & Price to manage the lettings at his own block of flats. He'd been satisfied with what they'd done for him, so he recommended the charity use them in future. This particular house was the first of ours to be handed over to the agency, and they had let it in the usual way. No problems, until Brandon's unfortunate death.

'After that the students left the house, hoping that the incident meant they could break their lease. Only, gradually, they realized it wasn't as simple as that and began to return. Walker & Price were trying to sort the problem out when they began to be targeted by negative publicity of all sorts. Because of this, the charity is having to consider whether it is right to continue to use them. It has been suggested we transfer to another agency.'

'So . . .?'

Ellie held up her hands and let them fall. 'Rafael wants to back Walker & Price, the other trustees disagree. I wanted to see for myself what the agency was like and found the partners in disarray, bombarded with hate mail, abusive phone calls, packages with nasty contents . . . and then the last straw was the smashing of the window. It looked to me as if Walker & Price might go under. Another agency had already offered to buy them out and the partners were considering the offer.'

'Thursday afternoon? You saw them both?'

'I left about teatime. I'm not sure when, exactly. I had a lot to think about. I walked home, nearly walked into a bus, not looking where I was going. I got a taxi home. Thomas was babysitting Fifi while Susan took Jenny to the dentist. I expect Susan can give you a better idea of what time that would be. Or Thomas.'

Ellie winced. Could her absent-mindedness give Lesley the impression that Ellie was an unreliable witness?

Lesley sat back in her chair with a sigh. 'So it would be mid-afternoon when you left? He was alive then?'

'Oh yes. Of course.'

'And Mrs Price was, too?'

'Definitely. I got the impression that she still had some reserves of strength to deal with the issue, but that he probably hadn't.'

'And their employee?'

'I don't think he was there. No, he wasn't. Mrs Price told me he was out on a job somewhere. I had seen him the day before, though. He was putting out chairs so that no one would get too near the shards of glass that were falling from the smashed window. May I ask what happened to Mr Walker?'

'Mrs Price and their employee left by the front door at half past five, leaving Mr Walker at his desk going through some paperwork. He'd stayed on because a client had promised to ring with a decision about buying a house that afternoon.

'Mrs Price tried to ring him that evening to discuss the future but he didn't pick up and she left a message. This morning she got there well before nine and opened up. There was no sign of him. Their young trainee followed her in, noticed a draught from the back door and found it hanging open. Mr Walker was lying in the yard behind the shops, dead. The door into the alleyway at the back of the shops had been forced open. The young man called the police and collapsed.'

Ellie drew in a long breath. 'You think someone tried to break in through the back gate after hours, thinking the shop was empty? That he disturbed Mr Walker, who was still working? You think Mr Walker went out to see what the noise was and got killed?'

'Looks like it. There's a builder's skip round the corner with all sorts of rubble in it; balks of timber, metal struts, broken bricks; you name it. All useful stuff for breaking into locked premises. The petty cash box was gone. Nothing else. It was in the top drawer of Mrs Price's desk. She was in such a state when she left work the previous night that she can't remember whether she locked her desk or not.'

'Do you know when Mr Walker died?'

'No. We've been doing house to house. After six o'clock the shops on either side would have been closed and the personnel gone home.'

'There are flats above . . .'

'Too early for people to be home from work. We did find a couple of people in, but they said they hadn't heard anything or seen anything unusual.'

'An opportunist burglar? Disturbed on the job?'

'Looks like it. That's what my boss thinks. There's been all that media interest, the hate mail, the graffiti, the smashed window. It looks as if a local yob thought he could break in and spot if there was any petty cash to lift.'

'I don't believe it,' said Ellie.

Lesley grinned. 'I'm not sure I do, either, but that's the official line. Look, give me something to go on. Otherwise . . .'

Ellie couldn't. 'The connection with Rafael . . . No, that can't be anything to do with it. As for the charity . . . No, no! Oh, this is impossible.'

'The connection with Rafael,' said Lesley, her grin disappearing. 'Tell me what you know.'

Ellie saw where this was leading and didn't like it, not one bit. 'He used their services, and so did the charity. He was all for backing Walker & Price. There's no other connection that I can see.'

'A quarrel about Walker & Price selling out? A disagreement about payment of commission? A tussle ending in an unfortunate death?'

Ellie was horrified. 'You think Rafael . . .? No, no! That's just not . . .!'

'No, of course it's ridiculous! Do you think I want it to be anything? I'm thinking of Susan—'

'You weren't thinking of him in connection with the death when you came here.'

Lesley flopped back in her chair. 'No, I wasn't. And yes, it is ridiculous. But now you've told me there was a connection, I can't ignore it, can I?'

Ellie shook her head. 'No, you can't. And you're warning me that if I interfere in any way, you will have to turn the

spotlight on Rafael because there's no one else in the frame
except your make-believe opportunist burglar, whom I don't
believe in and neither do you.'

Lesley said, 'We shouldn't be having this conversation, I
ought not to have told you as much as I have. The next thing
will be my having to ask you where you were after closing
time at Walker & Price yesterday evening.'

Ellie blinked. And tried to think. 'Thursday. Last night. Well,
I came home. I talked to Rafael about his interests in the flats
and Walker & Price. Then Thomas and I had supper and went
to bed. And that's it, really. How did Mr Walker die?'

'Can't tell you that.'

Ellie filled in the gap. 'You think he was hit with something
taken from the skip round the corner? What are you doing
about it? You said you'd done door to door. Checking to see
if any local criminals were seen locally? Enquiring about
the drug addicts to see if anyone was particularly short of
cash?'

Lesley nodded. 'All of that. Nothing so far. Early days. We
haven't got the autopsy report yet. That might help. Whoever
did it either wore gloves or wiped up after him.'

'You say "him". I wonder . . . That nice young mother, Lily,
the one from Hong Kong, thought the person on the motorbike
who graffitied the window a week ago might have been a girl,
because they were slender and not too tall. Could a girl have
done this?'

'I suppose so, if she were desperate. But why would a girl
who owned a motorbike want to rob the agency?'

Ellie said, 'Drugs? No. Druggies don't usually care about
togging themselves up in all the gear and riding a motorbike.
They'd sell the gear and the motorbike to feed their habit. I
don't think it can have been her. It must be some chance
burglar, or someone looking for what he can pick up. He must
have been disturbed by Mr Walker and a tussle ensued.
That fits the bill nicely,' said Ellie, 'and I still don't believe a
word of that. Do you?'

Lesley winced. 'The boss says it's a cut-and-dried case, that
we may never discover which of our local layabouts was
involved.'

'And you're not going to reopen the case of the student Brandon who died? No, I suppose not. In any case, I don't think any of the students own a motorbike.'

Ellie thought of the girl Patsy, who'd shown them around the students' house. Patsy definitely didn't have a motorbike. She had a bicycle. She'd said so. What about Mona, and the boy who was returning to the house? Imran? Was that his name? Did he own a motorbike? And if he did, where did he keep it? Not in the house, that's for sure. In the garden shed? A possibility. Should Ellie suggest it?

Lesley said, 'That case is closed. The students are off limits.'

Ellie hissed between her teeth. 'Are they? Oh. Lesley, if there's nothing wrong with the verdict of accident, then that's one thing, but if someone's pulling strings to make sure it's not questioned, then that's another. Somebody's son or daughter has been caught up in this mess and you're trying to tell me that they are to be protected at all costs? Let me guess. It's not Patsy; her parents live in Wales and she does some tutoring to make ends meet. Her friend Mona? Her parents live not too far away but there's a lot of them crammed in a small house so ditto; they haven't the influence we're talking about here.'

Lesley half smiled. 'I couldn't possibly comment. Go on.'

'Imran? No. He has the smallest room and pays the least rent. His background is not right for this because he's strapped for cash or he'd have a better room. Terry? No. He's got a girlfriend who lives locally and acts as if he were her property. No, the connection must be with Brandon, the lad who died. He didn't fit in with the rest. He sounds an unpleasant character, who made trouble where he could and didn't help with the washing up. His room has been cleared out carefully and conscientiously but even now it stinks of cannabis.'

'Dear me.' Lesley sat back in her chair. 'Go on.'

'It's Jocelyn, isn't it? Jocelyn was the leader of the pack. He organized the students into moving into that house. Brandon was his cousin, included only under pressure from his family. It doesn't sound as if they were on good terms. Jocelyn had the best of the rooms. He's the one who led the move out, and who told the others the rent had been paid. Only, he hasn't collected their share from the others, and they still face paying for utility bills and so on. Jocelyn has all the earmarks of a spoiled rich kid. It must be his father who plays golf with the high-ups, and it's he who's put the kybosh on any in-depth enquiry into Brandon's death. Am I right?'

A hesitation. 'Honestly, I think it was an accident.'

'Apart from the cannabis?'

'No, because of it. And because no one had a reason to want the lad dead.' Lesley gathered herself together and stood up. 'I think you're right in the case of Mr Walker even though there is a link – a very slight link – with the letting of the students' house.'

She drifted over to the window saying, 'I was assigned to the case of Mr Walker's death this morning. I conducted the first interviews with Mrs Price and the junior colleague, whose name is Archie, by the way. I organized door-to-door questioning and did the first two or three interviews myself. Then I was rung up and told not to waste police resources on what had been decided to be a street crime. Some piece of local shit set out to burgle the place without realizing Mr Walker was still on the premises and ended up hitting him a little too hard. The death will be dealt with exactly as it ought to be. Someone in the underworld will talk and we'll get the perpetrator in due course.'

Ellie swallowed some hasty words. Some years ago, she'd come up against a detective inspector with no manners and ears which turned bright red when he was under stress. Not knowing his name, she's referred to him as 'Ears'. The nickname had caught on. He'd been furious about it, vowing to get Ellie for something, anything, that he could possibly find. Rumour said he hadn't yet forgiven or forgotten.

'Ears' was now Lesley's boss. Any time Lesley brought up Ellie's name, it would be like flaunting a red rag to a bull.

Lesley spoke to the window. 'If Ears could pin something on you or the charity, he would. Meanwhile, I'm to be put on another high-profile job which has just come in. I was on my way back for a debrief to the station when you phoned, and I came here to see what you had to say. You understand why I can't take the matter any further.'

A very rude word popped into Ellie's mind, but she managed to suppress it.

Lesley tapped on the window. 'Your garden looks a bit of a mess.'

Ellie forced herself to say, 'Three children on the rampage. What do you expect? Susan is very apologetic. I'll get round to dealing with it soon.'

Lesley produced a social smile. 'Of course you will. You have green fingers. And the children have loved romping around out there, but the park's not far away and I expect they can let off steam there in future.'

She looked at her watch. 'I won't be mentioning that I visited you in connection with Mr Walker's death. You understand?'

'Only too clearly. Let me translate. You personally might have liked to investigate the death of Brandon more thoroughly but have been prevented from doing so by someone important pulling strings. Ditto the matter of Mr Walker's death. You can't do anything about it, so you've handed the nightmare scenario over to me to deal with, while warning me to be very, very careful whom I offend.'

'I couldn't possibly comment.'

Ellie gritted her teeth. 'What do you expect me to achieve? Am I supposed to kill Goliath and rebuild the temple before supper? I can't make bricks without straw.'

She'd mixed up three Bible stories there, but who cared?

Lesley remarked that the afternoon was brightening up and she hoped it wouldn't rain again till she got back to the station.

The sun had indeed come out. A rather weak sun. Ellie waved Lesley off and went to find Thomas. Her head was full of queries and doubts.

She found him on the phone in his den, chatting away to someone. Ellie took a chair and waited for him to finish. She told herself to calm down. Thomas would speak to her as soon as he could. A neat list of names and addresses was in front of him on a pad of A4 paper. He was talking to someone about Walker & Price? Perhaps he had found out something to help?

At last he put the phone down, looking pleased with himself. 'The local grapevine is a wonderful institution. I only had to contact one of my old parishioners who'd downsized locally to be given the names of other people who had bought or sold recently and what their experiences had been.

'There are three votes for Walker & Price; solid and honest, would recommend them to anyone. Five votes against Streetwise for being slick salesmen who would promise anything to get you signed up but overestimate the price you should get for your property and then have to reduce and reduce it to get a sale. Most annoying. Is that what you wanted to know?'

'I suppose so. Had they heard of the recent bad press that Walker & Price had been getting?'

Thomas consulted his list. 'Two said they had heard of it but didn't understand it. They thought maybe standards were slipping because Walker & Price had taken on this young chap who maybe wasn't best suited to work in the old way but was being seduced by the bright lights and flashy cars of the newer agencies. My contacts trust the old folk but didn't seem to like the youngster much.'

'Archie,' said Ellie. 'His name is Archie, and it was he who found Mr Walker dead, early this morning.'

Thomas looked at her, long and hard. 'Dead? I see. That was Lesley's car outside, wasn't it? What did she want?'

'She's been told officially that Mr Walker's death was the result of an opportunist burglar who found the old man still there after the time when he was supposed to have closed the shop and gone home. The police inquiry into his death will be confined to looking for the usual suspects, local layabouts, drug addicts, and so on.

'Lesley acknowledges there is a possible link between Walker & Price and the student Brandon's death but thinks that it is not worth bothering about. She informs me that her boss had been contacted by someone who sits on a committee with an important person who was pushing the accidental verdict for the student's death to save the boy's family from further grief. Lesley hinted that there might be a focus on Walker & Price's arrangements with Rafael and the charity unless we accept the official view.'

'She's passing the buck to you? Hoping you'll continue digging where she can't? That's blackmail.'

'Of sorts,' Ellie agreed.

They contemplated the problem.

Ellie became conscious that for some moments there'd been a thudding noise at the back of the house. The noise hadn't stopped, so she went to investigate. The banging was coming from the empty conservatory. Someone was trying to open the door from there into the hall.

Finally the door crashed open and a small procession appeared led by young Evan, fair-haired and solid, holding tiny Fifi by her hand. He said, 'Fifi got upset.'

Fifi didn't look upset. She looked as if she'd just been roused from sleep and wasn't sure which end was up. She was clutching her rather dilapidated Gonk in one hand. She released herself from Evan, stumbled forward to the nearest pair of legs, raised her arms above her head and said, 'Up!'

Ellie picked her up, and the child relaxed back into sleep.

Behind Evan came Jenny, who was holding her tablet, as usual. She went to Thomas. 'Where's telly?' Jenny did love her television, but there was none in the den.

Thomas picked her up and gave her a cuddle. 'What have you got on your tablet?' She showed him.

Midge the cat stalked in, worked out that no one had a lap to spare, jumped up on to the windowsill to sit in the watery sun and give himself a quick sprucing up.

Evan latched on to Ellie's leg and said, low down, 'They're shouting.'

'Ah,' said Ellie, moving Fifi into the crook of her arm so that she could put her free arm around the boy. 'You are a brave boy.'

'Fifi doesn't like it when they shout.'

Fifi actually didn't seem to care much, but Evan did.

Ellie said, 'Shall we have tea in our kitchen today?'

Evan confided, 'I wanted to go to Lin's house after school but Daddy said no, he couldn't be bothered to come out again to fetch me. I like Lin and I like his mummy and it would be nice and quiet there.'

If Susan and Rafael were having a row next door, then it was best for the children to make themselves scarce. Ellie tried to think what she could give them for their tea. Eggs? Chipolata sausages cut into two or three? Spaghetti Hoops followed by fruit in yoghurt, perhaps?

'Let's see what we've got for tea, shall we?'

Tea was chaotic, as they had no highchairs. Fifi sat on Thomas' knee which meant he couldn't help with the others. Jenny upset her cup of milk, and Ellie wasn't sure whether it was an accident or on purpose. However, it was second nature for Thomas and Ellie to deal with small children, so they fed them and then washed hands and faces. After that they read books and let the children sit in front of the telly to watch a suitable programme.

At long last Susan arrived; also by way of the garden and the conservatory. All three children ran to her for a hug and a kiss when she appeared, and all three spoke at once to tell her what they'd eaten and what books they'd been looking at. Susan looked flushed and heavy-eyed, and apologized profusely for her brood's presence.

Ellie and Thomas said it was nothing and they'd enjoyed it. But, after the hordes had departed, they didn't exactly admit to one another that they were not as young as they had been but they did decide to have a light supper, watch something mindless on the telly and call it a day.

EIGHT

Friday bedtime

Getting into bed, Thomas said, 'Do you know, I miss my own grandchildren but I didn't think about them at all this afternoon. Evan is a little soldier, isn't he? He sized up the situation and removed his siblings from danger. My heart goes out to him.'

'Jenny is so edgy. I see my daughter Diana in her, even though Jenny and Evan are as fair haired as she is dark. But I remember that Diana never listened to me. I loved her. I ached for her to love me, but she didn't seem capable of doing so. It was her father's influence, I suppose. He was always wanting more money, more kudos, more of everything.

He wasn't easy to live with but I did love him and he loved me in his own way.'

'You told me he'd had had a loveless childhood. People who've been brought up without love find it difficult to show it to others.'

'I know. I tried to show Diana love but she wasn't interested. She only wanted things. Expensive things. Money, money, money. She was never satisfied, whatever I did or said. I felt myself tighten up when she came near me, because she was only interested in me for what I could give her while at the same time criticising me for being slow and stupid.'

'You are neither.'

She tried to smile. 'Fine words butter no parsnips. I wish I'd been able to work out how to help her. She was never happy. She's always chasing a rainbow, but never finding the pot of gold at the end of it. I think Evan's going to be all right, but I see Diana in Jenny all the time.'

'Evan is a sunny soul and a natural leader. He gives affection to those around him and receives it in return. Jenny sees this and is tormented by the fear that no one will ever love her as Evan is loved. Don't worry that she's going to turn out like Diana. Remember that all three children ran to Susan when she arrived. She loves them unconditionally, and they love her. Maybe it's my job for the foreseeable future to help Jenny adjust to family life. To love her and build up her self-esteem. She's as bright as a button. I can see I'll have to hustle to keep up with her.'

Ellie nestled within his arm. 'You're a good man, Thomas.'

'Yes, yes. Meantime you'll deal with Susan and Rafael, sort out what's wrong there and find out who's responsible for Mr Walker's death.'

'If Lesley can't do anything, I don't see what I can do.'

'You'll think of something, I'll be your Dr Watson and do what I can to help.'

Saturday morning

No school. No nursery. The children were turned out to play in the garden. Thomas offered to keep an eye out for them while Ellie trundled off to the shops to buy one or two things.

She loved her grandchildren. Of course she did. But she was relieved to have left them behind as she walked along to the Avenue. She noted in passing that there were no lights on inside Walker & Price, and that there was a notice on the door saying they were temporarily closed, please ring such and such a number. Not surprising, really.

As she walked along, Ellie was stopped by various acquaintances who said they were delighted to see her back, and had she heard about the ructions in the Avenue? Yes, Mr Walker had been killed by some lout who'd tried to burgle the place, would you ever believe it, in this quiet neighbourhood?

Yes, Ellie would believe it. She gathered from local gossip that people thought this would be the end of Walker & Price, so sad, but the new people would be all into the latest notions which was not perhaps quite what the locals were used to but there, we have to move with the times, don't we?

Ellie wasn't thinking of using them, was she? In which case, Ellie should know that the number on the door went straight through to that young man of theirs, who was probably perfectly all right in his way, but it wasn't the same as dealing with Mr Walker, or indeed, with Mrs Price, was it?

Ellie nodded and agreed. She went to have a coffee in her favourite café and was pleased to see that they remembered her after all this time. They were delighted to see her back and would she like her usual? Which she would, indeed. It was very pleasant to live in a neighbourhood where you were known and your likes and dislikes remembered.

She got out Walker & Price's card and rang Mrs Price's mobile number.

Mrs Price did answer. She sounded ten years older than when Ellie had seen her a couple of days before.

Yes, Mrs Price could find time to meet with Ellie. It would be about the contract for the student house, wouldn't it? Ellie did understand that she, Mrs Price was hardly able to think constructively at the moment.

Ellie said she understood and didn't like to intrude but she was at the shops at that moment, and Mrs Price could hardly be feeling up to doing any shopping so was there anything Ellie could get for her?

Mrs Price broke down then and wept. But didn't break the connection.

Ellie waited, drank her coffee, looked at her watch and waited for Mrs Price to mop herself up.

At last Mrs Price mastered her voice. She said that Ellie was too kind but perhaps some breakfast teabags, the sort for hard water and a loaf of wholemeal bread from the bakery, sliced? Otherwise, she could manage. Did Ellie know where Mrs Price lived? She gave the address. Not far away.

Ellie finished her shopping with some strong cheese from the deli. She waved to a couple of people she knew but didn't stop to talk to them.

Mrs Price lived two roads along and up the hill, at the end of a cul-de-sac of three-bedroomed detached houses. Like the others, her house had a gabled roof, the front garden had been laid to lawn and there was a drive at the side occupied by a mid-range car. There was probably an extension out back for an enlarged kitchen.

A couple of passers-by showed some interest as Ellie went to the front door. Word had got around.

Ellie rang the bell and wondered what Mr Walker's place had been like. Was there a wife, children and grandchildren?

Mrs Price opened the door and ushered Ellie inside. The hall was dark but light streamed in through from the kitchen at the back which yes, had been extended in the modern fashion.

Ellie handed over her purchases and Mrs Price made tea. Mrs Price was in mufti, a baggy blue-and-white T-shirt over a navy denim skirt. The skin around her eyes was bloated from crying, her hair was a mess but she still attempted to play the hostess. She lumbered around, not quite 'with it'. A headache? She found the biscuit tin and opened it. It was empty. She apologized. 'I don't know what's the matter with me.'

Ellie said that a cuppa was all she wanted.

Mrs Price put two sugars in her tea and stirred it. She took a sip and then pushed the mug away from her, saying she never took sugar in her tea, and what was she thinking of?

Ellie patted her hand. 'Are you alone in the house?' Lesley hadn't mentioned whether or not Mrs Price had any family.

'Yes. I mean, no. I mean, my husband died last year and my daughter moved to New Zealand. I have one close friend nearby. She came round when she heard, but she's had to go back to her place to deal with the washing machine man who's due to make a service call. She said she'll come back as soon as he's finished. I rather wish she wouldn't, but she insists. She talks. You know?'

'I know. But perhaps it's good for you to have someone to make sure you eat and drink properly.' Ellie took Mrs Price's mug, emptied it in the sink, rinsed it and gave her another cuppa. No sugar.

Mrs Price managed a weak smile. 'Thank you. I'm sorry, I'm so . . . it was the shock, you see. I had to identify him. Closest relative nearby. Poor Charles. He was always so careful of his appearance and now . . . They say it was quick. I held it together. At least, I think I did. Then they said they'd send me home in one of their cars and I was pleased about that, because I think I'd have crashed my car if I'd tried to drive.

'I'm trying to think what needs to be done. Did I ring his son? Yes, I did that. I contacted my daughter as well. I thought she might come back for a few days, but of course she couldn't leave her job. It was stupid of me to think she could.'

Ellie nodded. When families lived that far apart, they couldn't leap to the rescue overnight. 'Did you get anything to eat?'

'Eat? No. I had a bottle of wine left over from . . . When did I last have someone over for supper? Yes, I remember. It was Charles, and he brought me some and I . . . I'm ashamed to say I finished it off in bed.'

A hangover, on top of shock and grief. 'You need aspirin?'

A faint smile. 'I did take some. I got up this morning and . . . Well, yes. Aspirin. But I still can't think straight. My name's Nancy, by the way.'

'I'm Ellie. Drink up.'

Nancy nodded, and did as she was told.

Ellie looked around. You can tell a lot about someone from looking at their kitchen. Ellie knew that empty worktops, immaculately clean, meant ready meals were the order of the day. Here there were a few dishes in the sink, a dishwasher left open, a slight disorder of used cutlery. A couple of used pans soaking in the sink. A well-used chopping block, a stand of spices.

There was a large fridge/freezer which meant Nancy probably did her own cooking. A geranium in full flower was on the windowsill and Ellie caught a glimpse of a tidy garden through French windows. Full of roses and not much sign of blackspot.

Ellie concluded that Nancy Price was normally well-organized and catered for herself with no sign of Alzheimer's.

There was a large box of tissues on the table. Ellie pushed it towards her hostess who took one, used it and apologized for breaking down. 'It's not like me. Usually I rise above things but this is . . . Must pull myself together. You've been very good. You've come about the charity. Of course. You'll want to know where this leaves the student house in the future and I'm sure we'll still be able to . . . but perhaps you'll want to change things now? I'm not sure. I'll have to look at the paperwork.'

Ellie said, 'No need to worry about that now.' *I must check with Stewart what our contract is like with them.*

Nancy pulled her top straight over her shoulders and ran her fingers back through her hair. 'I'm not quite sure how we're fixed. I mean, Charles and I did make our wills, years ago, leaving the business to one another, so I suppose . . . I don't think he's altered his, and I certainly haven't altered mine, though now I suppose I'll have to do so.

'If I'm right and I inherit Charles' share of the agency, then I can assure you that we will honour all our commitments. Young Archie has been hinting that we ought to take him into the partnership and he's bright enough but perhaps . . . Charles wasn't keen and I did have some reservations, but there, he's young and responsibility might settle him down. He's a good lad, really. He said he'd go in, see to the post, keep the agency running . . .'

But he hadn't, had he? The shop is closed. Do I tell her that? No, I think not.

Nancy blew her nose again. Her voice was thick. 'Charles had been talking about retiring next year. I keep thinking of how much he'd been looking forward to that. He was going to sell his house here and move to a smaller place near his son on the south coast. We'd had an offer for the business but it wasn't a good one and we were going to look around and . . . Why am I bothering you with our troubles?'

The doorbell rang. Nancy jumped a mile and knocked her mug on to the floor. There wasn't much liquid in it, but the crash broke the handle off.

Nancy gasped. 'My favourite . . .! Oh, no! But it's just the handle, isn't it? I've got some superglue somewhere; I know I have.' She got to her feet. She was shaking. 'Where did I put it? In the drawer under the sink? I know I used it last week for something!'

The doorbell rang again, sharply.

Nancy dithered. 'I don't know who that could be. Oh, maybe it's my friend from up the road. But no, she has a key. I did give her a key, didn't I?' She set off for the hall, calling out, 'Coming!'

Ellie wondered if she should leave. She got up from the table, looking around for her handbag, which she must have put down somewhere. A murmur of voices and Mrs Price returned with a tall, well-built young man; Archie, from the agency, armed with a folder. So he definitely wasn't keeping the agency open as promised.

Instead of leaving, Ellie picked up the mug and the handle from the floor and looked for the superglue in the kitchen drawers.

The newcomer glanced at Ellie and glanced away. Young men don't take any notice of older women, do they? Particularly one in an ancient blue shirt and skirt.

She knew him, all right, but he didn't know her from Adam. Or Eve.

In a tone of complete disinterest, he said, 'Glad you've got someone in to help you. She can be the second witness to your signature.'

Perhaps he thought Ellie was Nancy's cleaner? He had a rich, plummy voice. Private school? Moneyed background? Or someone who'd learned how to speak like it?

Nancy rubbed her forehead. 'What? Yes, she's been lovely.

But Archie, I don't think . . . Oh, do sit down. You're looming over me. Is everything all right at the agency? Something's happened? More vandalism? Did you bring the mail with you? Oh, sorry. My manners! Do you want a cuppa or something?'

'No, no.' He took Nancy's arm and guided her back to her chair. 'Sit down, Nancy. I'm in charge today, remember?' He took a seat beside Nancy, presenting his profile to Ellie. A good-looking lad.

Ellie wondered why he wanted Nancy's signature, and moreover, a signature that had to be witnessed? Ellie found the superglue. She washed the mug, angling herself so that she had a good view of what was happening at the table.

Archie bared his teeth in a false smile. 'Well, Nance, I can see this has knocked you for six. But, tell the truth, it's been a while since you've really been on top of things, right?'

Nancy took a tissue and used it on her eyes. 'It's been a bad couple of months, hasn't it?'

'And you're not getting any younger.' Archie held up a mina-tory finger. 'You did your best. I know that. Charles knew that, too. He would have bowed to the inevitable and sold out long ago if he hadn't relied on you to do double the work. That's true, isn't it?'

Ellie dried both surfaces and glued the handle back on to the mug.

Nancy said, 'Yes, he did talk about retirement. You remember that weekend he went down to Hastings and saw a flat he raved about . . .' She started to laugh. 'Until he realized there were no car parking spaces. The idea of Charles walking anywhere, instead of getting into his Jag! Oh, oh. I don't know how I can laugh when . . .' She sniffed and took another tissue. 'Ah well. At least his dying now means he doesn't have to give up his Jag. That really would have been the end for him.'

'Indeed.' Archie's rich voice sympathized. 'But he's gone. Much regretted. Poor old man. And somehow, the rest of us have to carry on. The world keeps turning on, day after day.'

Nancy said, 'I know. It's hard. I don't think I can face it yet.'

'That's where I come in, Nance.' He patted her hand.

Ellie ran the tap and started to wash up the few things that had been used. She cast sideways glances at Nancy, who was not, definitely not, up to much at the moment.

Archie turned to the folder he'd brought with him. 'So let's have a look at what we do next.'

Nancy shook her head. 'I don't really think—'

'There are some things we can't put off, Nance.'

Ellie began to dislike this young man intensely. His tone was changing from oily to harsh, revealing himself as something of a bully. Shortening Nancy's name to 'Nance' was another way of belittling her. Ellie noticed that Nancy hadn't like it, either. She'd blinked and removed her hand from under his.

Nancy said, 'Not today, Archie.'

'Yes, today. If we want the agency to survive, we have to act quickly. Rumours get around. The value of the property diminishes with every hour. The scandal has done us so much harm already and if we're not careful the student's family may decide to sue and take you for everything you've got.'

Ellie's hands stilled. This was an echo of what Lesley Millard had been saying. Someone, somewhere, was pulling strings to make sure the case of the student's death would be closed and kept that way. So why was Archie bringing it up now?

Nancy gasped. 'Don't say that! That's . . . awful! We did everything correctly, I swear it. The work was signed off by the town hall and—'

'Corruption, my dear Nance. It is being said that you bribed the inspector to—'

Nancy pushed back her chair. 'No! No, we didn't! We couldn't! You know we didn't! Has the world gone mad?'

'My dear Nance, you are being naïve. Such things are being done all the time. No need to pretend with me.'

'It's not pretence! Archie, I don't understand. Charles and I have been in business all these years, we've done everything by the book, I swear all the paperwork is correct.'

'Paperwork can be falsified. You aren't a child any more. You know that.'

Nancy prepared to stand up.

Archie caught her arm and pulled her down again. 'Calm down. However bad things look now, there's always a way out. You don't want to be mixed up in this silly affair. Let us assume it was Charles who cut corners. Well, what he did, dies with him. Cut your ties to the past, and you won't have to go to court or anything like that. You can take up bridge, or go out to live with your daughter in Australia—'

'New Zealand.'

'Wherever. Walk away from the whole nasty mess and take a well-earned retirement.'

Silence. Nancy looked at Archie as if she'd never seen him before. At the third attempt to speak, Nancy said, 'You're trying to tell me that Streetwise have renewed their offer to buy the agency? But they weren't offering anything near what it's worth.'

'My dear Nance, the price has dropped to floor level now. You can't expect anything else in view of what's happened. You should be grateful they're still interested. They're going to have their work cut out to start again and build up a decent reputation.'

Nancy shuddered. 'And you, Archie? What have they offered you? Am I right in thinking they've told you there'll be a place for you in their organization?'

'Well, of course they'll keep me on. There isn't any mud sticking to my name and I know the business inside out.' He laid some papers on the table in front of Nancy. 'Here you are. Your passport to the future. Sign and walk away from the whole nasty mess. There's enough here to give you a great holiday in Australia—'

Ellie said, under her breath, 'New Zealand.'

'You might even find you like it enough out there to stay,' said Archie. 'Then you can sell this old house, which you've been saying is too big for you nowadays and buy yourself something Down Under. Isn't that what you've always dreamed of doing? Now, have you got a pen? You can borrow mine, if you like.'

Ellie held her breath. Should she intervene? Nancy was clearly in no state to make an important decision about her future.

To interfere would be to come between Archie and his prey.

An inner voice refuted that. *Oh, come on, he isn't a predator and Nancy is an adult, capable of making her own decisions.*

To which Ellie replied. *Socks to that. She isn't capable of drinking a cup of tea without dropping it at the moment. Which means, I may have to interfere. But what to say?*

Before she could decide what to do, Nancy pulled the paper-work towards her and leafed through it. And then pushed it away, saying, 'That's a ridiculous offer. It would hardly cover the air fare, and it's a fraction of what Streetwise were suggesting earlier.'

'I know. But in view of what's been happening, it's very reasonable. I don't want to see you suffer, Nancy. You've always been very kind to me, and whatever Charles has done or not done, you shouldn't have to face corruption charges at your age. I can see a police investigation lasting for months, and then the income tax people will come sniffing around, thinking you've been cheating the Inland Revenue, and the social media and then the press . . . oh, won't they have a field day!'

Nancy looked at Archie in horror. 'You think . . . but . . . that's awful!'

'I know. I understand. Selling is the only way out. I know the terms are not what you'd hoped for, but under the circumstances. Here . . . use my pen.'

He pressed it on her, but she didn't open her fingers to take it.

Ellie thought, *I've got to interfere. Nancy is in no state to make a decision about her future, but what can I say? Dear Lord above, give me the right words.*

The doorbell rang, once, sharply. The front door opened and someone called out, 'Yahoo! It's only me! You forgot to take in the milk this morning. I hope it's not gone off yet. It's going to be another warm day, and I thought that, if you were up to it, we could . . . Oh, you've got visitors?'

A little bird of a woman appeared. She was all in brown and bore a distinct resemblance to a wren. She was having difficulty managing a bulging plastic bag and two bottles of milk. She didn't look safe to carry anything.

Ellie stepped forward to take the bottles off her and put them in the fridge. The little wren let them go without making any objection.

Nancy shook her head to clear it. 'Sorry, love. This is Archie from work. Business. But I'm not really up to it. Archie, I need to think about this. And I will. Yes, I promise. But not today. You keep the office open. I'll ring you later and we'll have another talk when I'm feeling more the thing.'

Archie was not amused. There was more than a trace of temper on his face. He said, 'Look, Nance. This is important. It's really crucial that you sign this today so that we can draw a line under this whole sorry business. I want to get back to Streetwise so that they can get cracking, change the locks, get the sign painters in, advertise that Walker & Price are no more. Otherwise . . .'

The little wren chirruped up. 'What's going on? Are you going to sell up, Nance? That's a bit sudden, isn't it?'

Nancy pulled and pushed herself to her feet. She looked worn out. She said, 'Nothing's decided yet. I don't know what I'm going to do. I ought to ask my daughter, I suppose. She could do with the money, if I sell, but . . . I hadn't thought it would be so soon, and so little. Tell the truth, I'm not sure if I'm on my head or my heels. Archie; sorry about this. I know there's a lot to be done but at the moment . . . Forgive me, but I think I'd better go and lie down.'

Archie pinched in his lips. He was furious and not hiding it very well. He gathered up his papers and put them back in the folder.

Nancy balanced herself, trying to stand straight. 'Leave the papers. I'll look at them later.'

Archie said, 'Look, I'll try to screw another thousand or so out of Streetwise. You have a rest and I'll come back this evening so that we can tidy up the loose ends, right? I'll let myself out.'

He stormed off, red flags flying on his neck and chin. He did have a nasty temper, didn't he? The front door slammed shut behind him.

Nancy swayed, hand to forehead and sat down with a thump. 'Oh dear! Now what! And he's taken the papers with him.'

The little wren dumped her bags and made for the kettle. 'A cuppa will cheer you up. I brought some biscuits, too.' She looked enquiringly at Ellie. 'You work with Nancy, do you?'

'No,' said Ellie. 'Well, sort of. There's been a business deal we're involved in but I don't think she's up to it at the moment.' She dried the last of the cutlery and laid them out on the tabletop.

Nancy made it to her feet again. 'Forgive me, both of you. I think . . . Perhaps a little rest . . .'

'I'll go,' said Ellie. 'I'll leave my phone number at home so that you can call me when you feel up to it.'

The little wren darted around Nancy. 'Now don't you worry about a thing. Why don't you go on up and have a nice lie down, and I'll bring you up something to make you sleep. There may be callers, people wanting this and that, there always are after a death, but I'll stick around for a while. I've brought my Kindle and my own teabags and it'll give me a chance to catch up on the latest in the Richard & Judy book club, right? Come on, then. Up the stairs we go to Bedfordshire . . .'

Nancy lifted her hands, helplessly, and allowed herself to be taken away. Ellie let herself out of the house, making a point of closing the front door quietly behind her and walked home trying to distract herself from thinking about Nancy, and Archie, and skulduggery in general.

It was a beautiful afternoon now the sun was trying to come out. She admired the clever planting of cosmos next to Lady's Mantle in someone's front garden. Such a pleasure to look at. Her own garden was a disaster area, devoid of flowers and littered with children's playthings. But perhaps having children playing in it was as good a use for a garden as flowers?

No, it wasn't. Oh dear.

That young lad, Archie, could bear watching. A bully on the make. Had he been made an offer he couldn't refuse by Streetwise after the death of poor Mr Walker? Or, perhaps . . . No that was a really nasty thought, but perhaps it ought to be examined? How long had Archie been aware of the threat by Streetwise to the small, independent Walker & Price?

Streetwise had been pretty prompt with a reduced offer to take over Walker & Price after Charles' death, hadn't they?

One should not even think that they might have engineered the problems that had recently beset Walker & Price. No, of course not.

What a horrible thought!

Ellie wondered if this had occurred to Lesley. No, wait a

minute; Lesley hadn't been looking into the matter of the prosecution of Walker & Price. That had been someone else's problem.

Ellie turned into her driveway and felt in her pocket for her keys. There was an expensive car parked between her and the front door. Now, who . . .?

NINE

Saturday, noon

A decorative blonde was sitting in the passenger seat of the car, checking her make-up in a compact mirror, while an otherwise unremarkable, somewhat thick-set young man was pressing Ellie's front doorbell.

Ah-ha. The plot thickens. Could this be, by any chance, the disappearing Jocelyn, the leader of the gang of students who had taken the house and then opted out of paying the rent?

So . . . why was he here? Trying to flannel his way out of his debt? Hoping to enlist the sympathies of the charity for the poor, impecunious students, who'd been forced to break their lease?

Er, no. Not if that car belonged to Jocelyn.

And that raised another question. How had he found out that she was involved? Who had given out her home address? Ellie had always tried to keep business matters and home life apart from one another and this looked like business to her.

The girl in the car was busily teasing out her hair and hadn't heard Ellie approach. So she jumped when Ellie said, 'May I help you?'

'Now look what you've made me do!' The girl smoothed back her carefully disarranged mop of hair.

'What!' The man swivelled. 'Hello! Are you Mrs Quicke? Sorry to call on you like this. Mona gave me your address.'

So Mona had managed to get in touch with Jocelyn? Or he with her?

Ellie wanted to say, 'And who are you?' Though she knew,

really. This had to be Jocelyn, the soft-voiced leader of the gang, who'd led the walkout.

'I'm Jocelyn Hallett. Could you spare a few minutes?'

The blonde bombshell opened the car door and swung her legs out. Legs which went on for ever. 'And I'm Peri. It's, like, "fairy" in Persian.'

Ellie could see that Peri's studiedly casual clothes were designer gear, her hair had been dyed, her breasts had been augmented and her lips Botoxed. Her eyes were a startling blue and her gaze ingenuous.

Ellie diagnosed stupidity in a pretty package.

The man was another matter. Not particularly tall, mid-to-late-twenties. Not a pretty boy, in fact not a boy at all. He was what people used to call 'plain'. He was on the plump side, no addict of exercise. Heavy-lidded eyes, a thatch of reddish-brown hair already thinning. Brains. Oh yes, brains aplenty. Could be charming, could be cold. Young, but old as the hills.

Several things became clear to Ellie.

The first was that this man would be a good match for Patsy.

Mr Walker had said that a doctor had taken the lease on the student house and paid the rent himself. That would be Jocelyn, wouldn't it?

Patsy's comments on Jocelyn revealed that she liked and respected him. She'd refused to go on a date with him, probably wary because of Brandon's lies about his cousin? Patsy had also said that Jocelyn had got his PhD at Harvard and only returned to this country because his mother was ill.

Now, was that a weakness in him, or a strength?

Ellie dipped her head in acknowledgment. 'Dr Hallett, do come in.'

Ellie let them into the house and crossed the hall into the sitting room.

Where was Thomas? Why hadn't he answered the door to the callers?

Ah, she could hear shrieks of laughter coming from the garden. A quick glance through the windows and she saw he was playing 'cricket', bowling to Jenny who was wielding a tennis racquet with fervour, while Evan danced around, yelling, 'It's my turn!'

Ah, Saturday lunchtime. No school, and no one to cope with

three small, active children except for an overtired mother and a father who'd gone to work? So, Thomas to the rescue. But where was little Fifi?

'Nice house,' observed Jocelyn, in an appreciative tone.

Ellie stiffened. She didn't ask her guests to sit down. 'I'm a trifle busy today. If it's about the rent at the house, it's best you talk to the agents.'

'Pretty fabric,' observed Peri, caressing a tapestried cushion. 'I like pretty things.' She plumped herself down on the settee.

Yes, thought Ellie. *You like pretty things and you also like moneyed men. Jocelyn is definitely a moneyed man. Old money? Possibly. But there's none of that sense of entitlement here which you often get with old money. On the other hand, he has a presence. One way or the other this man is already accustomed to the use of power. He also had some empathy.*

He understood he'd made a false step in his insincere comment about the house, and he acknowledged the reason why Ellie hadn't asked them to sit, or offered refreshments. He backtracked, fast.

'My apologies for descending on you, Mrs Quicke. I ought to have rung first.'

Ellie glanced at the clock on the mantelpiece. 'Yes, it's not precisely convenient to—'

'No, I can see that. It was thoughtless of me. May we start again?' A small-boy grin, admitting error and asking . . . No, expecting forgiveness. Ellie was interested to note the surface charm, but also to see that there was a hint of steel behind his smile.

Now that she had had a good look at him, she could recognize that he might be a pussy cat, oh yes! But one of the larger variety, say, a leopard or a lion? There was a certain drive which she'd observed before in people who are used to exercising power. In Kate, for instance. Yes, she could see why Jocelyn had been the natural leader for the students.

Ellie tried to work out why he'd come. 'I expect you've heard that I visited the house where you were living. I understand that you left soon after that dreadful accident.'

A sudden immobility. A flash of light from heavy-lidded, hazel eyes. He was remembering Brandon's death, wasn't he?

He said, 'My cousin, yes. A great shock. It upset us all but especially my aunt and my mother, who's rather fragile at the moment. I promised the other students I'd straighten out the financial side of things and I did. I paid the rent and utilities by direct debit. The others were to pay me each month according to the size of the room they had but in view of Brandon's death, I said I'd make up the difference, and I have done.'

'But . . .?' said Ellie.

'Something seems to have gone wrong and the agency doesn't seem to have passed on the news that all the bills have been paid and that they don't owe anything. Imran and Terry in particular are arguing they should still pay me, even if I have cleared the bills. They say I shouldn't have to pay for the last couple of months because of Brandon's death. Patsy and Mona agree. I'm aware that that tragedy doesn't invalidate the terms of the lease but they think that under such circumstances perhaps an agreement might well be reached, some proportion might be waived by the charity as a gesture of goodwill?'

In which case, he'd be due a rebate? Hmm. I may be wrong, but I don't think this is a question of a few hundred here or there to him.

Ellie said, 'I'm no legal eagle, but I would say that your suggestion has merit. You should put it to the agency.'

'That's where I've come unstuck. I've tried to contact them without success. Either the phone is not answered or someone says they'll ring me back, and fail to do so. I drove past there today and it looks as if they've gone out of business. Mona mentioned you'd been round there from the charity which owns the house, so I thought I'd look you up on the off-chance.'

Ellie was not amused. 'Your contract is with the agency, not with me.'

His eyes narrowed even more. 'I've heard the agency is going under. If that's true, have you any idea where that leaves me?'

Indeed. Now, where did you hear that about the agency, I wonder?

Ellie said, 'You're not thinking of returning to the house yourself?'

'Peri here . . .' He indicated the girl, who now had her emery board out and was concentrating on shaping her nails. 'Peri isn't enamoured of the idea.'

He sidestepped that nicely.

'Like you'd see me going near the place!' said Peri. She shuddered, prettily.

'Talking of the agency,' he said. 'I've just heard the news about poor Mr Walker. Shocking. I find it hard to understand the sort of random violence that did for him. A harmless old man disturbs someone looking for petty cash and is killed for it. A terrible indictment on our society.'

How did he hear about Mr Walker? Lesley told me, and I heard people talking about it when I was shopping in the Avenue but he's not the type to shop locally. Has Archie been in touch with him?

Aloud, Ellie said, 'Yes, it is shocking.'

She thought, *I don't believe you came about the rent. You were the tenant, you arranged for the others to join you, you paid the rent in full and I don't believe you are strapped for cash and need a rebate. So why have you come?*

Peri put her nail file away. 'Jossy, like, you said we'd only be a minute. You know I have to be at the hairdresser by two and you promised me lunch first, didn't you?'

Jocelyn's lips thinned, but he replied in his usual soft tones. 'In a minute. Mrs Quicke, to be quite frank, I could do with some help here. Patsy says she's heard the agency is being taken over by another firm with connections to your charity and that you will probably move to sell a house with such sad connections. Is that what you're going to do?'

Ellie joined up the dots.

Jocelyn had heard of Mr Walker's death but hasn't said how. He says he's heard the agency might close and be taken over. Mrs Price said Walker & Price had not taken Streetwise's offer seriously before he died, and it was only this morning that Archie had been pressing her to sign. So how did Jocelyn know about it?

I don't like this, not one little bit. I get the impression that someone in the background is directing events. There were those rumours Lesley Millard had heard which seemed to imply big money was moving behind the scenes in the case of Brandon's death and possibly also in the case of Mr Walker.

But this man is not in a position to affect council's decisions, is he? What do I know about him?

I know that his father got him to return home when Brandon died. His excuse; that his mother and aunt were in distress. Who is his father? Is he a councillor or a businessman? Is his father influential enough to pull strings in the council?

Was it his father who'd pulled strings to get a verdict of accidental death for Brandon? Was it his father who told Jocelyn that the agency was going under, and asked him to enquire about it? Is Jocelyn acting as his father's emissary now? If so, does it mean that Jocelyn's father is connected with the two events in some way?

He's mentioned the charity a couple of times. Why?

Behind the scenes . . . murky waters.

Time to test those same murky waters.

Ellie said, 'I do understand that you want to help your friends, but I'm afraid you've wasted your time, coming here. I have no idea what is going to happen at the agency. As you said, your contract is with them, and not with the charity.'

'I'm told you *are* the charity and only have to lift your finger for them to obey your slightest wish. You could set all our minds at rest.'

So he knew that, did he? He'd been researching me? Or his father had?

Ellie said, 'Blatant flattery will get you nowhere, young man. I suggest you put your case in writing to the agency.'

Peri was getting restive. 'Jossy, darling! Like, the table is booked for one. We really need to go.'

The lines of Jocelyn's face hardened. 'Give me a minute. I'm not quite done.'

There was a sudden clamour outside, clapping and whooping. The door into the house from the conservatory rattled open, and into the sitting room stalked Midge the cat, closely followed by tiny Fifi, dressed in dungarees and holding a spoon which she was licking in concentrated fashion. One of her shoes was half off, and she was limping.

Midge jumped up on to the table and settled himself for a nap in the sun.

Fifi collided with the first pair of legs that she met, put her spoon in her mouth, and lifted her arms to be picked up.

Jocelyn obeyed. Smiling. 'Well, well. Who do we have here? Oh, I see. This shoe's come off.' He seated himself on the nearest chair, positioned Fifi securely on his knee and dealt with the shoe. 'There, now. And what's your name, eh?'

Fifi was sucking her spoon and didn't answer. But she grasped a fold of his shirt and shifted till she felt more secure on his knee. She managed then to look up at him. What she saw seemed to give her pleasure for she treated Jocelyn to one of her most entrancing smiles.

Jocelyn smiled back.

She hit him with her spoon.

He laughed.

'One of your grandchildren, Mrs Quicke?'

'Fifi. Rafael's child.'

Was that slight tightening of his mouth? Did he know Rafael? What did he know about Rafael? Was Rafael mixed up in this affair . . . whatever it was?

Peri was not amused. 'Jossy, like, put it down! You don't know where it's been. And we really must go.' She tapped her foot, impatience twisting those overfull lips of hers.

His eyelids snapped. Again there came that flash of hazel. He didn't like Peri's attitude to Fifi, did he? Ellie would have taken a bet that he was going to drop his acquaintance with little sweetie-pie Peri as soon as possible.

'A beautiful child,' he said, carefully putting Fifi down on the floor and making sure she was steady on her feet before he let her go. 'Bye, bye, little one. Keep safe.' And to Ellie, he added, 'One of my oldest friends has two-year-old twins. They tell me I'm their favourite uncle.' He smiled to himself. Evidently he liked children.

Ellie picked Fifi up, and pushed the dark hair out of her eyes, while taking note that Jocelyn knew Ellie had more than one grandchild. So he had indeed been boning up on her, hadn't he? Why?

He stood up, facing Ellie, full on, giving her the respect to which he now felt she was entitled. 'I apologize for the intrusion. You are, of course, quite correct in what you say. No doubt things will become clearer in a few days' time. May I give you my card? It has my personal number on it.'

Ellie accepted it. 'Will you move back into the charity's house?'

'I don't know. Maybe. In time.'

Carrying Fifi, Ellie led the way out of the house and into the drive. Jocelyn helped Peri into the car and held out his hand to Ellie.

'Thank you.' He hesitated. He wasn't anxious to leave yet.

Ellie said, 'What were you researching for your PhD, Dr Hallett?'

'Bows and arrows against crossbows.'

'And which do you consider won?'

'Gunpowder.'

Ah-ha. He meant that the latest invention was always the deadliest? Iron Age weaponry was defeated by Bronze – or was that the other way, she'd never been sure about that – but whichever it might have been was in turn defeated by steel and so on through the ages. At a guess, he was now working on something to do with modern defence technology. Interesting.

She realized he'd been watching her to see if she'd worked it out.

She said, 'You were sent to see me on a fishing expedition. Why?'

He stared at her and through her. Finally he shook his head. Either he didn't know, or he didn't want to say. He got into the driving seat and drove neatly away.

Ellie returned to the house to find Thomas laid out in his La-Z-Boy, mopping his brow. 'Phew! You found Fifi, did you? I thought she'd come in this way. I'm too old for all this excitement. The others have gone in for lunch and we're invited, but I made our excuses.' He lifted his arms to take Fifi, who nestled into his shoulder and resumed her chewing of her spoon.

Ellie said, 'Tell all.'

'Big row, next door. In whispers. They were trying not to let the children know, so I took them into the garden to play. Little ones shouldn't have to listen to their parents quarrelling. In the end Rafael stormed off upstairs to his study in the attic and Susan called the children in for lunch.'

'Except for Fifi, who'd escaped by coming here.'

Thomas rolled his eyes. 'What are we going to do?'

Ellie rolled hers back. 'We tell Susan we've got Fifi, and have some lunch here. Give me five minutes and I'll be with you. I need to check something first.'

She went into her study, booted up the computer and asked it to provide information on the Halletts. Which it did. Pretty pictures of a handsome young man . . . and yes, one of Brandon, deceased, with only a short piece about his unfortunate demise.

Ah, now up came a man who was the spitting image of Jocelyn but carrying more weight and without so much hair. Sleepy eyes and all. Councillor Hallett; managing director of a firm of advanced technology; chair of this and that; charity donor; behind various worthwhile enterprises. He wore beautifully made business suits and yes, here he was in evening dress with a frail-looking wife at his side. She was wearing some very fine diamonds. Councillor Hallett was a man to be reckoned with.

So Councillor Hallett might well have been in a position to pull strings when his nephew died in such spectacular fashion. And Jocelyn was one of his marionettes?

Ellie sighed and went to make the lunch, only to be inter-rupted by the house phone ringing. As Thomas was cradling Fifi, it was Ellie who picked up the phone.

Somewhat surprisingly it was Kate, the charity's wizard finance director on the phone. She didn't usually bother Ellie with charity business at weekends, but saved any queries she might have for their meetings.

As usual, she was in haste. 'Sorry to bother you, but some-thing's come up. That agency, Streetwise, has sent a note round asking for a meeting tomorrow. They say they're in the process of taking over W & P and would like to confirm that we will continue business with them instead. It seems a reasonable solution. Can you make it?'

Ellie tried to make her brain work. Kate lived life in the fast lane and Ellie often felt she had to sharpen up when dealing with her. Now Ellie's mind flashed back to her conversation that morning with Nancy Price and remembered how pressing young Archie had been . . . almost threatening . . . followed by that mysterious visit from Jocelyn.

Ellie said, 'Kate, stop right there. Something's very wrong. Why the haste?'

'Streetwise point out that every day the business is not operating is money lost, rents not collected, and so on. I've asked Stewart and he's free tomorrow afternoon. We can work out a provisional agreement and—'

'No, no, no! Kate, wait a minute. Let me catch my breath.'

Ellie flumped into the nearest chair, and concentrated. 'Now, bear with me, my dear. I visited Mrs Price this morning and I can tell you that, shaken as she is, she is nowhere near ready to sell the business to Streetwise. For a start, they've offered her a derisory sum. That young salesman of theirs, Archie Something, he was there, pushing her to agree. He says Streetwise have promised to let him keep his job, so it's understandable that he's promoting their interests, but . . . No! I'm sorry, Kate, but I don't agree we should act in such haste. Mr Walker's not dead forty-eight hours and it feels as if the vultures are gathering.'

'Vultures?' Kate laughed. 'Come on, Ellie. I agree that yes, Streetwise are being a trifle quick off the mark, but that's the modern way. Yes, the speed at which they acted did take my breath away at first, but then I told myself I'm growing old, and need to shape up to the brave new world that's coming.'

Was this a dig at Ellie becoming too old to cope with the modern world?

Ellie said, 'Kate, I hate to disagree with you but something is seriously wrong with this whole business. I smell a rat.' She hadn't known she was going to say that. She waited for Kate to laugh her out of court.

Kate didn't. She'd known Ellie long enough to take her strange warning seriously. She said, cautiously, 'What sort of rat? A river rat? A sewer rat? King Rat?'

'King Rat. I think. Oh, I don't know. I feel that we're being pushed into something we may regret. Why all the haste? I sense some shadowy figures working behind the scenes to . . . Oh, I must be imagining things. I thought it might be a certain person who was masterminding . . . Lesley Millard did hint that pressure was being brought to bear to . . . Oh, I just can't make sense of what's happening.'

'Surely, it's a straightforward takeover of one estate agency by another.'

'Um. Yes. Maybe. I've just received a visit from Jocelyn Hallett, a most intelligent youngish man who used to live in the student house. He was on a fishing expedition in the same murky waters. I think he was sent by his father, who is some kind of business tycoon, to find out which way the charity is going to move, for or against Streetwise. And no, I don't understand why anyone like that would be interested, either. And to cap it all, I don't believe Mr Walker was murdered by a chance burglar.'

Silence. Kate said, 'Hold on a mo, Ellie.' She half covered her phone and Ellie could hear her speaking to someone at the other end, asking them to delay something for a few minutes. Then Kate was back. 'You're serious?'

'I don't know,' said Ellie, feeling miserable. 'I tell myself I'm making a mountain out of a molehill. I tell myself you've no need to listen to me as I'm a silly old woman who can't read a balance sheet without help.'

Kate's voice warmed up. 'In my opinion, your judgment of people is invariably correct and your value to the charity is beyond rubies. I have never worked with anyone who can see the whole situation so clearly, so . . .' Sniff, sniff. 'Now you've got me going all emotional.'

That made Ellie feel a little better. 'Can we delay meeting with Streetwise?'

'I'll say my diary is full for the first part of next week. Which, by the way, is true. That should allow things to settle down. Perhaps the police will find the murderer by then or Walker & Price will sign a deal with Streetwise. That will make life simpler.'

'It might be silly of me, but I'm beginning to think we shouldn't sign with Streetwise, however pushy and up-to-the-minute they are. If I have to justify that . . . Well, I don't think their way of doing things chimes with the objectives of our charity. They are all out for themselves and by definition a charity is out to help others and not just to make money. I do wonder . . . do you think we could help Nancy Price in some way? I mean, if she does sell, she ought to get a fair price for the business and not have to walk away with a fraction of what it's worth.'

'How could we do that?'

'Well, they're short-staffed, aren't they? Suppose I ask Mrs Price if we might send in one of our own people to help them out for a few days? We might perhaps offer to have a look at their books, which would give us all an idea of what they are really worth. I'm sure they're worth more than Streetwise are offering. And to be frank, I'd like to keep an eye on that Archie. I don't trust him.'

'We could offer to audit their books? Mm. That's not a bad idea, and it provides a good excuse to delay talks. Whom are you thinking of sending? Mm, mm. Yes, you mean young Nirav, one of Stewart's bright young men, don't you? I remember him. Sharp as a tack. He's taken some accountancy exams since he's been with us, hasn't he? Will you ask Stewart to release him, or shall I?'

'I have to get Nancy Price's agreement first. Oh, poor woman, she's hardly in any condition to make decisions about her future at the moment.'

There was a confused mumble at the other end of the phone and Kate said, 'Must go. I've got a call on the other line. Speak later.' The phone went dead.

Ellie reported back to Thomas, saying, 'I'm really not sure what I've got myself into.'

Thomas said, in his comfortable way, 'Sometimes I think of you as a knight in shining armour, riding out to do the Lord's business.'

Ellie giggled. 'Imagine me on a horse! In armour, too.'

They both took a moment to enjoy the vision. Then Thomas said, 'I'll take Fifi back to Susan and drive you round to see Mrs Price. Is she a churchgoer, do you think? Should I wear my dog collar, or play at being the chauffeur and sit in the car with *The Times* crossword while you talk to her?'

Ellie grinned. 'Under that beard of yours, who'd know whether you wore a dog collar or not?'

* * *

In the event, they couldn't get through to Nancy Price's landline or mobile telephone number, so after lunch Thomas drove them round there on the off-chance Nancy would agree to see them.

Ellie rang the doorbell and waited. And waited. Thomas joined her in the porch. Was Nancy going to open the door? Perhaps she didn't wish to be disturbed?

They were on the point of leaving, when the little wren opened the door and ushered them in. She led them into the kitchen, murmuring, 'I'm glad you came, she said you was a bit of all right, which is more than she is, poor dear. Neighbours have been around but she doesn't want to see them even though I think it might help. And this is your husband, is it? I think I've seen him about. Clergy, isn't he? I go to St Peter's, myself, but what I always say is, it doesn't make much difference which church you go to nowadays, whatever some of them say.'

She gestured to the open French windows leading on to the garden. 'She's out there, now. Gardening. It takes us different ways, doesn't it? She had a bit of a nap, and I got her to take some of my home-made soup that I knocked up for her, but we had to mute the telephone because it keeps ringing and she's getting those awful hate calls that make your skin crawl, they really do.

'And in between it's her daughter ringing and clients and all. And she's expecting to hear from the police, but how do you tell a call she wants to hear from those she doesn't? The problem is I'm due at my daughter's for tea today. I always go on a Saturday. I thought of saying I couldn't, but it's sort of what we do, every weekend. Only, I don't like to leave Nancy.'

'Yes,' said Ellie, responding to the unasked question. 'Now we've come, we can stay with her for a bit.'

There was a burr, burr sound. 'That dratted phone!' said the little wren. 'It never stops!'

'That's something I can deal with,' said Thomas. 'Can you find me something to write on and I'll take messages?'

Ellie stepped out into the garden. Nancy was kneeling on a crazy paving path. She didn't turn her head when Ellie approached but continued in a furious assault on some weeds that had seeded themselves between the stones.

There was a wooden bench a little way off. Ellie sat there and waited. She could hear Thomas speaking to someone on the phone inside the house. It was peaceful in the garden. Sparrows twittering.

Nancy grunted, sat back on her heels, got to her feet with an effort and came to sit beside Ellie. 'Got a cigarette?'

Ellie shook her head.

Nancy said, 'We gave up fifteen years ago; my cousin, my husband and I. My husband went back to it but we stopped, me and Charles. Only now, I keep thinking about starting again.'

Thomas appeared in the French windows. 'It's your daughter on the line, Mrs Price. Would you like—'

'No!' Violently. 'No, no, no!'

Thomas went back inside.

Nancy rocked to and fro. 'They've got at her. Told her if I don't sell now, there'll be nothing left for her to inherit. And she could do with a bit extra, of course she could.'

'And you said . . .?'

'I'd get back to her.' Nancy's breathing slowed. She folded herself over, holding herself together. 'What am I going to do?'

TEN

Saturday afternoon

Ellie didn't know how to answer that question. She said, 'We could always pray.' She didn't know whether Nancy ever prayed or not, but she herself got down to it straight away.

Dear Lord above, help! I don't understand what's going on, but it's left Nancy's cousin dead and her in trouble. I'm way out of my comfort zone here. Please can you help her, or show me how to help her?

Time passed. Now and then Ellie could hear the phone ring. Thomas would deal with that, wouldn't he?

Finally, Nancy relaxed with a long, slow breath. She leaned

back on the bench, closing her eyes and lifting her face to the thin sunshine.

Thomas tapped on the doorframe to attract their attention. This time he was carrying a sheet of paper.

Without opening her eyes, Nancy said, 'I'd forgotten God.'

Thomas said, 'He hasn't forgotten you.'

Nancy started and opened her eyes. Ellie could see her thinking, *Who is this strange man?*

Ellie said, 'This is Thomas, my husband. He's been dealing with the phone for you.'

Thomas said, 'I've taken messages from the following: your daughter, who wants you to ring back, and two newspapers. There were three identical hate messages, nasty. I think they're being sent to you automatically, perhaps every twenty minutes or so.'

'That's right. In the beginning at work, we were lulled into the idea it was safe to pick up the phone and then we'd get whammed with another series of nasty messages. You could time it. Every ten minutes mostly, occasionally they went for fifteen minutes. They must have found my private number.'

'I got on to the telephone people, asked them to block the calls but the caller is withholding his number so they can't do anything much about it. They advise changing your number. Two neighbours rang with offers to help including someone called Hugh, and a Charlie Walker—'

'Dear Hugh. But no, I can't talk to him yet. Charlie Walker is my cousin's older son. He'll be handling the funeral, I suppose. Nice boy. I'll ring him back some time. Nothing from the police?'

Thomas shook his head.

Silence fell. Nancy concentrated on her problems.

Ellie and Thomas waited.

Finally, Nancy said, 'I think . . . I'm not sure I'm up to it, but I think I want to fight.' And then, with a wail, she added, 'No, I'm not sure. On the one hand, I don't want everything that Charles and I have worked for over the years, to drift away. I object to being hounded by phone calls and our window being smashed and people wanting me to sell. I'm heartsick at losing Charles, but I can't see my way clear to carrying on.'

'Well,' said Ellie, 'I actually came to ask if you'd allow one of the bright youngsters from the charity to help you out in the office next week. At the very least he can man the phone for you and, if you like, he can take a look at your books and bring them up to date. He can assess your true worth in the market-place. That will give you some ammunition to fight Streetwise's attempt to buy your business at a knock-down price.'

Nancy's mouth dropped open. 'But . . . but Archie wouldn't want . . .?'

'I agree. I don't think he'd be at all happy about someone else coming in if he's that anxious for Streetwise to take over. But Nirav's on our payroll and not yours and will provide an impartial, independent report which can only help you decide what to do in the future.'

'Yes,' said Nancy, in an empty voice. 'I suppose that would give me a breathing space. I'm thinking of all the people on our books who are waiting for us to help them; people who want to move, or to sell. We mustn't let them down.'

'That's right,' said Thomas. 'Oh, and your neighbour said she'll be back from her daughter's this evening about seven as she doesn't like to think of you being by yourself, with that phone ringing all the time and people knocking on the door that you don't want to see. And yes, I can hear the phone sounding off as we speak, but I've left it switched to taking messages, so I'll deal with them in a minute. Anyway, your neighbour says either she comes here to stay with you tonight, or you must go to her.'

'No, no,' said Nancy, 'it's tempting, very. But no. I don't know if you can understand, but I need some time by myself. I'm used to being by myself. I need it. I'll potter about the garden and have something light for supper and watch some silly game show or other on the telly and go to bed early and not think about anything important till tomorrow.'

'All right, if that's what you want. I'll leave a list of people who've called so far, but I suggest you switch your landline phone to take messages till tomorrow. And forgive me, you may think it entirely unnecessary, but I'd like to put the police and our home telephone number on your mobile's speed dial.'

'I'm sure that's not necessary, but it's a kind thought.'

Thomas nodded and went back in to deal with the phones.

Nancy pushed herself to her feet and smoothed back her hair. Putting herself back together again. She even managed a social smile, saying, 'It's been good of you to come round but I'm all right now and I'm sure you have better things to do than stick around here.'

As Ellie and Thomas left, they heard Nancy bolt the front door behind them. Thomas drove them back in silence and parked in their driveway. Rafael's big car was there and the sounds from the open kitchen window spoke of a young family having their supper. No screaming or cat fights.

So far, so good.

Their own house seemed a little dusty, a little too quiet after the disturbances of the day. Ellie set about ringing Stewart to bring him up to date with what was happening, and to ask him to release Nirav to work in the agency the following week. They had a chat about Streetwise's offer to the charity; Stewart was rather inclined to take it, but Ellie persuaded him to wait on events.

Thomas suggested he cook supper but Ellie said she'd do it. She was restless and so was he. He drifted into his Quiet Room to pray but left the door open in case she needed him.

Ellie couldn't sit still. Recent events ran through her mind, over and over again. She kept getting flashbacks. She was standing in the road watching as the window of the estate agency was smashed. Over and over again.

She scolded herself. She hadn't witnessed that. She'd only been told about it. So why did she keep imagining it now?

All was quiet next door. That was good, wasn't it? Susan and Rafael must have made up their differences. Ellie would hear all about it tomorrow . . . Or not, as the case might be. It was wrong to interfere.

Thomas cleared up after supper. There was a spat of rain in the air. He went round the garden, picking up children's toys and storing them in the conservatory. They watched an hour's television. A game show. Ellie wondered if Nancy were watching the same thing. It was a lowering sort of evening, the nights were drawing in. They would probably go to bed early.

Ellie dillied and dallied, finding unnecessary tasks to do in the kitchen to while away the time.

Eventually Thomas said, 'What are we going to do about it?'

She brought out her fears and looked at them. 'The nasty phone calls Nancy and Charles received at work are now turning up on Nancy's home phone, right. This indicates to me that the person who was making them to the office, now has her home address and phone number.'

'Yes, but surely Nancy won't be listening to her messages tonight. She was emphatic that she'd be all right by herself.'

'I know, I know. But I'm remembering what happened to the agency. A brick through the window. Hate mail. Dogs' leavings. A spider. What if someone starts the same thing at her home?'

Thomas stared at her. He wasn't laughing. He was taking it seriously. That was the great thing about Thomas: he took her fears seriously.

His hand hovered over their landline. 'I switched her phone to messages only. Which means we can't contact her to see if she's all right?'

'You want to try her mobile, just in case?'

He tried it and shook his head. 'Voicemail. There's no way we can contact her. She wouldn't thank us for disturbing her, anyway. That neighbour of hers said she'd be round, didn't she?'

'Yes, and Nancy probably sent her away. Take no notice of me. I'm sure she's perfectly all right.' Ellie switched the kettle on. 'It's early but we've had a tiring day. A nice hot drink will settle us down before we go to bed.'

A ray of evening sunshine found its way into the kitchen, and then faded. Clouds moved across the sky. It was a dark evening. It would probably rain before morning.

Ellie paused with her hand reaching for their mugs. 'Thomas, I'm thinking the baddies – whoever they are – might up their game. Nancy is so near breaking point. They must realize by now that she's not taking messages on her phone. So what if . . . No, I know it's ridiculous, but what if a brick was thrown through her front window tonight? While she's all alone in that big house.'

He looked at his watch. 'If we phone the police, they could . . . No, they wouldn't take it seriously. Why would they? I think I'd better get round there, see if she's all right.'

She loved him that he would offer but could see the snags. 'What can you do? She's probably gone to bed early. She wouldn't let you in, anyway. You'd be reduced to sitting outside the house in the car all night, on the off-chance that someone might come along with vandalism in mind.'

Their phone rang. Thomas took the call. 'Nancy? . . . Yes, I see . . . No, no. You did the right thing to get them both, police and fire brigade. Now what else? . . . Yes, rouse your neighbours on either side. The more people around you, the safer you'll be. I'm on my way.'

Thomas crashed the phone down and reached for his jacket. 'Someone poured inflammable liquid through the letterbox and followed it with a lighted spill of some kind. She'd put the chain on so couldn't get out of the front door. Fortunately she hadn't gone to bed yet. She heard the whoosh as the fire ignited and threw buckets of water from the kitchen on the flames so it didn't take hold. Then she rang for help. I think she's managed very well, but now she's ready to collapse. I'll pop over, make sure the police take it seriously. I'll call you when I know what's what.'

'Wait!' said Ellie, but Thomas was already out of the front door, jangling his keys. She heard the car start up and leave.

Fine! Just like a man, rushing to help but not taking a minute to think what this means.

No, I'm being unfair. He's doing the right thing. He'll be better at coping with the police and fire brigade than I would be.

Nancy shouldn't stay there, alone . . . I should text Thomas, make sure he brings her back here . . .?

No, that's the wrong thing to do. If that house is left empty, it'll be torched again as soon as the police leave.

Sit down and think, Ellie!

She thought and thought. And all she could think of is that King Rat – whoever he might be – was upping his game.

It was King Rat who was behind all this, wasn't it?

But not the Halletts.

Or was it?

Think, Ellie. Think!

King Rat was someone of importance in the community or he wouldn't be able to influence decisions made by the police.

Ellie imagined Councillor Hallett in the role – a well-padded businessman with sleepy eyes. He was smoking a cigar and had a bit of a paunch. She wondered if he went around, chauffeur-driven, in a big car with aides toting his laptop and papers around for him as he wafted without effort from meeting to meeting. By helicopter? Yes, definitely. Private jet, too.

Oh really, Ellie. You're letting your imagination run away with you.

On the other hand, she imagined that Councillor Hallett was the sort of man who only need to lift a finger here, have a quiet word there, to be certain that his every wish would be obeyed.

King Rat didn't make abusive phone calls or torch houses himself. No. But he could have people who'd do it for him.

No, no! The Halletts are not rats. There's someone else moving in this . . .

The phone rang again. This time it was Kate, sounding taut with anxiety. 'Ellie, sorry to ring at this time of night, but earlier this evening I had a sort of social call from a woman I know who works for the council. She asked me if it was true that the council were talking about building a new community centre at the back of the old fire station. She said that at the council meeting last night they discussed making a compulsory purchase order on a street of condemned houses which some developer or other had recently purchased. And she named it. She was laughing because she said that the compulsory order meant a derisory price would be paid for the lot and the developer would lose out.'

Ellie reached for the nearest chair and sat down with a bump. 'You mean . . . our Ladywood project? The row of derelict houses the charity has just bought? No, it can't be!'

'It is.'

Ellie was silent. Thundering through the back of her head was the refrain, *King Rat is upping his game. And yes, he's behind everything that's happened; Brandon and Mr Walker's deaths, the takeover of Walker & Price and now . . . the charity's latest project!*

The charity was Ellie's baby, set up with an inheritance she'd received, to provide decent accommodation for those who couldn't afford market prices. It had performed so well that a while back they'd been left a large sum of money by a well-wisher. It was the biggest donation they'd ever had and they'd thought long and hard about how best to use it, eventually deciding to purchase a street of rundown housing which had been badly maintained and recently condemned as unfit for habitation.

Their architects had drawn up plans and they had obtained planning permission to renovate the housing: new windows and doors, electrics, plumbing, refitting kitchens and bathrooms. All to be redecorated and the common garden area behind to be landscaped. From what was presently little better than slum housing, there would be a street of affordable, modern, two- and three-bed houses to be let at very reasonable rates.

The builders had been briefed and their estimates accepted. Work was due to begin the following week.

'They can't do that,' said Ellie. 'We've got all the planning permissions we need. We've done everything by the book. We have, haven't we?'

'We have. I checked. I checked back through my notes. We've done everything correctly. My contact says that they've found some "discrepancy", which means the planning permission is flawed and can be disregarded.'

'You mean they've invented something . . .?'

'Sounds like it. Basically, they can do what they like. I've thought and thought about it. Can we object? No. It's their right to give or refuse planning permission.'

'But they can't rescind planning permission that they've already granted. Can they?'

'I'm not sure. Most people are not contactable at the weekend but I did finally manage to get hold of a councillor friend, and he said that yes, it wasn't generally known as yet, it had only just come up, but the proposal had met with general approval. So far it's just a proposal but it's scheduled to come up at the next housing committee meeting.'

Silence while Ellie digested this unpalatable fact.

Kate continued, 'You and I know that they could hold up proceedings for months if not years if we fight them over this. They'll insist this is the only possible space on which they could build their much-needed community centre and it doesn't hurt a developer, they'll say, to lose a slice of the profits. For the general good. And so on.'

'This is King Rat at work.'

Kate said, 'Yes, I daresay. The problem is the charity's options are limited. We've paid a whacking price for a street of houses which are not fit to live in as they are. We've paid for planning permission, architects' fees, organizing builders, etc. If we fight the council's decision, it will be throwing good money after bad. It's a bitter pill to swallow but my advice is to cut our losses, accept whatever sum they choose to give us and move our interests out of this borough for good.'

Ellie said, 'No, I don't think we need to do that. I rather think that if we appear to accept what they say, in a few days' time we'll be approached by Streetwise to say they've heard we're in trouble, and that they just might be able to pull a string here or there and get that decision reversed. Streetwise will expect us to fall on their neck, weeping with gratitude as we sign a contract for them to manage the project for us. And yes, as soon as we've signed, the council will drop their proposal.'

Kate thought it through. 'If you're right, I suppose we could sign with Streetwise in order to save the project.'

'No. Definitely no. Absolutely not. I've been looking at the way they work and it stinks. They are not a good match for a charity – too pushy by half. Look, I can't prove that they are behind all the unfortunate things that have happened to Walker & Price, but I suspect that they are. Had you heard Nancy Price's house was firebombed this evening?'

'What!'

Ellie told her what she knew.

Kate was shocked. 'All that pressure on a woman who's already been knocked down by her cousin's death and the persecution at the agency? I think of myself as being a hard-headed businesswoman, but no, if Streetwise are behind this, I definitely don't want to tie us down to working with them. But are you sure? I mean, they're a small but up-and-coming business. I looked them up. They're basically a two-bit agency run by some bright young things who like to fast-talk clients

into paying too much for their properties. They only have two
shops and neither of them are in the town centre. In some ways
I thought they'd be good for us, push us into the next century
and all that. But, how could a two-bit agency like that pull
strings in the town hall?'

Ellie couldn't think straight. The Halletts were involved in
this somehow. But how? She said, 'Kate, can you do something
for me? I think someone big is behind Streetwise. Possibly
someone who has the same surname as one of our student
friends. Can you find out?'

'If you think it important. Give me their names.'

Ellie gave them.

Kate said, 'Any preference?'

'Yes. Jocelyn Hallett. I don't think it's him, though it might
be, but it might be someone in his family.'

'I know a Councillor Hallett, highly respected, was mayor a
couple of years ago, wealthy, does a lot of good, on the board
of this and that charity. You don't think he'd be involved in
something like this, do you?'

Ellie sidestepped Kate's question to say, 'What's he like?'

'A quiet man, does lots of good by stealth. I believe he was
offered a gong a while back and refused it.'

'A *what*?'

'An honour or some sort. A title or an MBE or something.
But no, he avoids the limelight.'

'You've met him? You like him?'

'Yes to both. Ellie, this is not your King Rat.'

Another vote against it being Councillor Hallett.

'I agree it sounds unlikely. But would you ask around, just
to please me? We need some ammunition to help us decide
how to deal with Streetwise. Can we hold an emergency
meeting of the charity? Could you clear your diary for Monday
morning?'

'No, I don't think . . . Well, yes. All right. I'll see what I can
do. Yes, I agree this is an emergency. Count me in.'

It was late. Ellie went to bed because what else was she to
do? She decided she'd better take her mobile phone up to bed
with her. She hardly ever used it, much preferred the landline,

but this situation was different. Thomas might call her. Or someone might try to push something flammable through the front door.

She prayed for a while, which calmed her. Then she dozed off but couldn't sleep properly.

Thomas rang her at one. She started awake and reached for her mobile. 'What's happened?'

'Just to let you know I won't be back tonight. The police have just left, and so has the fire brigade. They say the house won't burn down now. Nancy threw enough water into the hall to float a battleship, probably far more than was needed in her anxiety to make sure the fire wouldn't start up again. The water's spread into the surrounding ground-floor rooms. Every step you take, it's like paddling at the seaside.

'Some neighbours turned up and between us we managed to prop up the remains of the front door and wedge a step ladder behind it so no one can get in that way. Nancy's little friend – whose name is Abby, short for Abigail, by the way – took her off to spend the rest of the night at her place. I volunteered to stay here in case the fire starts up again. Nancy wouldn't leave unless someone stayed.'

How like Thomas to put himself out for someone else.

He said, 'It'll be an insurance job. New front door and carpets throughout the ground floor for a start. As for the wear and tear on Nancy . . . well, she's tearless. Numb. Confused. Are you all right?'

'Yes.' Ellie didn't feel there was any point telling him about the new threat to the charity at this time of night. He'd got enough to worry about. 'Will you get some sleep?'

'Sure. I'll be back home for breakfast. I said I'd take a service tomorrow morning. Can't remember where for the life of me. Someone's wife's ill and they asked me to take over at short notice. Can you look it up for me in my diary? I'll take the service then pop back here afterwards, see how Nancy is, organize a builder to replace the front door. Some of the neighbours have promised to come round tomorrow to help.'

Ellie slept, in snatches.

ELEVEN

Sunday morning

Thomas returned for a shower, breakfast and a change of clothing. He put his filthy, wet shoes in the conservatory to dry out, observing they were probably ruined and might as well go straight in the dustbin.

Around mouthfuls of scrambled egg, he said, 'I spent the night on the settee in the sitting room with all the windows open to alleviate the stink emanating from the hall. I'd always been told that things will look better in the morning, but in this case, the extent of the damage is even more shocking than I'd thought. The hall is a stinking hellhole with a sodden carpet underfoot. Everything the fire touched is a blackened, hardly identifiable mess. They may be able to save the carpets in the other rooms but I doubt it. I swept some of the water out of the front and back doors so we're not paddling any more, but every step you take, the carpets go "squidge".

'Nancy's friend, Abby, came round to collect this and that for her. She said she'd given Nancy some hot milk to take to bed with her. She said the milk might have had a sleeping pill dropped into it, so Nancy would probably not wake up till later that morning. Abby was as shocked as I was by the state of the hall, and said she'd try to get back later to start on the clear up.

'Then one of Nancy's neighbours turned up to help and we looked at the front door together. We decided there was no way it could be repaired and the immediate problem was how to make the house safe. He said he'd go back home and try to raise a builder to deal with it today. Nancy has some good neighbours which says a lot about the woman herself. I hope you don't mind, but I said I'd pop back and see what I could do to help later this morning. I'll take some rubber gloves and my old wellington boots to change into.'

Thomas drained the coffee pot, collected various bits and pieces for the service, left the house, came back for his boots and some rubber gloves, and finally left for the local church.

Ellie cleared away the breakfast things and sat down with the telephone to make some calls.

The first was to Patsy at the student house. She was pretty sure Patsy would be an early riser, and so she was.

'Patsy, this may sound a strange question, but is everything all right at the house? Have the other students returned yet?'

'Why, Mrs Quicke . . .! Yes, Imran and Terry are back and we're all fine. At least, we're rather anxious waiting to hear about the rent, but otherwise . . . Oh, you don't mean that stupid flier pushed through our door, do you? How did you know about that? I mean, it's just some joker. Even Terry and his girlfriend thought it was funny. Honestly, some people need their heads examining.'

Ellie told herself to keep calm. 'What sort of flier? What did it say?'

'Advertising us as a brothel, of all things. Every house in the street received one. Fortunately most of them know us and think it's a laugh, but we're having to put on the chain when we open the front door because you'd be surprised how many men have come calling.'

Patsy laughed. She was taking it in her stride.

'Did you tell the police?'

'I rang them and reported it. They didn't seem interested. They haven't been round to see us or anything. Why? What do you know? You sound as if you were expecting something bad to happen.'

Ellie sidestepped that one. 'Has Jocelyn returned?'

'No. The others want me to text him again, but I . . . I don't want to bother him. Do you think he'd care?'

'Yes, I do. I think if Jocelyn returned, you'd have no more trouble.'

'Why? He's not been responsible for this. No way!'

'Agreed. Give me an hour. I'll see if I can get hold of him. I promise to ring you back.'

Would Jocelyn be out of bed at ten on a Sunday morning? Ellie fished out the card he'd given her and rang his smartphone, hardly expecting him to answer. As expected, her call went to voicemail. She left a message asking him to ring her urgently and scolded herself for thinking he would.

He rang back within five minutes. 'Mrs Quicke? Something's happened?'

'Yes, quite a lot.' She filled him in on the problems Nancy Price was experiencing, moved on to giving him the problems the charity was facing with the council, and finished up with the tale of the student house being advertised as a brothel.

'What!' A confused sound. Had he dropped the phone? Then he came back to her. 'Sorry. Clumsy of me. You were saying . . .?'

'The house is being advertised as a brothel. Patsy's holding them together. She said she hadn't wanted to bother you, but I said you needed to know what's happened.'

'Do you really think that I . . .? No. I am not responsible for any of this.' He repeated the words, his voice going deeper. 'None of it.' He was not only disturbed, but also angry.

'Agreed,' said Ellie. 'It's not your style. But you know how to stop it.'

'That statement is . . . almost . . . libellous.'

'Perhaps. But it's true, isn't it? Everything that has happened can be linked in some way to you and to the charity.'

'Including council decisions? Including the projected takeover of Walker & Price by another small estate agency? That's ridiculous.'

'I don't think the people at the top have been involved in throwing bricks or delivering fliers. I think that the little people who work for them heard the boss wanted to replace Walker & Price with another agency and they took it into their heads to earn some brownie points by helping him to get rid of Walker & Price. They didn't ask the boss. Perhaps he knew what they were doing. Perhaps he didn't. But the little men enjoyed upsetting the lives of other people and once they'd started their programme of destruction, they became excited and things got out of control.

'First they concentrated on Walker & Price: pushing nasty things through the letterbox; graffitiing the exterior; making obscene telephone calls; and finally smashing in their front window. I don't know whether Mr Walker's death was connected with that behaviour. That's a horrific thought and I don't want to entertain it. So for the moment I'm discounting that.

'They've now taken to the same tactics to try to break Nancy Price, which has culminated in firebombing her house and leaving her homeless. Their latest trick is to distribute fliers advertising the student house as a brothel.'

'A brothel! No, there's no possible connection. I can't believe that!'

'The police were informed. Whether they'll take action or not, I can't say. And no, so far the student house has not been targeted for anything except the claim that it's a brothel. That's unpleasant enough for the students, isn't it? How long do you think Terry and his protective girlfriend will put up with callers wanting to book a prostitute?'

'Mrs Quicke, you can't really think I had anything to do with arson or these fliers?'

'No, I don't. But I do think you know something about it and could stop it if you chose to do so. So I'm asking you, what are you going to do about it?'

He said, slowly, 'You want me to move back there.' It wasn't a question.

'Yes,' said Ellie. 'And to make it known to . . . whoever . . . that you have done so. That should keep the students safe. At least, I don't think the little men would have a go at you. Would they?'

'You forget that the little men don't always report back. Little men, as you say, may well be out of control.'

'Understood. But you know someone who can sort them out.' Again, it wasn't a question. 'Time is of the essence, Jocelyn. Last week they managed to close down Walker & Price. They moved on to advertise the student house as a brothel, and last night they firebombed Nancy's house. What are they planning for the students today?'

A long pause. She could hear him breathing, softly, not hurried. He was a man with good self-control.

Jocelyn had been sitting on the fence until now. Whose side was he going to come down on? Ellie thought, she hoped . . . had she read the signs wrongly?

He said, 'I assume Patsy is coping?'

Ellie punched the air. She'd guessed right. She said, 'What do you expect her to do? Faint?'

A faint, very faint, chuckle. He broke the connection.

Ellie found she was smiling. Jocelyn had decided whose side he was on. He would make a good ally.

Now . . . she sighed. She had to arrange a meeting of the trustees for as soon as possible, and sort out Rafael and Susan, and she didn't know which of those was going to cause her the most trouble.

Sunday morning, continued

First Kate, who rang to confirm she'd cancelled her trip to somewhere or other, so that she could attend an urgent meeting at the charity's offices. Ellie asked if Kate had learned anything more about the Halletts.

Kate said it was rumoured Councillor Hallett had plans to retire and take on more charity work, that he was supposed to be the person who had given a lot of money to the local hospital for some special equipment or other. Kate concluded by saying that that was ironic because his wife was currently being treated there.

'No tie-up with Streetwise?'

'Lord, no. Why would there be?'

'I know, I know. It doesn't make sense, and I wouldn't keep on about it if Lesley Millard hadn't hinted that someone in authority put pressure on the police to play down Brandon's death, and I'm not at all sure they haven't done the same thing with the murder of Mr Walker. Also, every way I turn, there is Jocelyn Hallett, who definitely knows more about the situation than he should.'

'You don't think he's the bogey in the background, do you?' Amused.

'No, I don't, but . . . Well, thanks for listening to me. See you tomorrow.'

Ellie turned her attention to the name of the next person on her list, who was the charity's general manager, Stewart.

Stewart had to be filled in on what had been happening.

He argued a bit, but he did eventually agree to clear his desk to attend. And, after some pushing by Ellie, he also agreed to getting young Nirav from the tenancy department to spend some time at Walker & Price's agency to see what was really happening there.

The remaining trustee who needed to be notified of what was happening was Rafael and, after the way they'd parted company, Ellie knew that was going to be more difficult. It wouldn't do to pull rank. Perhaps, although she didn't feel like doing so, she ought to apologize for interfering in his private life?

She wondered how Jocelyn would cope with such a situation and smiled. She thought he'd use soft words and sympathy. He didn't pull rank because everyone respected him and he didn't need to raise his voice to get things done.

Well, that seemed to have worked in the student house, so perhaps it would work here as well. After all, it was no skin off her nose if she had to grovel a bit to get Rafael moving.

She went out into the garden and along to the house next door, hoping to catch him alone. It was a nice sunny day and the children would probably be playing out in the garden. Yes, the French windows were open and Rafael was on one of the pair of sunloungers on the patio keeping an eye on the children, who were sitting on a rug in the shade of the trees, and taking no notice of him. Little Evan was turning the pages of one of his picture books and showing Fifi how to look under each flap. Jenny was absorbed in one of her digital games. There was no sign of Susan.

Rafael was talking to someone on his phone when he saw Ellie. He clicked off his phone, scowled his disapproval of her visit, but finally decided he'd better be civil. He half rose from his chair to say, 'Can I help you?' And subsided into it again.

That was, almost, rude. Well, actually, it was rude.

Ellie managed a smile and took the chair next to him. 'Dear Rafael, Thomas and I have been racking our brains how to help you. You must be so worried about Susan, so near to her term. If she was to miscarry now . . . It doesn't bear thinking about, does it?'

He blinked. Ellie could see it hadn't occurred to him that

Susan might miscarry at this stage. He hadn't given much thought to her welfare recently, had he? And Ellie would take a bet that that phone call he'd been making was not about work, but to a certain little lady who'd hung on his arm and given him a kiss at the student house.

He said, 'Susan's resting and I'm spending some quality time with the kids.'

That's not all that you were doing, not at all. But we won't argue.

Ellie sighed deeply. 'Oh dear, oh dear. So much has been happening. I don't like to add to your worries, but I suppose you'll be mad at me if I don't tell you and you find out afterwards.'

He gave her a narrow-eyed look. She'd overdone the 'little old lady' bit, hadn't she?

She assumed a more decisive air. 'I'm calling a special meeting at the charity tomorrow morning at the office and I hope you'll be able to make it. The charity is in trouble because . . .'

She went through the list, ticking the problems off on her fingers one by one. The attacks on Walker & Price, the death of Charles Walker; the abusive phone calls transferred to Nancy's home, the pressure for her to sell at a derisory price and the firebombing; and now the news that the council had rescinded planning permission with all that that entailed.

Rafael was shocked. 'What does Kate say?'

'She's conflicted. On the whole I think she thinks it will be cheapest in the long run for us to roll over and let Streetwise tickle our tummies.'

A fleeting grin. 'You won't go for that. You think Streetwise are behind all this?'

'I thought someone was behind Streetwise and I thought I knew who it was, but I was wrong about that. Yes, I do still think Streetwise are responsible for what's been happening and that they will turn their attention to us – to you and me – if we don't go along with what they want. It's illegal and frustrating but I don't see how we can prove that they are the ones who've been doing all the damage. I don't want to do a deal with them, but I'm not impartial on the subject of Streetwise.

When it comes to a vote, I shall have to stand aside and let the rest of the board decide.'

'I'm with you. We can't give in to threats.'

'It's not just threats. Did you hear that someone's been posting fliers through letterboxes, advertising that the student house is really a brothel?'

Rafael shifted in his chair and Ellie realized that of course he knew about that. Mona had put him in the picture, hadn't she? She'd probably expected him to fly to her side and carry her off on the saddle of his white horse. And that, of course, he'd been unable to do. Ellie wondered how he'd talked his way out of that one.

He knew he'd been caught out, but years of slightly dodgy dealings had trained him to put on an innocent-but-concerned face. 'Yes, Mona told me. Terrible! I advised her to go to the police and cry on their shoulders.'

Ellie told herself not to smile. She said, in well-simulated surprise, 'But you said you hadn't given Mona your number.'

He *knew* that she *knew* he'd lied, but he wasn't going to admit he'd been at fault. He produced a beautifully timed sigh of regret. 'I was sure I'd given her a wrong number. I don't know how she got it.'

Liar. But no great harm done. Mona is perfectly capable of looking after herself.

Ellie said, 'I wonder, do you want to whisk Susan and the children away to safety somewhere?'

He hadn't thought of that. His face went blank and his breathing slowed as he considered what she'd said and what might lie behind it. He reddened, and his fists clenched. 'They wouldn't dare!'

Ellie didn't even bother to raise her eyebrows. Of course they'd dare. Look what they'd been up to so far, and it was no good saying they didn't know where Ellie and Rafael lived because the names and addresses of everyone at the charity were in the common domain. And they mustn't forget that Rafael had given Mona their details, too.

His breathing quickened. 'If they so much as lay a finger on my . . .!'

'Abusive phone calls,' said Ellie. 'Firebombing the front door.'

He shot upright in his chair. 'We have no fire escape. The children sleep at the back . . .!'

'Yes,' said Ellie. 'I don't think even Susan could get all three out using that wooden staircase of yours in the middle of the night.'

He was breathing fast. 'We must get police protection!'

'On what grounds? That you know someone who has recently received the attentions of an arsonist? No, I don't think Streetwise will turn their attention to us as yet. They will wait to see how we react to firebombing at Nancy Price's house. Only if the charity turns Streetwise down will they start on us. I don't think it's necessary to alarm the students because Jocelyn will take care of them.'

'Wait a minute. Patsy said he was the student who got them organized. At the time the name didn't ring a bell, but . . . if it's the same one . . .? Yes, I suppose it might be. Unusual name. I think I came across him sometime . . . some charity event at the town hall? No, the man I met was much older, not a student. His father, maybe? Didn't the girls say Jocelyn was the first to leave the student house?'

'He did leave and now I've asked him to return. I think he will.'

'But, why should he? Ellie, I don't understand. You can't think this Jocelyn's responsible in any way for what's been happening?'

'When I checked with him, he denied that he was in any way involved.'

'Well, then.'

'Think Mafia. Not that this is Mafia; I don't mean that. Think of a family that has power and influence locally. Think of their connections in the community, the way their tentacles reach out and surface in unexpected places. Think of Jocelyn as someone who has such connections. I admit I don't know how he's connected to King Rat – not through his father, but perhaps through an old schoolfriend? Someone he feels he has to protect? I believe Jocelyn is innocent of wrongdoing and was shocked when I filled him in on what's been happening. Now, tell me what such a man would do when a Mafia-sponsored tide of nastiness reaches his doorstep?'

'The father or the son?'

'I got Kate to look into the father's background because I thought it might be him who is behind Streetwise but it doesn't look as if he is, so I can't prove anything. However, Jocelyn has decided – I think, I hope – to protect the students by returning to live with them. Probably because he has a fondness for one of the students.'

'Mona? Yes, of course. She's quite something.' His tone indicated that he really had no interest in Mona. And, he probably hadn't.

Ellie didn't comment. She didn't think Jocelyn was interested in Mona; or Mona in him, come to think of it. 'I'm hoping that the waves Jocelyn will make by returning to the student house will cause King Rat – whoever he is – to ask what's been going on, and to rein in his troops. I think that should give us a day or so to regroup and think what's to be done next.'

'You say we're safe for the moment, but what if we decide to turn Streetwise down? Then the threat of action against us becomes very real. Do I find somewhere for Susan and the kids to go? But where? Who would take them in? And for how long?'

Ellie was pleased to see that he was really worried. 'We'll discuss our options tomorrow at the meeting. Now I'm going to see how Susan is.'

'She's resting. She asked not to be disturbed till lunchtime.'

Ellie had to accept that, so returned home to find Thomas in the kitchen, peeling sodden pieces of paper one by one out of a malodorous lump and trying to flatten them out.

He said, 'I know this looks like the contents of someone's waste-paper basket that's been dumped in the sink. Actually, it's gold dust. Can you manage to get some lunch ready while I'm using the table?'

Ellie said, 'In a good cause, yes.'

While she built sandwiches and heated soup, Thomas explained. 'I arrived back at Nancy's to find her helpful neighbour – nice man, practical – at screaming point on his phone because this was the umpteenth builder he'd tried and failed to get out to replace the front door on a Sunday morning. We talked it over and decided to take measurements which he'd take to the nearest DIY place to get something, anything, to make the house safe for the time being.

'Abby had also returned. She said Nancy had woken up but agreed to stay where she was in bed today, which proved that she was pretty poorly, poor dear. Abby said that if I was there to help, would I please make myself useful and take the remains of the carpet and coats which had been hanging up in the hall out to the garden at the back so that Nancy could decide later what could be kept, which frankly we both thought was not a lot.

'There was one of those thin, old Turkish carpets covering most of the hall floor. Fortunately it hadn't been nailed down. It was sodden. Most of the water had now drained away or been swept out of the ground floor, but the carpets were all still wringing wet. Abby was using a mop to collect water, which she then wrung out into a bucket. And talk! She never stopped. I suppose some kind of hose might have pumped the water out quicker, but if you don't have a hose, the next best thing is Abby with a mop.

'So I took armloads of stuff out to the back to dump it, while she complained that the place wasn't fit for Nancy to live in till it had been completely redecorated; with which I agreed, not that she was listening to anything I said. She went on to tell me how many years she's known Nancy, that they'd seen one another through both their husbands dying, and it was only to be expected that Nancy's no-good daughter in New Zealand was going to want her pound of flesh . . . And that was when that bright young man from the agency showed up with his briefcase, demanding to speak to Nancy.'

'Ah-ha,' said Ellie, ladling out mugs of hot soup. 'Young Archie, on the dot.'

Thomas said, 'I thought he was supposed to be working for Walker & Price, but he didn't act like it.'

'If I've read the situation aright, Archie was their junior salesman, but he's recently been informed that he'll keep his job, possibly with a bonus, when Streetwise take over. He's got divided loyalties. Cheese sandwich, do you?'

'Sure.' Thomas looked puzzled. 'The thing is when he first

came up the path he was, well, smiling to himself. Which surprised me a bit, because even from the road you could see there'd been a spot of trouble. Then he stopped where he was and his face changed. You know how you meet someone bereaved in the street and have to adjust to look sympathetic?'

'I do. Do you want some chutney with the sandwich?'

Thomas nodded and continued, 'Archie said, "What's been going on here, then?" He didn't wait for an answer. He took me for a builder, I think. He said to me that he needed to see Nancy, straight away. That's when Abby popped up from behind me in the hall to say he couldn't see Nancy as she was in bed, suffering from shock. That didn't stop him. He said he had to see her on a most important, urgent matter and he tried to step over the threshold, at which point I took a step sideways and somehow got in his way. He came over all red and tried to get round me but the more he tried to dodge, the more I dodged, too. He was pretty well dancing with impatience. I could just imagine him bursting into a sick woman's bedroom and insisting she sign his papers!'

Ellie grinned. 'Nancy wasn't even at home. She was at Abby's.'

'A fact that we didn't share with him. Anyway, Abby thrust me aside and started scolding him. She's got a good command of language, most impressive. How dare he come round bullying a widow woman who was poorly in bed, and so on! He opened his briefcase and showed me the papers, saying that he'd make it worth my while to take them up to Nancy and get them signed. Abby lost it. She told me to stand aside. I did as she said and she threw her bucket of dirty water all over him and into his briefcase. All over his papers.'

Ellie laughed out loud. 'Abby deserves a medal.'

'She does. She screeched at him to look what he'd made her do, and how it came to something that a poor widow woman was being tormented by furies. At least, I think it was furies she said. It might have been "thieves". Young Archie stood there, shaking with rage. Dripping. He upended his briefcase and his papers fell out, all in a stinking wet bundle, and he didn't know what to do next. His mouth moved, but no sound came out.

'Abby swept up the sodden mass of papers, dumped them in her bucket and told me to take them out to the rubbish bin. He yelled that she couldn't do that because they were important and he had to get them signed that morning. Abby put her hands on her hips and told him to get lost or she'd fetch the police. She picked up her mop and thwacked at his shins. He screeched, and she screeched, and I backed into the house and took the sodden mass out to the kitchen and hid them under the sink in case he managed to get past her . . . which he didn't.

'He yelled that I must give him back his papers or he'd have the law on me. He actually managed to get round Abigail and started after me down the hall, until she hooked his leg from behind with her mop and brought him down. Before he could scramble to his feet again, she shouted to me to ring the police as we'd found an intruder breaking into the house. That's when he finally gave up and left. He picked up his briefcase and limped off down the pathway, shaking his wet trousers out, trying to pull his shirt away from his body, with Abby following him all the way, calling him a cat's cradle and a tin-eared toy dog and a mess of potage, and I don't know what else.

'He got to the kerb, and there was this girl waiting for him on one of those small motorbikes—'

'What?' Ellie dropped the plate she'd been about to put in the dishwasher. She said, 'A girl waiting for him? On . . . what?'

He blinked. 'I said. A motorbike. You know. Not a Harley Davidson. One of the smaller models.'

'Oh!' said Ellie, sinking on to a stool. 'Oh, no!'

TWELVE

Sunday lunchtime

Thomas suspended operations on his sandwich to stare at Ellie. 'Whatever's the matter?'

'A girl? On a motorbike. Really?'

'Of course I'm sure. She took off her helmet to shout at

him.' He half closed his eyes, remembering. 'Fair hair, cut short. Fair skin. Slender build in black leather. Leather gloves. Tallish.'

'Oh!' said Ellie. 'That matches the description of the person who daubed a nasty word on the window at W & P's last week. A young mother I spoke to actually saw the girl do it but was too far away to get the licence number and wouldn't recognize her again because she was wearing black leathers and a helmet. Did Archie arrive on the motorbike?'

'Um. Not sure. I didn't notice this girl until after he'd been seen off by Abby. You mean, was this girl waiting for him while he tried to get into the house? Yes, I would say she was.'

Ellie groped for the truth. 'We knew that Streetwise had made Archie an offer to keep his job when they took over Walker & Price, but we had no idea he was friendly with a girl who was actively involved in their persecution. I suppose I ought to say "allegedly" involved, but it feels right to me. It looks as if Archie sold out to Streetwise while still working for Walker & Price and it follows that he aided and abetted her in what she was doing. Allegedly doing. Or did he only get together with the girl after she'd defaced the window?'

Ellie shook her head at herself. 'No, that's not likely, is it? Though I suppose it's possible.'

Thomas also shook his head. 'I suppose there may be other girls who ride black motorbikes?'

'What are the odds on that? All right, it's not proof positive that he was working for Streetwise while being paid by Walker & Price, but it looks very much like it. Oh, poor Nancy! And Charles as well! They gave Archie a job and look how he's repaid them! He must be feeling pretty confident that his future looks rosy if he can use the biker girl to get him to and from Nancy's house. I wonder why he isn't driving himself? Perhaps he's lost his licence for some reason?'

Ellie reached for a pen to make a note to herself. 'I'll ask Nancy. She'll know.'

Thomas grinned. 'I can tell you that the biker girl wasn't best pleased to let him on to her bike when she saw how wet he was. There was quite an argument as to whether or not she was going to allow him to ride with her, but eventually she let him get on the back of the bike and off they went. I've got the licence number.'

'We must give it to Lesley. She can trace the girl from that and get her for defacing Walker & Price's window. I wonder if she was responsible for the other nasty things that have been happening there?'

Thomas said, 'That's a nasty thought. Anyway, as she drove off, Nancy's kindly neighbour drove up with a door tied on to the roof of his car, having collected a friend who knew how to fit it. Abby made them tea, I rescued the sodden papers and brought them back to see if we could dry them out and read them. Anything been happening at your end?'

'Yes, indeed.' Ellie updated him on the latest with news of Kate's phone calls, and what she herself had done to get Jocelyn to move back into the student house.

Thomas said, 'You're sure Jocelyn is on the side of the angels?'

'Oh yes. He . . . he *feels* good.'

He grinned. 'I don't think that comment would be acceptable as a reference in a court of law, but it'll do for me.'

'I'm not ruling him out completely. I like the man, but his actions don't always seem to tie up with what I had expected of him. For instance, why did he flee the student house so quickly after Brandon's death? Because his mother's dying and needed him? Well, yes . . . Why am I not convinced? What's more, Patsy wasn't convinced by that argument, either.

'Another thing; why didn't he respond immediately to Patsy's texts about the rent? He says he arranged with Walker & Price to pay everything himself, but they don't seem to have passed that information on to her. All right, I'll give you that he might have spoken to Archie about it, and Archie failed to pass the message on. Oh, I don't know. There's something going on between Jocelyn and Patsy that I don't understand. One minute I think he's serious about Patsy and the next . . . Why is he blowing hot and cold?'

'I couldn't say. Ah. Look at this.' Thomas pointed to the rescued papers, which were drying out nicely. The ink on the printed sheets was intact but where someone had edited the text in biro, the water had leached almost all the colour from the page.

Some items were easy to identify. There were two copies of a computer-processed bill of sale for Walker & Price, with spaces left for signature of both buyer and seller. Presumably this was what Nancy had been expected to sign.

Ellie was curious. 'How much were they planning to buy the agency for?'

'Not enough.' Thomas grimaced, carefully separating damp sheets one from one another with a knife. 'Here it is. Five thousand pounds. Enough for her air fare to New Zealand, perhaps?'

'Not enough for all those years of hard work, and nothing like the value on the open market.'

'Mm. There's something else here. Walker & Price are giving Streetwise the right to manage all properties currently under contract to them. Which includes the student house, I suppose?'

'Over my dead body.'

Thomas said, 'It might be legal, if Nancy signs it.'

'Doesn't the charity have to agree?'

'I think you'd better get a professional opinion on that.' Thomas turned to some more papers. 'Nothing legible. A draft of some sort, I think. Too waterlogged to read.'

Ellie was poring over another sheet of paper. 'This is a draft, too. With what looks like handwritten corrections in blue ink on it. Only, the blue is mostly disappearing. It's a draft for the bill of sale which you've got there, only . . . yes, they've included the address of the student house. And that's the only property which they've given the address for.'

She looked up. 'So why did they take the address out of the final version? Answer: they wanted Nancy to sign it without realizing that this is really all about who controls the management of the student house. Tell me I'm imagining things.'

Thomas didn't answer. He was frowning over a different piece of paper. 'Look at this. It's a list of addresses, mostly in London. Are these the other properties which Streetwise have on their books? No, wait a minute. That can't be right. The last one on the list is the Ladywood project, the latest acquisition

by the charity, the one you've just been told is to be compulsorily purchased by the council.'

Ellie took it from him. Was that a draught from the back
door? No, it was firmly closed. She shivered. She said, 'It's a
list of all the properties the charity owns. Which means that
Streetwise are not just aiming to take over Walker & Price or
the student house. They're after the charity.'

She blinked. 'No, that's stupid. How could they possibly be
after the rights to maintain and let all the charity's properties?
No, no. That's far too big a proposition for even the ambitious
Streetwise. Isn't it? I mean, why on earth would we let them
do that?'

Thomas was staring at another piece of paper. He thrust it
at Ellie, and went to open the back door, to let some air into
the room. He said, 'We thought this was a small-scale spat
between two estate agencies with very different agendas, but if
I'm right, whoever is at the back of this is now widening the
scope of their activities and yes, they are now intending to
attack the charity itself.'

'No, no.' Ellie could not believe that. She. Simply. Could.
Not. Believe. It.

Thomas said, 'Look at the timeline of what's happened.
First came the attacks on Walker & Price; small-scale at first,
they escalated until it was clear Streetwise wanted to buy
them out. But, like the tidying away of Mr Walker's death
which was supposedly at the hands of a random burglar, there
was also pressure to play down the death of the student at
the charity's house. I have to ask: in whose interest was that
done?'

Ellie let her shoulders rise and fall. The answer seemed to
be Councillor Hallett, which was nonsense according to what
everyone knew of the man.

Thomas continued, 'I'll ignore the fliers claiming the students
are running a brothel for the moment, because I can't see how
that fits in. It sounds like a student prank which misfired. But
I'm beginning to wonder if these people – maybe Streetwise,
or whoever is at the back of them – can also be aiming to get
the charity's redevelopment project cancelled, making everything the charity has invested in that property practically

worthless and therefore vulnerable to a takeover. Look at this paper. What do you see?'

With reluctance, Ellie looked at the list of names on the paper. She didn't want to look. By some fluke this piece of paper had not been soaked as thoroughly as some of the others and most of the words were legible.

The content? A typed list of names half obscured by someone – or perhaps more than one person? – doodling over them in different colours.

The names were listed in alphabetical order with addresses attached, and some had a comment, or a tick in red biro beside them. Yes, she recognized one or two names, but what was the connection between them? Ah yes, she saw it now. They all worked for the charity or were connected with it in some way.

Ellie's name and address was on the list, but not ticked.

Thomas' name had been crossed through, three times, in red. The biro had slashed through the paper there.

Kate, their finance director, was included in the list, as was Stewart, but neither of their names had been ticked. Stewart's name had been followed by someone with a blue biro writing the words, 'Not yet!'

Pat – who had been Ellie's part-time secretary for many years – was featured and her name had been ticked. The remark by Pat's name was 'Yes!' Pat had actually stopped working for Ellie some time ago so . . . what was that about?

Last but not least was Nirav, the clever lad who worked for Stewart in the lettings department, and who was being seconded to help out at Walker & Price the following week. His name had been double-ticked while Red Biro had marked his name not only with another 'Yes!' but followed by two stars.

Ellie couldn't make sense of the doodles. There were all sorts of scribbles. Blue Biro had drawn a children's version of a house and Red Biro had drawn an expanding explosion.

Ellie felt rather sick. She said, 'These are papers that Archie was carrying, but he didn't make the list, did he? No, because he wouldn't know who worked for the charity. We know that the bill of sale originates from Streetwise so presumably that's where this list comes from, too? It's a horrible thought, but I see they're interested in people who work for us. I see they've made Nirav their number one target?'

Thomas said, 'Think about Walker & Price, and Archie. Streetwise got to Archie, didn't they? I think they promised him the earth if he helped them to bring down Walker & Price and he fell for it. We don't know exactly how much of the persecution was down to him, but he was certainly thinking more of what Streetwise could give him when he pressed Nancy to sell, than he was of what she would be wise to do. Is it possible they're now going after Nirav, presumably hoping they can seduce him into working for them, too?'

Ellie could see what an asset Nirav would be to Streetwise if he could be bribed to work for them. It made sense to go after him instead of one of the principals.

If Nirav were offered a large sum of money or if his family were threatened, then how would he react?

Ellie said, 'Do you think they've got to him already? We can't have him attending the meeting tomorrow if he's already been bought and sold.'

Thomas muttered something about Ellie being in denial.

She ignored that. She had something much more important to do than worrying about doodles on a draft.

She reached for the phone and got through to Stewart. As general manager, he would know how Nirav was doing. Once through, she said, 'Sorry to trouble you on a Sunday again, but something's come up. I know you've asked Nirav to work in the Walker & Price office next week. Did that cause any problems for you?'

'No. He's a good lad, saw the point of getting a look at their books before we decide what action, if any, to take. As a matter of fact, at our next meeting I intend to recommend him for a rise in salary.'

'Has he asked for one?'

'No. Well, not openly.' Stewart laughed. 'What he did was, he came to me recently saying he'd been headhunted by some agency or other, that he'd considered their very attractive offer, but before making a decision he wanted to know if we thought he had a future with us. He's taken on more responsibility of late, and developed an excellent rapport with our builders whom, as you know, can be somewhat temperamental. I said he'd done well – which he has – that we hoped he'd stay with us and that I'd put in for a raise for him.'

'Which agency?'

'What? Oh, he didn't say. Does it matter?'

Ellie thought it mattered a great deal.

Stewart went on. 'It did cross my mind that he'd invented the offer so as to give him an excuse to ask for a raise, but no; I think it was genuine. He said that he wanted to stay with us but he had to look out for his future as his wife is newly pregnant and they're going to have to find a larger flat or even a small house soon. I congratulated him on the forthcoming event and we talked about what this would mean for him.

'I said we'd be happy to help him find a suitable house and we discussed various possibilities we have on our books at the moment. We also talked about him taking paternity leave. I was going to suggest that we take on someone he can train up to help him with his workload and act as his assistant in future, and he said that he could always work from home part-time when his wife gave birth. I said I'd raise the matter at the next meeting, but of course this Streetwise business has rather put that on the back burner.'

Ellie thought that Nirav was a high-flyer and his first loyalty would always be to himself and his family. This time Stewart had offered him more than the opposition and so Nirav would stay with the charity, but he would probably leave to work in a bigger organization in due course.

Ellie said, 'You've already asked Nirav to work with Walker & Price next week and that stands, but a lot has been happening on that front, and he'll need briefing before he goes there. Let me bring you up to date, too . . .'

There was a lot that Stewart didn't know about the bigger picture, and how the emphasis seemed to be shifting from the destruction of one estate agency to an attack on the charity itself.

She had wondered how Stewart would react at hearing that he was on a list of possible targets but scheduled for later on. Ellie had thought he would be worried about that, but he laughed. He was a very well-grounded man, content in his job and with his young family.

Ellie decided not to remind him of the inconvenient fact that he had once endured a miserable few years married to her ambitious daughter Diana, who had left him to bring up their son, who was now – heavens, how could that be! – about to apply to the university of his choice. No, Ellie would not remind him of that.

Sidetracked into thinking about her daughter, Ellie realized she didn't even know where Diana might be living at the moment.

It was ridiculous to even entertain the thought that Diana . . .! Stop that thought before it took hold!

Ellie kept looking down at the Streetwise list. If you were of a suspicious turn of mind you might have tried to make out a 'D' in one of the more convoluted doodles by Red Biro.

She pushed the paper aside. Think, Ellie! Think!

Nirav had been double ticked, and they now had confirmation that he'd been approached with an offer he wasn't supposed to refuse. Nirav had been level-headed enough to see that he was better off staying with the charity, who could offer better accommodation, paternity leave and a raise. Streetwise – if it was them, and surely it must be them – had miscalculated there.

The question was; who else had Streetwise approached? Her hand hovered over the phone. She could ring Pat, the part-time secretary she used to have before she went to Canada. But no, Pat had moved away some time ago, hadn't she? Devon? Cornwall? If she'd been approached, she wouldn't have had anything to offer Streetwise.

Ellie rubbed her forehead. She was probably running a temperature. 'I think I might have a nap this afternoon.'

Thomas said, 'I don't think that will help.'

She didn't want to listen. 'Of course it will.'

'That list was made up by someone who didn't know that your secretary had stopped working for you some time ago. They've been out of touch for a while, haven't they?'

Ellie didn't want to listen. 'You're imagining things.'

'Why is my name crossed out three times? She's never made any bones of disliking our marriage.'

'You've no grounds for saying that.'

Thomas said something inarticulate and removed himself to his Quiet Room. He was going off to pray.

Prayer was a good idea. Except that Ellie didn't seem able to calm herself sufficiently to pray.

Come on, Ellie. It can't be Diana behind the campaign to discredit Walker & Price and nibble away at the charity. Of course, that idea made sense in a weird way, as Diana always thought she had an inalienable right to whatever piece of the action she came across, whether she deserved it or not. She had asked – no, demanded – that she be appointed a trustee of the charity. That idea had quickly been kyboshed by Ellie, Kate and Stewart. Was this her way of trying to force her way in?

Diana had got through several fortunes in her time. Her late – and latest – husband had left her nothing but debt and when last heard of Diana was trying to get the charity to buy her another estate agency. Running an estate agency was really the only skill she had. Which might have been why she was attracted to Streetwise . . . if that was where she was working now.

Stop right there! Diana couldn't possibly have anything to do with all this. No.

Back to basics, where was Streetwise getting the money from to launch this campaign?

Which took Ellie back to Jocelyn. Could the Halletts possibly be involved? No, she'd been wrong about that, hadn't she?

Thomas loomed in the doorway and waited for her to acknowledge his presence.

She reached out to him. 'Sorry. Sorry. You're right, of course. I still can't quite believe it, but . . . No, it has to be her.'

'You haven't heard anything from her since we got back? For some reason I got the impression she'd gone abroad.'

'Susan next door told me Diana left a couple of expensive presents for the children soon after we went to Canada but didn't want to see them. She was expensively dressed and went off in a limo with someone.' Ellie caught her breath on a sob. 'She didn't even want to see her children! How could she!'

Thomas sat and put his arm around her. 'They are much loved now. They have a stable home and are doing well.'

Ellie reached for the phone. 'Perhaps, if Diana's just got back from wherever it is she went, she'll have been in touch with her children? Yes, surely she'll have done that. I'll check with Susan.'

Thomas shook his head. 'You know that Diana cuts her ties with anyone who might hold her back in her climb up the ladder. Didn't she dump her first child on Stewart, and leave Evan and Jenny with Susan as soon as it was convenient? She didn't want the hassle of looking after any of them, did she?'

Ellie couldn't cope with this. Diana was self-centred and in financial difficulties; yes. But if she were back in town, surely she must have got in touch with her children again?

Ellie dialled Susan's smartphone and got through straight away. 'Susan, my dear. How are you feeling?'

Judging by the clattering of pans, Susan was in the kitchen. She sounded distracted. 'I'm OK, Ellie. Had a good rest. Just doing the kids' tea.'

'I won't keep you a minute. Have you by any chance heard from Diana lately?'

'What? No. Or rather, I've just this minute taken delivery of a couple of boxed games bought from Harrods, both intended for far older children. I assume they're from Diana but there's no message, no money and both Evan and Jenny need new shoes. I must admit I'm feeling rather cross about it. I told Rafael I'd have to sell the games on eBay or something, but Rafael says to keep them and he'll up my allowance.'

Ellie tried not to grit her teeth.

Oh, Diana! How could you!

'Susan, my dear, you should have said. You manage beautifully, but children do cost money. We'll have a session together next week; you, me and Rafael and see what can be done to help. So you haven't had anything direct from Diana? Do the children miss her, do you think?'

'No, I don't think they do. There's been such a big change in their lives since they came here, what with Evan going to big school and Jenny starting at nursery. He's a little soldier, and Jenny is beginning to trust me enough to come for a cuddle every now and then. Aaargh! My back! I'm a bit achy today. I really do need some help in the house. Rafael's suggesting we should all go away for a holiday by the sea. As if! With me not a fortnight from my due date.'

There was a cry of alarm from one of the children, and Susan hastily ended the call, with a quick: 'Must go!'

Ellie recounted to Thomas what Susan had said.

Thomas reflected, 'So Diana's back and, from the evidence of the papers we've rescued it seems likely she's involved in some way with Streetwise's attack on Walker & Price and may be behind the other things that have been happening, too.'

Ellie fought a rear-guard action and said, 'No, no way! She wouldn't have arranged for bricks to be thrown through windows, or fliers advertising the students' house as a brothel. Nor the firebombing of Nancy's house.'

Thomas said, 'My dear, it was you who said the King Rat didn't get involved himself but had little people to carry out his wishes rather too enthusiastically.'

Ellie shrugged and sought for a tissue so that she could blow her nose. She didn't want to believe it! And yet she had a sneaking feel that yes, Thomas was right. Diana might well have conceived a plan to upset Walker & Price. Nasty phone calls, dogs' doodahs thrust through letterboxes, and also . . . Ugh . . . the spider. Ellie had to admit that it was, perhaps, the sort of petty aggravation that might have appealed to Diana.

She said, 'Diana wouldn't have killed Mr Walker. No way!'

'Agreed. It might have nothing whatever to do with her.'

'You don't believe that. You think it all ties up.'

'I think that the police would have done some door-to-door enquiries along the shops. They would check the footage on any security cameras which had been installed there. I wonder if they'd managed to find any footage indicating a visitor who might have been trying doors on the off chance? But no, the intruder caught Mr Walker in the yard at the back of the shops, didn't he? I doubt if there were any security cameras there.'

Ellie thought about what else had been happening. 'I suppose – I hope – that the police will take the arson attack at Nancy's house seriously? Surely they must investigate that?'

'Yes, but if there were no witnesses they won't get far.'

'Surely they must see that it ties in with the persecution of

Walker & Price? If no one else will explain about that, then I will.' She drew the phone towards her and dialled Lesley's smartphone. Engaged. Voicemail.

Ellie left a message. Surely Lesley would see the point of further investigation now?

THIRTEEN

Sunday afternoon, continued

Ellie finished clearing up the meal while she waited for Lesley to ring back telling herself that Thomas was completely off track. Diana couldn't. Wouldn't. Impossible!

Lesley rang back ten minutes later, but was no help at all when Ellie asked her about the problems at Walker & Price, culminating in Mr Walker's death. 'Sorry, Ellie. I've told you already it's been decided that it's a local yob-type burglary gone wrong and they've not changed their mind on that. Very sad and all that, but we're not wasting much time on it. There aren't any security cameras in that stretch of the Avenue, and in any case we think the burglar came in through the alley at the back and there's no cameras there.'

'There's been other things happening, though. Do you know about . . .?' Ellie had a feeling she was fighting a losing battle but forced herself to carry on.

It didn't help that Thomas had now received a call on his mobile, and was walking up and down, listening to someone with a high voice complaining about something.

Ellie went through her list of events to wind up by saying, '. . . and now the charity is under attack. Lesley, surely you can see a pattern emerging?'

Lesley was having none of it. 'You're imagining things, Ellie. People do fall off balconies in a drunken haze, and they do get clobbered by a yob looking for money for a quick fix. The fliers advertising the student house as a brothel? Surely that's a typical student prank. I hadn't heard about the firebombing of Mrs

Price's house. I'm not on duty this weekend and the case will
be handled by someone else. I expect they'll find it's a disgruntled customer. We'll get them in due course. Probably.'

Ellie had one more go. 'And the charity?' She couldn't bring
herself to say she thought Diana might be involved.

'Surely you know that developers are not generally loved
and the borough council will be applauded for taking the
Ladywood project over. They know best what's needed in that
area. Now, if you don't mind, I've plans for this evening.'

So that was that. Ellie put the phone down, feeling completely
zonked out.

Thomas, however, had finished his call and was trying to get
her attention. 'That was Abby on the phone. She'd gone round
to Nancy's to put the heating on and open the windows to dry
the place out. The neighbours had installed a new front door
and given her the keys but, as she went in, Archie leaped out
of the bushes and forced his way in after her. He wanted the
paperwork he'd brought to the house yesterday.'

Ellie said, 'Yes, of course he would. He's had to report he's
lost them, and his boss won't be at all pleased, especially if
they realize the annotated entries might fall into the wrong
hands.'

'Indeed. Abby says he's half out of his mind. He demanded
to see Nancy. Abby tried to tell him Nancy wasn't there and
he must leave, but he rampaged through the house, upstairs as
well as down, calling for her. Abby told him she'd flushed the
papers down the toilet and Nancy had gone to a hotel somewhere and, if he didn't go, she'd call the police. Finally he left,
saying he'd be back and she'd better find out where Nancy has
gone and be ready to give him the information.'

'Abby deserves a medal.'

'Yes, but she's beginning to realize she's out of her depth.
She doesn't want to leave Nancy's house with all the windows
and doors open to dry out, but she doesn't want to stay there,
either. She's locking up and returning to her house but she's
worried that Archie will ask around till he discovers where she
lives and then he'll turn up there to harass Nancy.'

'How is Nancy doing?'

'She's got herself up and dressed and says she wants to go

home to start sorting out the insurance which, Abby says, Nancy is really not capable of doing yet and what can we suggest?'

Ellie looked at Thomas, feeling helpless. 'She must ring the police if Archie turns up again.'

There was a thump on the door from the conservatory, and the door was eased open to allow young Evan to enter, towing little Fifi and with the cat Midge behind them.

Fifi went straight to Thomas and lifted her arms. He bent down to pick her up, and she turned her head into his shoulder.

Thomas exclaimed, 'Ellie, her little heart's racing. Evan, what's happened?'

Evan stated, in a voice which defied the tears tacking down his cheeks, 'Fifi doesn't like shouting, so I brung her here.'

Quite clearly, he didn't like shouting, either. Ellie and Thomas both turned their heads to listen to whatever might be going on next door. And yes, someone was banging doors and shouting. Oh dear.

Ellie gathered the boy into her arms. 'I don't like shouting, either. Is Jenny all right?'

'She's hiding. I said, "Come next door", but she wouldn't.'

Five years old and Evan is protecting the younger ones. What are Rafael and Susan thinking of, to fight before the children?

Oh, dear! Of course they're at odds with one another. Rafael wants Susan to take the children away, and she will be thinking he's doing that so that he can go on flirting with Mona . . . and neither of them will understand the danger they may be in.

Ellie went into granny mode. She washed the children's faces, located the biscuit tin, and gave one to each child. Fifi relaxed and nibbled away, safe in Thomas' arms. Evan said he would in a minute, but could he . . .?

Ellie diagnosed the problem and took him to the downstairs cloakroom to deal with it. In the old days Evan had used a small potty, which fortunately was still there, but now he used the adult toilet and could reach the taps on the washbasin! He was growing up, wasn't he?

Once that was over, though, he climbed on to the chair at Ellie's side and accepted a biscuit and a mug of milk.

Fifi nestled in the crook of Thomas' arm while she drank

her milk. She even managed a tiny, very tiny smile at Thomas. Ellie handed out more biscuits. She could hear Susan's voice in her head, saying that the children eating biscuits now would spoil their appetite for supper but this, Ellie decided, was an emergency.

Finally, Fifi recovered enough to sit upright, and then slither down to the ground. She didn't bother to speak. She had Evan to do that for her. He said, 'She needs the potty.'

Was she potty-trained already? Could be. She was a fastidious little lady but it transpired she couldn't get in and out of her dungarees without help. Ellie coped with that, and then led the children to the ottoman in the sitting room, into which she'd stowed all the toys which Evan and Jenny had been accustomed to play with before Ellie and Thomas had gone to Canada.

Evan straight away hauled out the box containing the plastic train set which had been his favourite in the past. Thomas got down on the floor, with only a groan or two – had he put on weight, recently? Ought he to stop using the car and walk everywhere? – to help Evan fit the toy railway lines together.

Ellie wondered what was it about railways that attracted the men to it? But in this case, Fifi seemed equally absorbed by it. That kept them both happy.

The noises from next door abated, but there was still the occasional banging of doors to be heard. The children didn't seem to notice, but they did look up at Ellie and Thomas every now and then, to make sure they'd not been deserted.

There was another shove at the conservatory door and in stomped Jenny, fair curls bouncing. She was grinning, pleased with herself. Ellie held out her arms to the little girl, who accepted a kiss but didn't return it. She'd been holding something, which she now put on Ellie's lap.

Evan looked up and said, 'That's Raff's mouse from his computer. He'll go bonkers!'

Jenny leaned against Ellie, and grinned. 'Watch telly?'

Ellie didn't know what to say or do. She could read the script only too well. When Susan and Rafael had started rowing, the children had been distressed. Evan had taken the wisest course and removed himself and Fifi from the scene. Jenny had responded by striking back at Rafael and removing his computer mouse, without which he was unable to operate.

Jenny was proving herself to be her mother's daughter, all right. You didn't land a hit on Diana without her fighting back. Jenny was the same.

'Jenny? You've found Rafael's mouse, have you?' said Thomas, getting to his feet with some difficulty. 'We'll get it back to him later. Meanwhile, come and help me with this railway track. You see, I want to make the railway go over the bridge here, but I can't seem to find the right pieces for it.'

Jenny considered the problem. Then she went to sit down beside Fifi and delved into the box of bits and pieces to find the parts she needed to complete the task.

Ellie and Thomas withdrew to the kitchen, leaving the doors open so that they could hear if the children needed them.

Ellie said, 'I can't bear it. It wrings my heart to have them in such distress. I want to cuddle them and keep them safe for ever. I know that there are other people out there in the big world who are in trouble and distress but all that now seems unimportant. Our priority is surely to look after the children?'

Thomas shook his head. 'It's not as simple as that. If I'm right, *you* are at the centre of this affair. No one but *you* could draw all the various events together and make sense of them; the war on Walker & Price, the death and consequent abandoning of the students' house, and the charity's Ladywood project, which was intended to benefit so many people. They're all connected. If you turn aside, then King Rat's plan will succeed. Remember; all that's necessary for evil to triumph, is for good men to do nothing.'

'But the children . . .!'

Thomas said, 'My joints are telling me I'm too old to sit on the floor. We need help. What about the girl who helped Susan out before?'

'That nice schoolgirl? She's doing A levels. We can't ask her. No, no. I'm sure we can cope between us.'

'No, Ellie. I can see the temptation, but it's not sensible. Yes, we can help with the children from time to time, and we will. That goes without question. But we are not as young as we were and we cannot do as much physically as we used to do.

We need someone else to help out with the children, not just for Susan's sake, but for ours. And lastly, you have been given a different task to perform, which only you can do. You have to deal with Diana. You know that, really.'

Ellie glared at him. She didn't want to listen to this, she really did not.

Yes, she knew in her bones that she couldn't cope with three active children under the age of six. Now and then, yes. For the odd hour. She also knew that Susan needed help here and now. For a start, who was going to look after the children when Susan popped out her second baby?

She said, 'I don't know who to ask.'

Thomas' phone rang, and he picked it up. And listened. He said, 'I'm handing you over to my wife.' And did so.

Ellie accepted the phone with reluctance, only to hear someone babbling away in a high voice. '. . . so Abby and I locked ourselves in, but he went round and round the house, waving his papers and Abby rang the police and someone came round and had a word with him, and he's retreated to the end of the road, but I can see him from here. He's sitting on the front wall of my house, watching this place. Obviously I can't stay here for Abby's sake, so I can't think what to do. And then I thought I'd get a taxi to—'

'Nancy?' said Ellie. 'Is that you?'

She saw that Thomas was checking that he'd got his car keys. Was he going to ride to Nancy's rescue? She should go with him.

No, she couldn't. She couldn't leave the children who were playing next door.

Dear Lord, help!

'Yes, that's me. I'm at Abby's. Who is that? I thought I was speaking to Thomas.'

Ellie took a deep breath. She couldn't see far ahead, but she could see a little way. It was time to take up arms. By opposing the enemy in one small matter, perhaps the next step would become clear.

She said, 'This is Ellie. Now listen to me, Nancy. Thomas is coming to fetch you but to avoid trouble, can you alert one of your nice neighbours to help, too? If he could hang round until

Thomas arrives, the pair of them could then escort you back to your place? Archie won't take on two large men, will he?'

'Well, no. But I can't stay at home. At least, Abby says—'

'Take your time. If Archie sees you've got a bodyguard, he'll leave you alone. Collect any business papers you might need, and either put your valuables in a safe place or bring them with you. Pack a couple of bags with clothing, and toiletries.'

'I can't just abandon everything. The business, we'd be letting people down. I have to reopen sometime but . . . what on earth am I to do about Archie? I can't trust him any longer, can I?'

'No, you can't. I wonder if your helpful neighbour, the one who got you a new door, might be able to help you there? You need the locks changed at the agency. Now. Today. Can you ask him to do that for you? And don't tell Archie. You don't want him tampering with your customer's affairs, do you?'

'I suppose it would be sensible to change the locks. Yes, I'll see if Hugh can do it for me. He got me the new door, and he's offered to help but . . .' Doubtful, but considering the matter. 'I don't know whether I'm on my head or my heels. For one thing, it's going to cost . . . But that's not important. Yes, of course I can pay by card, or Hugh will. Then I can go to a hotel, somewhere.'

Archie will follow her when she leaves. He's not going to give up easily, is he?

'Nancy, you said he's sitting on your front wall. Did he come on a motorbike?'

'What? No, he hasn't a licence. Lost it some months back. Drink driving. No, I can't see any motorbike. He hasn't got one. He comes by bus. His girlfriend has a motorbike. I think he mentioned once that she was giving him a lift to a gig or a rave some way off.'

Ah-ha. So that explains the link between Archie, the girl who defaced the agency window, and what's happening now. I wonder if she's employed by Streetwise?

'That's good. If Archie's no means of transport, he won't be able to follow Thomas when he brings you back here.'

'To you? But I thought, a hotel, maybe or—'

'Listen, carefully. The problems you've been having at Walker & Price are only part of a series of mishaps which I've been trying to make sense of for the last few days. There's going to be a big meeting of the charity for all those concerned tomorrow, when we'll try to work out how to deal with it. I'd like you to be present. We have a spare room here or . . . Are you any good with small children, by any chance?'

'Well, yes, but . . . I mean, I used to see my grandchildren every week and I must admit I miss them since they've gone to New Zealand. But—'

'All will be explained. I'm shutting this phone off now as Thomas will need it. He'll be with you very soon.'

Thomas took his phone back, kissed the top of her head, and prepared to depart.

She caught him up in the hall. 'I've just thought. Can you get a couple of shots of Archie on your phone and send them to me?'

'Will do. God be with us.' He left.

Yes, indeed. Now there's something I said just now . . . What was it? It's Shakespeare, I suspect. Something on the lines of defeating the enemy simply by opposing him. Not sure how that works. Um. Well. Maybe. Worth a try.

She checked on the children next door. Fifi had burrowed into the cushions on the settee and was fast asleep. Evan and Jenny were working on the layout for the toy train. Evan was setting out the station and some trees around it while Jenny was building a flyover. Clever Jenny. Evan hadn't thought of that. Perhaps Jenny would become an engineer.

Back to her own phone went Ellie, scrabbling around for once well-known numbers. Ellie had never learned to drive, and over the years had come to rely on a particularly helpful taxi driver . . . and it was his daughter Coralie who had helped Susan out when Diana had dumped her children on her. Yes, everyone kept saying that Coralie couldn't help now because she was doing her A levels, but Ellie was on a roll and thought it worth a phone call to check.

'Is that Sam, the taxi man?'

'Mrs Ellie, is it really you? I was passing your house only last night and wondering if you were back yet and thinking then that Mrs Susan, she must be near her time. Coralie was only saying she hoped to hear from you soon . . . A-levels? My

Coralie? Well, we had hoped she might stay on and do them, but it's not for her and she left school the moment she could legally do so. She was looking after a coupla kids that was causing ruckus for a woman down the road for a while, and then the school persuaded her to go back and try again, and she did, but it weren't no good. She's not cut out for that life.

'Besides which, she's got herself a boyfriend and is out all hours with him, no matter what we say. Work? She tried that nursery that your little ones were at, but the woman there drove her crazy with her "do this" and "don't do that!" So she's been hanging around, working a bit here and there, shelf-filling at the local supermarket and the like. She'd be thrilled to help you out, though. When do you want her to start?'

'Now, this evening. Oh, Sam; that would be wonderful. You really think she'd like to come? Yes? That's brilliant! So much has been happening. I'll fill her in when she arrives.'

Praise the Lord. Oh, my! Oh my!

Tick that off on the list.

Next. Check on the children. Fifi hadn't moved. Evan and Jenny were both still absorbed in their tasks. Back to the phone. Find the number of the next person she wanted to talk to.

Ah-ha! Ping, ping! Is that my phone?

Thomas had sent her a picture or two?

Problem: Ellie had recently been persuaded to upgrade to a smartphone. Thomas had shown her how to do this and that and she understood she could now do a whole raft of things which she hadn't been able to do in the past. She had resisted getting all sorts of apps on the basis she wouldn't remember what they were for. But, given time and reference to the notes Thomas had made for her, she could send and receive calls, take a picture of something or someone and even access pictures sent to her.

She stared at the smartphone now, her mind awhirl with possibilities. She could do it! Of course she could do it! You swiped this and dabbed that and . . . No, she'd got that wrong.

She sent up an arrow prayer. *Dear Lord! This technology . . .!*

She knew a way around the dilemma. Of course she did. She could unload whatever was on the smartphone to her computer and see what she'd been sent. She gave a quick peek into the living room. Evan was running the train up and down a piece of track. Jenny had managed to turn the television on. Fifi was still asleep.

Ellie left that door open, crossed the hall into her study, and turned on her computer. She was never sure whether or not it would respond . . . Fingers crossed, it did.

Amazing. It wasn't annoyed with her as it often was when she failed to understand the way it was designed to work.

Now, how did she access the photos on her smartphone? Up came the photos Thomas had just taken. Yes! Young Archie, taken unawares. No motorbike in sight. He looked slightly frazzled. Good. Long may that last.

While Ellie had transferred the photos from her smartphone to the computer, she used the extension of the landline phone in her study to speak to the next person on her list.

'Is that you, Patsy? This is rather hush-hush. Can you take the call in private? Oh, sorry. Yes, it's Mrs Quicke here. But would you mind not telling people who it is who's ringing you?'

Patsy said, in a remote voice, speaking to someone in the room beside her. 'Just the family! I'll take it upstairs.'

Sounds of merriment in the background. More sounds of someone climbing the stairs, a door opening and shutting. Silence except for Patsy's breathing.

'Yes?' she said.

Ellie said, 'Judging from the noise below, you were celebrating.'

'Yes. Jocelyn rang to ask if we'd mind if he moved back in. Of course we said he could. Mona's going to stay where she is in Terry's room and Terry says he doesn't mind going up to where Brandon was.'

That made sense. Ellie had thought it might be Terry – who liked experimenting – who was the one who'd been trying out the cannabis Brandon had left behind. He'd left a distinctive trace in the air at the top of the house which was far too recent to have been left over from the infamous party.

Patsy went on. 'Imran's back already, in his own room. We may or may not bring someone in to take Brandon's place. Jocelyn came round straight away with his stuff and he's ordering pizzas all round for a feast this evening. His latest girlfriend keeps ringing him up to protest that he's deserting her. He showed us a picture of her. Glamour puss. This one's a brunette, by the way. Talons for nails and Botoxed lips.'

Ellie grinned to herself. 'I don't think you need to worry about her. She's camouflage.'

'He needs camouflage?'

'Yes. You know he does. You've done the same thing, haven't you? Refused to go out with him and told him you had a boyfriend back in Wales. You two have been taking things slowly. Quite right, too. But if Dr Hallett has told anyone in the house about himself and his family, he's told you.'

'Ah, you worked that out, did you? He makes out he's just an ordinary research student for this one last year. He's got a contract for a year's work to keep him occupied. All terribly secret and high-flying and so on. He doesn't talk about it, but we all know.'

'That's good news. But Patsy, this case is not over till we find out who's at the back of the bad things that have been happening. I think it's someone who has a connection to Jocelyn. Can you help me out there?'

'You mean Brandon's death? No, I can assure you—'

'I know, I know. Accident. Bear with me for a second. That's not the only thing that's happened recently, and I'm only able to link them together because Jocelyn seems to know more than he should about them.'

'What things?' Subdued.

'The estate agency he used was subject to a series of nasty happenings in an effort to make them sell to a competitor. When petty annoyances failed to get the desired result, a brick was thrown through the shop window, and then one of the partners was found dead. And no, before you start, it might have been a random burglary gone wrong, done by a local man on drugs. But what was definitely not an opportunistic crime was the subsequent arson attack on the one remaining partner who is being pressured to sell out.'

'That had nothing to do with us.'

'Have patience. Your tenancy of the house and the flyposting in the neighbourhood are collateral damage. If I'm right, the protagonist is not attacking you, but the charity which owns your house. The reason he or she went after the estate agent was that the charity had signed a contract for Walker & Price to represent their interests in the matter of your house. So, if they can take over Walker & Price, the new agency can use that contract as a lever to work their way into the charity itself.'

Patsy scoffed. 'What nonsense!'

'Yes, it would be, if I hadn't been told that influence had been brought to bear to play down the two deaths – Brandon's and Mr Walker's. I mean, why bother, if they were all that they were supposed to be?'

'But—'

'I dislike coincidences, don't you? Next, a most unpleasant discovery; the young salesman, Archie by name, at Walker & Price, so very helpful, has been hounding Nancy Price to sell to the second estate agent. And I mean, hounding. And lastly, I learned last night that the council is thinking of rescinding permission for the charity to develop a street of condemned housing which we had bought and intended to redevelop for affordable housing. The charity paid the market price for it, have spent a fortune on architects, surveys, etc, and were intending to start work tomorrow. Only now, at this last minute, the council say they want to compulsorily purchase the site for some other use, and they offer peanuts. This could ruin us, too.'

'This is ridiculous! Jocelyn would never—'

'No, of course he hadn't anything to do with it, nor with the firebombing of the house belonging to the owner of the estate agency which means she's now homeless and her business is in ruins. Nor did he have anything to do with the death of Mr Walker. But Jocelyn does know something. He admitted as much to me. He's moving back in an effort to protect you.'

'This is nonsense. I'm going to end this—'

'Wait. I'm sending you a photograph of a man who is in this business up to his neck. I think he may have been the one who put the fliers through the doors in your street. Can you ask around, see if anyone recognizes him?'

Ellie eyed her computer. Now, how exactly did she do that? She'd done it before, of course she had. Thomas was much better at this modern technology than she, and he actually liked taking photographs and sharing them with his family. She was doing this all wrong. She was all fingers and thumbs. Did she have to finish her phone call before she sent the photo?

How embarrassing; she was going to ask Patsy how to do it. Uh-oh. Patsy had ended the call.

Now, try again. Archie's picture is on screen. Share . . . Patsy's phone number. The picture went. She hoped.

Would Patsy ring back? No? Oh, dear.

Now what? Wait for her to ring back or . . . No, check on the children. Jenny had turned the volume on the television up to deafening, Evan was in the kitchen, climbing on to a chair to reach the biscuit tin and Fifi . . .? Where was Fifi?

Ah, she was in the downstairs cloakroom, in some distress as she tried to undo the clasps on her dungarees, in order to use the potty.

Ellie dealt with Fifi, Evan and Jenny in that order. The phone rang and she couldn't remember where she'd left it. It rang and rang. Jenny showed all the signs of going into a major tantrum. Evan kept repeating the word 'Biccy!'.

Fifi wanted to be lifted up and held close.

Ellie found her phone.

Oh, the television! 'Turn it down, Jenny!'

Jenny didn't. Ellie tried to answer the phone while cradling Fifi on her shoulder and failed. It dropped to the floor. Ellie could hear a disembodied voice saying, 'Hello? Hello?' but couldn't get down to the floor to pick it up with Fifi clinging to her.

Where were Rafael and Susan?

Where was Thomas?

Was that the front doorbell? Jenny started to scream and stamp her feet. She closed her eyes, opened her mouth, and let fly. She had a good pair of lungs on her. Evan managed to reach the biscuit tin and pull it off the table and on to the floor. The lid came off the tin . . . it had always been temperamental, but Ellie had liked the picture on it . . . and biscuits scattered all over the place.

Fifi burrowed into Ellie's arms. She did not like noise, did she?

The doorbell again!

Perhaps Thomas was back and had forgotten his key? No, she remembered he'd checked that he had his keys before he left. Perhaps it was Susan . . .? But no, Susan would have come round by the garden.

Ellie had a nasty thought. Something was wrong next door. Susan or Rafael ought to have been round to check on the children by now.

Ellie got herself to the front door and managed to pull it open.

FOURTEEN

Sunday teatime

A strange girl stood in the porch. Bright pink jacket, enormous hoop earrings, black leggings, corn-rowed hair and a big smile . . . which faded as she heard the noise Jenny was making, and saw that Fifi was trying to make herself small in Ellie's arms.

There was a crash from the kitchen. What had Evan done now?

Ellie gasped, 'Coralie! I hardly knew you. How you've grown!'

'Give her here,' said Coralie, taking a willing Fifi into her own arms. 'And is that naughty Jenny making all that noise?' She stepped past Ellie, crossed the hall, and collected Jenny with her free arm. 'There, now! What you in such a state for, eh?'

Jenny opened her eyes, hiccupped, recognized a superior being and closed her mouth. Her colour faded from scarlet to its usual pink. She hit Coralie's shoulder and yes, almost managed a smile. 'Telly!' she said.

Coralie freed herself somehow, long enough to turn the television off – oh, blessed peace! – only to resume her hold around Jenny. Ellie wondered how on earth did Coralie do that? She hadn't grown an extra arm, had she? Perhaps those who looked after children grew a third, invisible arm?

Now that the telly was off, Ellie could hear a phone ringing, somewhere. But where? Ah, it stopped.

'Remember me?' said Coralie to Jenny. 'I'm Coralie, which rhymes with "Come to me". Now, let's go and find out what your naughty brother has been up to, right?'

When Coralie said 'naughty', it sounded like an endearment. Jenny certainly took it as such.

Coralie put Jenny down on the floor but continued to hold her hand, while she said to Ellie, 'Dad told me you was in trouble. Where's Susan? I tried next door, but there wasn't no one in, and no lights on nor nothing.'

'I don't know!' said Ellie, 'I'm dead worried, tell the truth. I'd better go round there, if you can watch the children for a mo.'

Something hit Ellie's thigh. Evan, handing her a smartphone. He had biscuit crumbs round his mouth and a biscuit in his left hand. He looked up at Coralie and thought about it. Did he remember her? Perhaps he did? He was a serious little boy. Suddenly, he grinned. He sang, not too much off key, 'A fox went out . . .'

Coralie sang along with him. '. . . one starry night! We used to sing that in the bath, didn't we? What a clever boy you are to remember Coralie. Now, let's get everyone cleaned up and sitting at the kitchen table, and we'll see what we can cook for our supper, eh?' And then to Ellie, 'You look frazzled. You can leave me with them while you have a cuppa, right.'

Ellie dithered. 'I was going to cook a joint for tonight's supper, but . . . I haven't even thought about—'

'We'll do fish fingers or pasta,' said Coralie, sweeping the children into the kitchen before her. 'Which would you prefer, kiddies?'

Ellie didn't think the children would like to be called 'kiddies', but they didn't seem to object. Coralie had the magic touch, didn't she?

Ellie's phone went off, and she jumped a mile.

'I've been ringing and ringing . . .' A male voice. Who was it?

'I tried on the way to the hospital, but . . . never mind that now. The thing is, they're going to keep her in, bed rest, they think they can stop it, because it's a week early. She's objecting like mad, but I said she had to think of the babe, and . . . Ellie, is that you? I don't know what to do about the children.'

It was Rafael.

She said, 'It's all right, Rafael. Relax. The children are here with me and Coralie's arrived and is going to look after them. Susan can stop worrying.'

'I've been going half out of my mind, not knowing what to do, to whisk her off to hospital, or put her to bed. Then she had a show and I panicked, I couldn't think of anything but getting her there and I knew you and Thomas were around and I did try to ring you but—'

'We're all here and doing fine.' Ellie's brain went into overtime. What if this . . . or that? She said, 'If they keep Susan in, would it be all right for me to ask Coralie to move into your spare room for tonight?'

'Yes, of course. That is, I don't know if the bed is—'

'Relax. This is Coralie we're talking about. I think you can safely leave it to her to do the right thing. Are you going to stay at the hospital?'

'I'm biting my fingernails, can't think straight. What if . . .? No, of course everything's going to be all right. I'll let you know what . . .' His voice died away, and then he clicked off.

Ellie wanted to tear over to the hospital. She wanted to ring him back and demand details. She wanted to do something, anything. Poor Susan! But she was only a week early. The baby would be all right if he was born now. If only . . .!

Ellie told herself to calm down. Rafael was at the hospital. Susan was in the best possible place for her at this moment. Ellie had other calls on her time. She couldn't go rushing to the hospital to act as mother when she had three little ones needing attention, not to mention the problem of Archie and Nancy . . . Oh, my goodness! Ellie had forgotten Nancy. She must be in quite a state, but surely Thomas would rescue her and . . . was the spare room bed made up here?

Calm down, Ellie. Think. Put your priorities in order. The children.

Ellie listened out. Joyful noises and squeaks of children happily making a mess came from the kitchen. The television was blessedly silent, but somewhere a phone was ringing. The landline in her study? Ellie got there just before the caller hung up.

It was Patsy. Agitated. 'Mrs Quicke, I've been trying and trying to ring you back. That photo you sent me. Where did you get it?'

'My husband took it this afternoon. It's of a young man called Archie, who used to work for Walker & Price but whom we think has thrown in his lot with Streetwise, their competitor. He was waiting outside Nancy Price's house this morning, trying to bully her into selling the estate agency. Do you know him?'

'Yes. I'm sorry to say, we do. Can you tell me how you've come across him? Has he actually broken the law?'

That was a strange question. But Patsy wouldn't ask without good reason. Ellie tried to think straight. 'I don't know that I can prove anything criminal. Would circumstantial evidence do you?'

'Yes. Feel free to use the word "alleged".'

'Very well. You know I'm involved in the charity which takes condemned properties and turns them into affordable accommodation? Yes, this is relevant. Do you want some details?'

'Yes, please.'

Ellie went on to explain the problems affecting Walker & Price, for whom Archie worked . . . the suspicion that he'd switched loyalties to work for Streetwise. She added that Archie had lost his driving licence some time ago and had been accepting lifts from a girl who rides a motorbike. A girl answering to that description was seen defacing the window of the agency, and she'd been accompanying Archie around while he tried to bully Nancy Price into selling the agency for a pittance.

Ellie said, 'I have personal knowledge of all that. Now for the "alleged" bits. I think it was either he or she who set up the nasty events which brought W & P to its knees, and I believe it was either Archie or his girlfriend who firebombed her house last night. And, if you want to let your fancy roam, then you might think it worthwhile checking in your road to see if Archie or the motorbike girl were responsible for posting the fliers which advertised your house as a brothel.'

'Anything else?' A stony voice.

'Jocelyn knows something about this, and the knowledge is tearing him apart.'

'How could he possibly be involved?'

'I don't know! Through an old friend, perhaps? Someone he cares for and is shielding? I thought at first it might be his father because someone in good odour with the council has been pulling strings to shut down police enquiries on the death of Mr Walker. The latest blow is that the council has rescinded the permits for the charity to develop that rundown street we bought. Councillor Hallett appears to be on the side of the saints, so . . . does Jocelyn have a friend or contact who could fill the bill?'

No comment on that. 'Anything else?'

'Yes. I don't think whoever started this campaign – King Rat, as you might say – actually firebombed Nancy's house or killed Mr Walker in person. He or she probably didn't think it through. He or she may simply have expressed annoyance that their takeover bid for Walker & Price was not welcome, and this annoyance was picked up by someone who took the hint to harass the people who were obstructing the boss's wishes, and who ran away with it. They probably thought a little hassle here and a threat there would do it, and when it didn't, they got more and more creative.'

'Jocelyn wouldn't.'

'No, of course he wouldn't. But he knows something. I believe he knows who King Rat may be. I believe he doesn't know how to stop what's happening except by moving back in to protect you and the others. Patsy, I need to know who or what it is that he's protecting. And I agree, it's probably not his father who seems to be squeaky clean if a bit of a bully.'

There was a long, long silence. Finally the girl broke it. 'Jocelyn said that this last year living with us has been the happiest in his life. Apart from the first few weeks when Brendon was being a pain, we were all really good friends. Quite often we'd all sit in the back room or the garden and chat of an evening. Sometimes I'd chat with Mrs Jermyn over the fence. We all went to Jocelyn with our problems.'

'Even you?'

'I didn't at first. Not for a long time. But when I understood that he was interested . . . He was such good company and . . . Only, you see, I'd promised my family that I'd go back home and teach when I got my MA. So I told him how it was with me. My father and mother are not well and my brothers have married and moved away.'

'And Jocelyn said . . .?'

'A married woman can teach anywhere, and that her husband's job might mean flexible working conditions.'

'Ah. He sort of proposed and you sort of promised to consider his proposal while pointing out the problems?'

Patsy gave a sad little laugh. 'Yes, I thought that was what he meant but then Brandon died and he left and I was so angry with him that I said . . . things.'

'This is all about family, isn't it? Yours and his.'

Ellie thought, *And mine. The pressures, the guilt, the levers of power.*

Patsy said, 'Families, yes. Mine is straightforward enough; even in this day and age in my family the boys go out into the world and the girls stay home to look after their parents. It's much the same for Jocelyn, except that he's drawn the short straw, being the one needed to stay at home. He was an afterthought, you see, arriving ten years after his elder brother, Avery. Avery took after his mother's side of the family, being tall and good looking. I don't think his mother ever loved Jocelyn. She handed him over to a nanny to be brought up and she laughed when Avery poked fun at Jocelyn. Nowadays you'd call the name-calling and sly jokes "abuse".

'Jocelyn was and is pretty bright, but no matter how well he did at school, his parents didn't seem to notice. It was always Avery this, and Avery that. They were outraged when an aunt left her fortune to Jocelyn and not to Avery. Even now Jocelyn's apologetic about having money.

'He doesn't complain about Avery's treatment of him, by the way. We only understood what had been happening because Avery used to visit us occasionally after we moved in. He was oh so smooth and oh so deliciously, fashionably handsome. With a snake's tongue! He'd come in and yell for "Fatso!" or "Baldy" and make jokes about overweight puddings. He'd tell us tales of how Jocelyn as a toddler had been slow to talk and stammered. Brandon was the same but easier to ignore because he told such stupid lies about Jocelyn that nobody believed them. Also, he didn't have Avery's presence.'

Ellie said, 'That's horrible.'

Patsy half laughed. 'That's family for you. Avery thought we'd laugh at his "jokes" but we didn't, and eventually he stopped coming. Jocelyn doesn't think himself hard done by. He sees that his brother's charm and good looks ease his path through life and he says "that's life" and gets on with it.'

Ellie understood. 'It's that inner strength and tolerance which made Jocelyn the hub of the group?'

'Yes. Once we'd made it clear to Avery and Brandon that we were Jocelyn's friends, everything went along much better. Actually, we made Jocelyn practise saying, "Oh, grow up, Avery!" We made him say it over and over until he started laughing and . . . well, it got to be a catchphrase. Every time one of us did or said something stupid, we'd say, "Oh, do grow up, Avery!" It helped.'

Ellie said, 'Yes, I can see that Avery's words must have hurt, and your teaching Jocelyn how to stand up to his brother must have helped. I suppose Jocelyn had that parade of totties to prove to himself – and to you – that he could get a girl in spite of what Avery said?'

'I was never quite sure, but yes, I suppose it was just that. Avery" evil, you know. He makes my skin crawl. He took Mona out a couple of times. The second time she came back in tears. Her breast was black and blue where he'd grabbed her. He's a nasty piece of work. I suppose I ought to say "allegedly", but I won't.

'We had some quiet months until one evening in May Jocelyn followed me out into the garden with a bottle of wine and a couple of glasses. He hardly drinks at all normally, but that night he did. He said the cancer treatment his mother had been undergoing had failed and that the tumour was inoperable. He said she hadn't long to live. She wanted constant attention and reassurance. Avery said he wasn't able to spare much time to be with his mother because he was going through a second divorce and had to attend to his business affairs. His father said he'd do early mornings and evenings and could Jocelyn return home and do the rest.'

'The tyranny of the weak?'

'Yes. Oh, Jocelyn saw it all quite clearly. He knew his mother really wanted Avery beside her but that if her favourite wasn't available, then Jocelyn would have to do.'

'But he didn't go home?'

'Well, there was a problem. He'd contracted to do this research job for a year and wanted to continue with it. He said he recognized that he was being selfish, that he owed everything to his parents and could see their point of view.'

Ellie said, 'Humph!' Loudly.

Patsy replied, 'Agreed. I pointed out that he was managing to fulfil his work commitments with ease. He has a fine brain, you know. He's had some job offers already which would make anyone else weep with joy, but he wanted this one last year before deciding in which direction to go. He covers up his serious nature with his idiot-about-town act. It had taken me a while to see through it—'

'Because of the way Brandon and Avery treated him?'

'Well, yes. Anyway, we talked it through and Jocelyn decided to carry on with his research job but spend almost every afternoon with his mother fetching this, and doing that; most of the time I think she just needs someone to listen to her complaints. He allowed himself one evening a week to take out a totty but then he'd burn the midnight oil to make up for it. He managed pretty well until that terrible evening when Brandon fell out of the top window. After that, Jocelyn's mother and his aunt staged a scene, begging him to go home. His mother's temperature shot up and . . . Oh, you can imagine it, can't you? So back he went.

'I understood in a way but I was also angry with him for giving in. I said he was a Mummy's boy and other things. I wish I hadn't. He said he'd sort out the lease for us. Something went wrong there, but he's promised to deal with it.'

Ellie looked at her watch. What time was it? Patsy was giving her some good stuff, but Ellie couldn't concentrate. Coralie seemed to be coping well in the kitchen, but poor Susan! And where were Thomas and Nancy and . . . She pulled her mind back to the present.

She said, 'All right. I get the picture. So who is the villain, the father or the brother Avery?'

'Avery the brother. Jocelyn admires his father for switching from business magnate to charity and council work. He made his money in communication technology. He's supposed to be shedding his workload by handing the business over to Avery. He doesn't intend standing for re-election to the council, but hopefully will continue with his charity work. He seems to be on the side of the angels.'

'Avery's been married twice? What's his current situation?'

'Not sure. I believe he's toting around another wealthy, Botoxed woman. Somebody with money. An heiress or something. Mama and Papa Hallett are anxious for Avery to produce children, and hopeful this latest woman will be able to do the deed.'

Ellie's brain wasn't in good working order. She was trying to deal with three sets of problems at once, and not succeeding. But she did say, 'You wanted to know where I got the photo of Archie from. Does that mean you recognize him?'

A long pause. Then: 'I'll get back to you on that.' And off went the phone.

Ellie looked at her watch again. Where was Thomas? And what was happening with Susan? And where was the bedlinen for the spare bedroom?

Sunday evening

Thomas' car turned into the driveway and parked, closely followed by another vehicle which Ellie didn't recognize. Thomas helped Nancy out of his car on to the driveway, while a complete stranger got out of the second car.

Incredibly, Nancy was smiling.

Thomas opened the boot of his car and took out a couple of large suitcases. The strange man did the same from his car. The three of them were laughing and chatting, very much at their ease. Nancy retrieved a laptop and a tote bag from the back seat of Thomas' car. And yes, she was still smiling.

What on earth was going on?

Ellie could have screamed with frustration.

How could they lark about when the world was tumbling down around our ears! What about Susan? What about the firebombing? What about the children?

She threw open the front door and stopped short.

Thomas had a black eye and a cut on his cheekbone, while the stranger had a large plaster on his forehead. Both men showed signs of having been in a roughhouse. Bloodstains, crumpled shirts. And big grins.

Nancy was flushed and bright-eyed. The two boys hadn't been fighting over her, had they? No, of course not. Ridiculous!

Thomas carried in the two suitcases, stopping to kiss Ellie's cheek as he passed her into the hall. 'Home is the traveller, home from the sea. Metaphorically speaking, of course. Nancy, do come in. Let Hugh bring in the rest of your stuff. Ellie, this is Hugh. He's the kind neighbour who got Nancy a new door yesterday and has offered to help take all her valuables out of the house.'

Nancy beamed at Ellie. 'You're so kind, Ellie. Everyone's so kind. I can't believe how kind everyone is.' Nancy was hyper. She was riding high but actually on the verge of tears. The moment she relaxed, tears would come. Yes, here they came.

Ellie said, 'You're safe here. Come and sit down. Cup of tea in a minute.' She ushered Nancy into the sitting room, only to be brought up by the sight of the children's toys all over the carpet, at which Nancy started to giggle . . . and so, after a minute, did Ellie.

Tears forgotten, Nancy helped Ellie shovel everything back into the ottoman while the men piled the luggage in the hall and joined them. Hugh was a big man, very like Thomas in build. Also bearded, a little younger, perhaps. In his fifties? Casually but expensively dressed. Wedding ring.

Ellie turned on the men. 'You've been fighting?'

They both grinned. Thomas said, 'Young Archie got a bit pushy. We told him to leave Nancy alone, but he was beside himself. Lost it. Started shouting that she had to sign his papers today, that minute! We closed the new front door on him. He tried to kick it in. Hugh went out to reason with him, and the lad took a swing at him. I remonstrated, so he picked up a stone from the garden and threw it at me. Wham!'

Hugh laughed. 'That's when Thomas here picked the lad up and carried him, screaming, to the road and dumped him there. Was he surprised! And when he got to his feet and was going to charge us again, he found most of our neighbours, including Abby, of course, had come out to see what the shouting was all about. Abby phoned the police and when he objected, we told him to sit down and be quiet. And he did.'

Thomas grinned. 'Well, it helped that another of the neighbours – no names mentioned – had armed himself with a cricket bat and said that in his opinion, Archie could do with a good thumping. That's when the lad thought he might scarper, but we formed a sort of circle of bodies around him, and he sat back down again. There wasn't a scratch on him, but Hugh and I were bleeding freely, which made quite an impression when the police arrived.'

Hugh nodded. 'They asked if we wanted to charge Archie with assault, and I wasn't sure but Thomas said yes, because the lad had been warned off before, and couldn't be trusted not to do it again. There was a general chorus of assent from all of us, so they took Archie off in a police car for further questioning and Thomas and I have to go down to the station tomorrow morning to press charges. Which we will.'

'Archie hit me first,' said Thomas, happily. 'I didn't hit him back. I just picked him up and shook him about a bit.'

Ellie said, 'My heroes! Tell me, was the girl on the motorbike hanging around? He's got no other transport.'

Thomas and Hugh looked at one another.

Hugh was doubtful. 'Don't think so.'

Thomas said, 'We ought to have checked. I didn't see her, but I wasn't looking.'

Nancy patted streaming eyes. 'I'm not crying. I'm happy. Really I am. Hugh was wonderful. And Thomas. And Abby said we ought to have photographs of the damage they'd done to the men before she took them into her kitchen and cleaned them up, and so we took photographs of everything: the injured boys, the new door, the damaged house, the blood and the stone that Archie threw.

'Hugh said we ought to take photos of the damage to the window at the agency, too. Archie had taken photos when it happened, but . . . well, I don't know what's got into him, I really can't believe that he . . . But I do realize he's changed so much from what he was that . . . And he didn't give me any

pictures of what happened at the agency so on our way here
we diverted to the agency to take some more shots of the closed
notice at the front just in case Archie . . . Well, I really can't
rely on him any more, can I? You know, I really thought he
was going to kill Hugh!'

She reached out her hand in Hugh's direction. He caught it
and held it tightly.

Hugh may be wearing a wedding ring, but he's carrying a
torch for Nancy! Uh, oh!

Nancy continued, 'I can't believe how well everything's
turning out. Hugh's son has been unhappy working for a tourist
firm in the city. I've known him since he was a baby and he's
a good lad. He's helped us out in the past over holiday times
and now he's going to leave his old job and come to help me
restart the agency, and if it works out, I'm to make him a partner
and oh, I keep thinking of the moment when Archie threw that
stone when I thought . . .!'

Hugh did the right thing. He sat beside Nancy and put his
arm around her in a manner most unneighbourly. She closed
her eyes and relaxed against him.

Ellie, wide-eyed, looked a question at Thomas, who said,
'Widow and widower, brought together by a strange set of
circumstances.' Thomas was smiling.

He needed a cold compress on that eye!

Ellie began to relax. If Thomas approved, then all was well.
And, she could hear the children playing in the garden, with
happy little screams, and Coralie's voice urging them on . . .
and the telephone ringing. Her smartphone?

She'd put it down somewhere? No, it was in her pocket. 'Yes?'

Rafael, gabbling. '. . . so I can't . . . only . . . the children . . .'

'Slow down. Say that again.'

'Susan. Is. In. Labour. They couldn't stop it!'

'Susan's in labour? Oh, but . . . look you must stay with
her. We'll look after the children. Relax! Coralie's here to
help.'

Confused noises from the other end of the phone. Was he
crying? He must realize he's responsible for Susan going into
labour early, and for leaving the children unsupervised. But
now was not the time to scream at him.

Ellie said, loudly and clearly, 'Rafael, you've behaved like an idiot but there'll be time to grovel later. The children are all right here, and your place is with Susan. So get on with it!'

A mumble. He killed the call.

Ellie faced three puzzled faces. 'Next door. Susan's gone into labour. I said we'd look after the three children.'

Nancy shifted, sitting upright. 'Oh. Well, that's . . . You can't be expected to look after me as well. Look, I can manage. I'll go to a hotel—'

Hugh was about to protest but Ellie got there first. 'Nancy, not to worry. I've arranged for someone to look after the children. We have a spare room en suite upstairs. Hugh will carry your things up for you. Straight ahead on your right at the top of the stairs. I'll find you some bedlinen to make up the bed. You have a little rest and come down in a while, when we'll have a nice quiet meal together. There's no need for you to make any decisions for the time being.'

Thomas said, 'You'll stay for a meal too, won't you, Hugh? I usually cook at weekends, so when you've seen Nancy settled you can join me in the kitchen and we'll put something together. But first, I'm going to print off the photographs we've taken.'

FIFTEEN

Sunday evening, continued

Ellie saw Nancy and Hugh go upstairs and Thomas retreat into his study. Then she went out through the still bare conservatory into the garden where Coralie was supervising the children at play. 'The thing is, Coralie, I know it's a lot to ask but could you possibly stay overnight? Susan's gone into labour. She won't be back tonight and Rafael's in no fit state to look after himself, never mind three lively children. You could sleep into their spare bedroom, if you can find bedlinen.'

Coralie thought a bit. 'I can doss down on the settee next

door. Only thing is, I was seeing the boyfriend this evening. He's good with children, really likes them, is thinking of doing a course, paediatrics nurse or something. Same as me, would you believe? I thought of it first, but it's right for him, too. Would you mind if he came round to help me?'

This was a halfway decent offer. But. 'Thomas would be upset if you and your boyfriend . . .?'

'Granted.' A big grin. 'My mum and dad, too. They think I'm too young. It's true we get a bit hot and bothered now and then, but no, I said we need to get some qualifications before we tie the knot and it'll be in church with Thomas doing the serious bit and a big party after. We both want that. We've agreed to hold off for the time being. Tell you what; I'll give him a ring, fill him in on what's happened. I'll sleep upstairs to be near the children and he can have the settee downstairs. He can go round the parents' place first and fetch me a tooth-brush and stuff, and then he can help me get the kids bathed and put to bed. Best to keep to their routine.'

'You might have trouble with Fifi. She knows something's up. She's been popping round to see that we're still here.'

'She's a knowing one. Old for her years. Likely she's not been parted from her mum since she was born.'

With that arrangement in place, Ellie returned to her own house and climbed the stairs to find Nancy and Hugh in the spare bedroom, sitting on the bed, he with his arm around her. Ellie busied herself finding bedlinen which she now remem-bered had been put in a chest on the landing. This gave Hugh the hint that he should leave Nancy in safe hands and go down to help Thomas cook.

Nancy helped Ellie make the bed. Well, Nancy tried to help, but really just stood there with a pillow in her hands.

Nancy said, 'You must think that Hugh and I . . . Yes, it is sudden, except that it isn't, not really. He was my husband's best friend, and I used to sit with his wife when she was dying and the other way round. We've always got along well but we didn't think of each other that way for ages, not till long after we were left alone and lonely. It's been gradually coming on for about a year. A couple of times he asked if I felt that perhaps someday we might . . . and I said it was too soon, but maybe.

When I saw Archie throw that stone, I realized Hugh might be killed and it hit me how important he'd become to me.'

'That's good,' said Ellie.

'Yes,' said Nancy, 'but then I had another thought.' She let Ellie take the pillow off her. 'I've always known Archie had a temper. Every now and then dear Charles used to take Archie outside to cool down when he got into a state about something but now . . . Oh, when Archie threw that stone, I suddenly thought . . . It's a horrible thought! But what if Archie lost his temper with Charles that night, when they were left alone to lock up? What if . . . I don't want to think about it, but suppose . . .?'

Ellie had been wondering that herself. 'We'll make sure the police know what we suspect.'

Nancy dissolved into tears again. 'I'm all right, really I am. Just . . . Well, it's wrong to be so happy about Hugh while I'm so wretched about the house and . . . I'm so grateful to everyone, and so . . . mixed up. Do you know what Abby said to Archie? She called him a toerag and said that for two pins she'd put him over her knee and paddle his bottom.'

'Yes, yes.' Ellie persuaded Nancy to sit down, took off her shoes, and pushed her to lie down. 'Tell me what was wrong with the lease for the student house.'

'Nothing was wrong with it. Dr Hallett wanted to rent a house for himself and some other students for a year. He said he'd pay the rent up front and he in turn would collect an appropriate amount, including their share of the utility bills, from the others. He said he wanted to offer the rooms at below the current rate to students who would otherwise struggle to get to uni.

'He'd already offered a room each to a Patsy Something and her friend Mona, whom he'd met at some charity function or other. He said the girls had had a bad time with an uncaring landlord last year and they were finding it hard to get a decent place with London prices being so high. He asked me to find four other students in similar straits. We picked four names out and they all accepted. Then he got back to us saying he had to include a cousin who'd been having trouble at home, so we adjusted the list accordingly.

'After that unfortunate accident when his cousin died, Dr Hallett got in touch and said he'd be responsible for any utility bills that came in after that, and he checked that he'd paid the rent up to the end of the academic year. I asked Archie to handle it, but now I'm wondering if he did. When the students started emailing us with their queries, I didn't know what to say so I referred them back to Dr Hallett. Nice man. Looks sleepy but isn't.'

She yawned mightily. 'I thought he might have his eye on either Patsy or whatever her name is, this Mona. The others he picked were all men.'

Ellie drew the duvet up over Nancy. 'Have a little rest. We'll wake you in time for supper.'

Nancy clung to Ellie's hand, and then let it go. 'Thank you. Bless you.'

Ellie released herself, drew the curtains and skittered down the stairs wondering what to do next. Pleasant noises were coming from the kitchen. The zizz of cans of beer being opened. The men were enjoying themselves, weren't they? Out she went through the conservatory into the now deserted garden. No sign of the children, or of Coralie. Toys left around. *Hope it doesn't rain. Pick up one or two, can't carry any more.*

Ellie went through the open French windows into the big living room next door, which was empty. Chirruping sounds came from the hall and stairs beyond, and there were Coralie and a smiling, chubby young man not much taller than her, taking the children up for their night-time routine: bath, bed and books.

Coralie waved with her free hand, as she had Fifi – half asleep – over her shoulder. Evan had his favourite Hippo toy with him, and Jenny . . .? Jenny stopped halfway from one step to another and swayed . . . only to be caught up by the young man and lifted high in the air. Jenny hated to admit it when she was too tired to cope. She usually refused to be carried until she dropped to the ground with exhaustion.

Coralie waved to Ellie. 'We're fine!' and continued up the stairs.

Reassured, Ellie reversed back through the big living room, along the patio and through into the conservatory, only to hear the front doorbell ringing.

The men in the kitchen were taking their time shifting themselves and Ellie got there before them, only to find another car in the driveway.

Jocelyn had arrived with Patsy.

He'd parked neatly enough but Rafael wouldn't be able to get his own car in as well when – and if – he returned from the hospital.

'Sorry to trouble you,' said Patsy, eyes flashing fire and wild mane tossing, 'but this idiot here says he needs to consult with you before we go to the police.'

By 'this idiot' she meant Jocelyn, who was indeed looking as if he'd rather be elsewhere. He said, 'What she means is, we need to pool our information.'

Ellie waved them through to the living room, introducing Thomas and Hugh as they went. 'My husband, the Reverend Thomas, and this is Hugh, Nancy Price's good neighbour. As you can see, they've become acquainted with Archie's fists and are prepared to press charges against him. I wonder, do you have any additional information about him? Were the photographs I sent you of any use?'

Patsy nodded and seated herself on the settee with Jocelyn next to her. The others found seats nearby.

Patsy looked at Jocelyn, who started as if he'd been pinched. He said, 'I suppose we have to start at the beginning. When we moved into the house we decided that we would have regular meetings and have votes to deal with day-to-day problems. After Brandon died, we had a meeting and agreed not to mention that he'd been using drugs to the police because his family – in particular his mother, my aunt – was distraught. In retrospect, that was the wrong decision. We thought his death would be the end of it. But it wasn't.'

Patsy nodded.

Jocelyn continued, 'It's my fault that all this happened. It was I who brought Brandon into the house. He's a cousin, my aunt's only son and I knew he wasn't to be trusted. He talked the talk but never took responsibility for anything he'd done. My aunt had been rescuing him from awkward situations since he was twelve when he learned how to steal from shops and resell on eBay.

'He's kept our family solicitor busy since he was fifteen and almost killed a young lad on a bike by driving my aunt's car when he was drunk. He stole from his mother and mine. He's cost them both dearly in terms of money and worry. He scraped into uni somehow but dropped out within six months. Drink, drugs and debts. My father sent him to an expensive rehab place for a year and he came back swearing he'd turned his life around.

'At first he did appear to have done so. He even got a job in a car showroom. Six months on and he wanted another stab at uni. My family put pressure on me to let him have a room in our student house. My aunt was in seventh heaven. At long last, blah, blah. I wasn't that hopeful. I told him that if he transgressed, he'd be out within the hour. He complained that it was wrong of me not to believe in him. Anyway, he did behave himself at first.'

Patsy said, 'Except that he said nasty things about you behind your back.'

Jocelyn shrugged. 'Par for the course. He did seem to have turned over a new leaf at first.'

Patsy explained, 'At first, yes. But. You see, Mona and I had known one another for ages and we got on well with Imran and Terry. We were in and out of one another's rooms. We didn't always lock our doors.'

Jocelyn sighed. 'Then one day Imran complained he'd lost his travel pass; he couldn't think how. He had to pay for a replacement. Bad luck, we thought. Then Patsy found Mona in tears. She'd lost the only bit of jewellery she had: the diamond earrings her godfather had given her for her twenty-first. Brandon had been drinking heavily of late. And I *knew*! I just *knew* that he was up to his old tricks again.

'We convened a meeting and I had it out with him. Brandon wasn't even apologetic. He handed over the pawn ticket for the earrings, saying that I could redeem the items for Mona and that Imran's travel pass had gone to a good home. I could have throttled him. I was going to throw him out there and then, but he pulled a masterstroke. He said that if I went to the police he'd tell them I smoked cannabis and kept a stash in my room.'

Patsy said, 'He was so convincing! Terry suggested that he

and I search Jocelyn's room. We found a stash in a shoe at the back of a cupboard. Brandon was triumphant. Jocelyn looked as if he'd been poleaxed.'

Jocelyn groaned. 'I tried weed once when I was at school and had a bad reaction. But who'd believe me if my roommates didn't?'

'So we had to decide what to do. The thefts swung it against Brandon. If he could steal from us, he could do anything. Jocelyn abstained but the rest of us voted that Brandon should leave that day. Only Brandon begged for a second chance. He said he'd been going straight. He said how he'd struggled not to slip back into his old ways. He said he'd been clean for ages but a friend had tempted him to go to a gambling club and he'd lost and hadn't known how to recoup his losses. And so on. We were idiots. We gave him a week to find somewhere else to go.'

Jocelyn looked grim. 'I asked Brandon where he'd got the weed. He said someone had left it in his room and he hadn't known how to get rid of it. He said he thought he'd seen me meeting a drug pusher at the end of the road, so it was only right that he'd left it in my room. I didn't believe him, but these soft-hearted fools outvoted me and gave him more time to create havoc.'

Patsy wasn't happy about it now. She said, 'I know, I know. We ought to have listened to you. But it was Brandon's birthday that weekend and he swore he'd leave the following day.'

Jocelyn said, 'So we come to the night of the party. I put in an appearance early for form's sake, then went back down to put my earphones on and do a couple of hours work. I could feel the reverberation as people pounded up and down the stairs but tried to ignore it. Eventually I took a break and looked at the clock. It was well past one and the noise from up above was deafening. The police had warned us before to keep the noise down and I thought our neighbours would already be on their phones to complain. So I went up—'

Patsy said, 'And met Mona and me coming down. I'd not stayed at the party but done the same as Jocelyn; put my earphones on and got down to some work. I was going to turn in at midnight but as soon as I took the earphones off, I could hear the noise upstairs. I went up to tell them to keep the music down. The room was full of people I didn't know, who told me to mind my own business. I could smell cannabis but it wasn't that bad and they had all the windows open, so . . . I chickened out. I left. I wish I'd called the police then and there, but I didn't.

'I got ready to go to bed thinking I'd have to put ear plugs in or I wouldn't sleep with all that racket going on. Then Mona knocked on my door. She asked if she could doss down with me as it was too rowdy up top for her to get to sleep. Remember she was in the room next to Brandon's, up at the top? I held the door open to let her in and a strange man barged in from the landing, dead cold sober, wanting to sell us some drugs, saying he'd some specials for us, at a good price. I flourished my phone and told him to go as I was calling the cops. He gave us a load of language but he did leave. That's when Mona and I decided we had to do something. We didn't want to be mixed up with a drugs bust and maybe get sent down from uni. So we went down to ask Jocelyn to help and met him coming up.'

Jocelyn said, 'Not that I'm much good at crowd control. If we'd got Terry and Imran to help, we might have made an impression but neither Terry nor Imran would answer when I knocked on their doors. So I went up there and shouted and no one took the slightest bit of notice. And the smell of cannabis! I tried to work out where the speaker might be so that I could turn it off, but there was a lot of shouting going on, and a sort of tidal wave of people avoiding the flying fists of a wild kid, who was whirling around, high as a kite. Then I got knocked sideways and before I could get to my feet, someone shouted "man overboard!" and turned the speaker off.

'The dancing stopped, bit by bit. I got up and saw everyone was looking towards the window. A couple were hanging over the balcony. You could hear everyone breathing. Someone laughed. Someone else said it wasn't funny and Brandon couldn't have survived the fall, could he? It took me a few seconds to work it out that someone had fallen out of the window. Suddenly, everyone began to push past me and run down the stairs. I couldn't believe how quickly the room emptied.'

Patsy nodded. 'We were right behind Jocelyn but cut off from him by the press of people rushing past us and down the stairs. Jocelyn yelled something like, "Downstairs!" and we followed him down the stairs and out into the garden.'

Jocelyn said, 'And there he was. It was obvious he'd accidentally fallen from the balcony and killed himself. Patsy called for an ambulance. Mona fetched a sheet to put over him. Patsy roused Terry and Imran who'd put in earplugs and gone to bed. Terry and I slipped away upstairs to make sure the drug pusher had gone and not left any telltales behind. Which he hadn't. The windows were still open and the smell was dissipating, so we decided not to mention drugs when the ambulance and the police came.'

Patsy said, 'We couldn't see that mentioning drugs would do any good. Brandon's death was an accident. His mother and aunt would mourn him and it seemed best to let them think he died while he was on his way to turning his life around. Mona helped me pack up his things for his family before we left.

'Since we returned to the house, I've gone up to the top floor a couple of times and each time I thought I smelled cannabis. I thought it must be left over from the party, though it's seemed to get worse as time went on. I don't understand it because we'd left the windows open, but . . . there it was. Maybe we need an exorcism or something.'

Jocelyn lowered his eyelids. Ellie guessed that he knew what had happened there. He'd gone up there with Terry, who enjoyed experimenting, to make sure the place was clean. Terry had then put the stuff somewhere from which he could retrieve it later – and enjoy a smoke himself.

Patsy said, 'We were all in shock. The police! Our families were distressed. Jocelyn's mother and aunt were in such a state! All our families were. We scattered to the four winds. But over the following weeks reality crept in, and we realized we'd have to do something about the rent and the utility bills. We tried ringing the agency but they said only that the rent had been paid and they'd get back to us about the utilities. They didn't. And none of us were happy where we were, so we came back, one by one. Even Jocelyn.'

Ellie looked hard at Jocelyn. Surely it was time he owned

up to having been responsible for the rent and utilities for the whole year? But no, he lowered his eyelids again. He wasn't prepared to speak out yet.

Patsy continued, 'We thought it was over and done with until this evening, when you, Mrs Quicke, sent me a photograph of someone we recognized. Or rather whom Jocelyn recognized.'

Jocelyn said, 'It was the lad who was fighting his way through the others at the party. I can't swear that he was the one who actually pushed Brandon over the edge. There were too many people in the way. And he'd disappeared – as had everyone else – by the time the ambulance men and the police came.'

Patsy said, 'Mrs Quicke, is this the man you called Archie, the one who you say has been responsible for so much else happening recently? I hadn't consciously remembered him from the party because there was such a crowd, most of whom I've never seen before. When I looked at the photo you sent me, I thought it rang a bell, so I showed it to the others. Mona and Jocelyn said they recognized him straight away.

'To make sure, we ran off some copies and called on some neighbours in the road. We showed them the photo and asked if anyone had seen this man pushing fliers through the door. And one of them had, and another said he was with a girl on a motorbike. If that's any help. So you were right, and this Archie was mixed up in all the other things that have been happening as well.'

Jocelyn washed his face with his hands. 'Mrs Quicke, you wanted to know who I thought was at the back of this spate of troubles. You pointed out that a number of events had a common thread: there were the problems at the estate agency and the death of one of the partners; the persecution of Nancy and the arson attack; the advertising of the student house as a brothel; and finally the way the council are thinking of revoking planning permission for the charity to develop a rundown site. And yes, I agree there is a common denominator here.

'You say that the Reverend Thomas and Hugh here are pressing charges for assault against Archie. Good. If the police have remanded him in custody, then that should neutralize him for the time being. Surely that's enough?'

'No,' said Ellie. 'We know he's not been working alone so at some point he's going to scream for help to the girl on the motorbike who's been helping him, but it isn't her who has the clout to sway council decisions, does she? No, he and she will point the finger at the people behind all this. How will he or she react to their scream for help?'

Jocelyn said, 'The prime movers will plead ignorance. They'll be genuinely horrified to hear that some carelessly spoken words of theirs might have led to arson and worse.'

Patsy wasn't having it. 'That's not enough, Jocelyn. Help us out here. You know your family is involved in some way. It must be Avery, who has somehow tricked your father into playing along. Who else could have brought pressure to bear on the police to play down Mr Walker's death, or have got the council to consider changing their mind about the charity's next project?'

'There is nothing to connect my father with—'

Patsy struck that out. 'Not your father. Avery and his new woman. And, I agree, there's no evidence to connect them with Archie and his girl – except their mobile phones. If Archie and his girlfriend have texted their bosses and received texts back acknowledging what they're up to, that might give the police enough to act upon.'

SIXTEEN

Sunday evening, continued

Jocelyn rubbed his tired eyes. 'You think my father is involved. Not so. Oh yes, he did, rightly or wrongly, ask the police to consider the grief Brandon's death caused the family. But neither he nor I knew anything about this Archie who might or might not have contributed to my cousin's accidental death. Likewise, my father knew nothing about the problems at the agency or about Mr Walker's death until you, Mrs Quicke, told me about them and I – somewhat reluctantly, I might add – passed the information on to him.'

Patsy prodded him. 'Come on. You know it's Avery.'

'I don't *know* anything of the kind. It's true he's short of money. He's been at me to make him a loan, a big one, but I have plans of my own and well, I have turned him down. You see, he's been married and divorced twice and has made some big purchases: another flat, a small business. He's planning another wedding which will also be expensive. He's shown my mother a photograph of this new woman which he'd taken on his smartphone. Apparently she looks like Cruella De Ville, all black and white. Does that mean anything to you?'

Ellie felt a jolt of recognition. She had hoped . . . oh, she had hoped Diana hadn't been involved but the description was spot on for her estate agent daughter who was indeed a black-and-white person, immaculately turned out.

Ellie managed a stiff, 'Yes, that could be my daughter, Diana. Did he buy Streetwise for her?' She felt for her hankie. She'd tried not to believe Diana was implicated. She'd gone through the same reasoning as Jocelyn. Her daughter Diana couldn't possibly have intended the dreadful things that had happened and neither could Jocelyn's brother . . . No, of course not. But . . .

Diana attracted wealthy men who could give her the lifestyle to which she thought she was entitled, and she did know how to run an estate agency. It would be only too like her to get a position in an up-and-coming agency, to take it over, and then look around for some way to bring in more money.

Over the years Diana had milked her mother of money time and again, but her judgment was poor and every time her efforts had led to losses. Ellie had put inherited money into her charity, which had prospered and attracted further donations, but Diana had never rid herself of the idea that this money really belonged to her.

She said, 'Avery and Diana. That's the link.' She knew she sounded desolate. As did Jocelyn. How far can you go to protect a member of the family who breaks the law?

Thomas said, 'Hold on.' He was consulting his smartphone.

'Have a look at this. The estate agency that's been trying to take over Walker & Price is called Streetwise, right? Let's see if there's any information on the internet about them.'

Everyone except Ellie now took their smartphones out, too. Where had she left hers? In her study, perhaps?

Hugh found something first. 'Facebook. Some award or other, bright young things aiming for the stars, welcoming a new manager who is somewhat older than the rest of them. Mrs Quicke, is this your daughter?' He held out his phone for Ellie to see.

She looked. It was Cruella de Vil all over again.

Ellie nodded. Her throat was dry. She said, 'So now we know. An ambitious estate agent teams up with someone who knows all the right people and who can do her favours. Is there a picture of the youngsters who work for Streetwise?'

Jocelyn was the next person to find something. 'There's three youngsters working for Streetwise. Two young men, one girl.' He held up his smartphone for Ellie to see. 'Is this the blonde who's been going around on her motorbike helping Archie?'

Ellie waved his phone aside. 'I've not seen her. Ask Thomas; he has.'

Thomas looked and said, 'Yes, that's her. I don't recognize either of the young men. Do you, Hugh?'

Hugh shook his head.

Patsy held up her hand. 'I've just thought; Archie is in custody but she's still out and about, isn't she?'

Ellie said, 'That makes me feel nervous. What will she do when she hears that Archie's been arrested? Neither Thomas nor Hugh noticed her this afternoon when they were rescuing Nancy, but she might well have been lurking in the under-growth. Even if she wasn't there, surely she's the person whom he'd have screamed to when he was taken into custody?'

That made everyone look around, uneasily. Ellie got up to close the curtains against the darkening of the day.

Patsy said, 'If he phoned her, surely the first thing she'd do is to pass the bad news on to her boss at Streetwise. She wouldn't take any action on her own, would she?'

Ellie said, 'She acted on her own when she defaced Walker & Price's window. I suspect she set up those nasty phone messages and maybe she's the one who threw the brick through the window, too. She's been involved with Archie, ferrying him around, throughout. The question is: was he the one giving orders to her or was she getting instructions from her boss at Streetwise?'

There was an uneasy silence. Then Patsy got to her feet and looked at Jocelyn. 'We ought to be getting back. We should warn the others to look out for her.'

Everyone stirred. Watches were consulted. There was a general move out to the hall when there was a thump on the door into the conservatory, and in came the tiny figure of Fifi, dressed in pyjamas, carrying her Gonk. She was sobbing, 'Mumma . . . Dada . . . Mumma . . . Dada.'

Patsy was nearest and swept the child up into her arms. 'There, there, little one. There, there. What's your name?'

Ellie caught the pleased flash from Jocelyn's bright eyes and thought, *That's the last test passed. He knows now that Patsy will be happy to bear him children and to love and care for them.*

Thomas was nearest to Patsy. He reached for the child. 'This is Fifi. She's our sort of grandchild, living next door. Her mother's in hospital having another child at this very moment but there's someone at home supposed to be looking after her.'

Ellie said, 'Giver her here. I'll take her back. How did you get away from Coralie, Fifi? Bedtime for you.'

'Mmmmm,' said Fifi, allowing herself to be cuddled. 'Mumma? Dada?'

Jocelyn started. 'What's that?' He ran for the hall. 'My car alarm?'

Ellie hadn't heard anything, but Thomas and Hugh followed Jocelyn into the hall. Thomas pulled the front door wide open and the faint hooting became a piercing scream.

The sky was rapidly darkening, threatening rain.

Jocelyn's car was indeed sounding the alarm.

Thomas' car was nearest the house and seemed to be all right, as was Hugh's which had been next to arrive. Jocelyn's car was nearest the entrance and now a fourth car was trying and failing to turn into the driveway.

The latest arrival must be Rafael, home from the hospital.

His attempt at entry had disturbed a dark figure which was currently bending over the hood of Jocelyn's car. He or she had tried the car door and set off the alarm?

A car thief?

The driver of the latest car to arrive – Rafael? – turned up his headlights, illuminating a slender figure in biker's gear in the act of throwing something . . . a can . . .? Into the bushes which lined the perimeter.

A heart-stopping pause.

A pinpoint of light.

A brilliant flash. Woosh!

Flames engulfed Jocelyn's car.

For a second the arsonist's figure was outlined in black by the flames.

The girl biker? Archie's friend and accomplice?

If so, she'd been caught in her own fire trap. She stepped back, arms raised, screaming thinly as the flames reached out to her.

Jocelyn's car screamed, too.

Ellie could see Rafael, parked between the gate posts, getting out of his own car.

Jocelyn plunged out of the house, shouting, 'Call the fire brigade!'

Thomas was already on his phone. Hugh, too.

Ellie turned away to shelter Fifi from the harsh brilliance of the burning car and was herself sheltered by young, strong arms. Patsy, of course.

Patsy was on her phone, too. 'Fire service and ambulance, yes!'

The blonde biker had misjudged the amount of petrol she'd thrown over Jocelyn's car, or not stepped back quickly enough when she'd set it on fire. She'd been caught in the flames herself.

She'd taken off her gloves to stroke a match! That was the pinpoint of light we'd seen, just before the car went up in flames.

Her hands had been caught in the fire.

Where was Jocelyn? Out there? Trying to rescue something from his car?

Thomas was shouting. Hugh, too. Thomas dashed back past Ellie into the kitchen.

Hugh yelled at Ellie, 'Fire extinguisher?'

Ellie shook her head. They'd never thought of having one.

Thomas rushed out into the drive, carrying a bucket of water . . . and disappeared around the first two cars.

Ellie stifled a scream. *No, Thomas! No!*

The arsonist was throwing herself about, struggling to get her helmet off, which was stupid because it was probably saving her head from the fire.

Flames licked around her leather-clad body.

Leather withstands fire, doesn't it? She's not in any danger, is she?

Out of the darkness a figure appeared behind her. Jocelyn, taking off his jacket to throw over her. Thomas appeared beside him to throw his bucket of water over the girl.

She staggered away from them. She was beyond reason, throwing herself around, arms flailing the air, screaming.

The men shouted at the girl to stay still, but she was beyond hearing them.

Fifi whimpered.

Hugh shouted, 'Fire brigade coming! I'll take a couple of pictures!'

Patsy's voice was strained as she spoke on her phone. 'Yes, that's the address. Hurry! If the flames reach the tank . . .!'

If the flames reach the tank . . . There'll be the almightiest explosion!

Dear Lord! Thomas! Jocelyn! Help!

Jocelyn had disappeared from sight. Where had he gone?

Thomas reappeared, rushing back to the house, chin on shoulder. 'Ambulance! Call an ambulance!'

Patsy yelled back. 'On its way! Where's Jocelyn?'

Jocelyn's car burst into a fireball as the flames reached the tank. The flash of light seared everyone's eyeballs.

Everyone recoiled. Fortunately Thomas had reached the house by that time and Hugh had gone into the sitting room . . . too late! But Jocelyn? Where was he? And the black-clad girl? There was no sign of her.

Now Hugh's car was on fire, too.

Ellie began to pray. *Oh, dear Lord! Oh, my Lord!*

The cars burned brightly.

Pray! Pray! Save Jocelyn! Oh dear Lord, let no one else be injured!

'What's happened! What's happened?' Nancy, shaking with fear. Descending the stairs, holding on to the banister. 'Is that a fire out there? Hugh? Where's Hugh?'

'I'm all right,' said Hugh. He abandoned his smartphone to put his arms around Nancy. 'Are you all right?'

Where was the girl?

Where was Jocelyn?

Patsy was holding herself together. Just. She was still speaking into her phone. Her voice had gone all high on her. 'Yes, please do hurry. There's at least two people injured. Jocelyn went to help and . . . Yes, you turn left from the main road and . . . Yes, that's right. No, the fire is not on the road, but in the driveway.'

Ellie's phone rang. In her pocket?

Fifi was burying her head under Ellie's arm, and moaning, 'Dada! Mumma!'

Patsy staggered. She made it to the hall chair and let herself down on to it, but still managed to keep talking to the fire brigade. 'Yes . . . Can you see the flames?' She dropped her smartphone.

Thomas pushed Patsy's head down between her knees. 'You're not going to faint. Take a deep breath . . . in . . . and out. That's it.'

Ellie fumbled one-handed for her phone, which was still ringing. Rafael's number came up on the screen. Was he all right?

He was shouting, 'Ellie! Pick up! For God's sake! What's happening? Are the children all right?'

Fifi stirred in Ellie's arms and lifted her head. 'Dada?'

'Yes, it's Daddy. You'll be all right, now.' And to Rafael: 'We're all OK. Where are you?'

'On the street. What are all those cars parked in the driveway? I leant on the horn to make them let me in, and the nearest car went up in flames! And then some clown appeared and told me to move my car back out into the road to let the fire engine in. What the hell is going on?'

Ellie thought, *Jocelyn must be the clown who told Rafael to back out. At least it looks as if they're both safe, thank God!*

And yes, here comes the fire engine, drowning out even the noise from the two car alarms. Is that an ambulance as well?

Ellie could hear Rafael burbling on, but the noise . . .! She shouted, 'Rafael, calm down. The children are fine. Is Susan with you? Where's Jocelyn?'

More shouting from Rafael, gradually becoming more intelligible till Ellie could make out the words: '. . . so quickly! A fine boy, a thatch of black hair and a temper . . . looks just like Fifi . . . can't believe . . . my son! . . . Home tomorrow.'

Fifi lifted her head. 'Tom-Tom's come?'

Ellie was fully aware that she was in the middle of a crisis, but couldn't resist asking, 'Rafael, is the baby called Thomas? Won't be it awkward to have two men called Thomas in the family?'

Ambulance hee-hawed. Police cars screamed.

Flames lit up the driveway.

And all Ellie could think of was, what the baby was to be called. How absurd! She looked around her. And where, oh where was Jocelyn?

Hugh was holding Nancy tight, and saying, 'There, there!'

Nancy was sobbing. 'Not fire! Not again!'

Rafael said, 'No, not Thomas. Of course not. Must go, move the car away. Firemen arriving. Police, too. What the hell is all this about, anyway?'

Fifi said, firmly, 'Tom-Tom. My baby bro.'

Ellie sighed. If Fifi said he was to be called Tom-Tom, then that is what he would be called, no matter what name was put on his birth certificate. Fifi herself had a long string of complicated names but was never known as anything but Fifi. And so it would be with Tom-Tom.

The noise outside reduced itself to the merely thunderous. Foam blanketed the cars, stifling the flames. The car alarms finally died the death.

Silence reigned, of a sort.

Two paramedics were busy in a corner under which laurel bushes had thrived till that afternoon. Ellie averted her eyes from what might be happening there. The paramedics heaved up a slender figure and placed it on a gurney brought from the ambulance. Ellie couldn't see if the girl was still wearing her helmet or not.

Now another intrusive noise. Yes, more police were arriving. The odd flame flickered here and there on the two damaged cars. Foam surfed around the wrecks. Tortured metal crackled.

More dark figures, helmeted and jacketed, worked around the wreckage of the two cars. Thomas' car appeared to be unharmed.

Jocelyn appeared, jacketless, making his way slowly, slowly, round the cars and back to the house. He was limping. Had he sustained burns?

Ellie said, 'Patsy, he's all right!'

Patsy lifted her head. Tears stood out on her cheeks. 'He's safe! Really safe?'

Hugh coaxed Nancy into the sitting room. 'Look, my car doesn't matter. That can be replaced. The great thing is, you're all right, and I'm all right and . . .'

Fifi had fallen asleep in Ellie's arms now she was assured that her father was safe.

Ellie felt very tired. Her arms were aching. Fifi was small for her age, but she was weighing Ellie down and . . . she needed to sit down. No, she needed to put the kettle on. After this, everyone would need hot drinks and then food.

There should be biscuits in the tin, provided Evan hadn't eaten them all. Possibly there was some cake in the freezer, which they could defrost in the microwave?

If only she weren't too tired to move.

Thomas took Fifi from Ellie. The little one didn't even yawn. Well, she trusted Thomas, didn't she? Thomas said, 'Ellie, go and sit down before you fall down.'

Patsy was occupying the hall chair so Ellie dragged herself to the stairs and sat down there, flump. She really must make an effort. She ought not to be sitting down when she needed to get to the kitchen and start feeding the five thousand.

Jocelyn appeared in the doorway, looking a trifle less put together than usual. One side of his face was reddened, one leg of his jeans had been singed by fire, but his eyes were wide open.

Patsy shot up from her chair.

Jocelyn opened his arms wide, and they became one.

Ellie noted with interest that Patsy would be taller than

him if she wore high heels. She also saw that neither of them
would care.

He said, 'Will you—?'

She said, 'Yes, of course I will. Idiot!'

Oh, praise be!

Two police appeared in the front doorway – a burly man and
an even bigger woman, followed by a fireman and one of the
paramedics from the ambulance. The fireman put Jocelyn's
jacket on the table. It was rather the worse for wear . . . as
indeed, was practically everyone present.

The policewoman had her chin tucked into her shoulder,
communicating by her shoulder phone with the station.

The fireman said, 'Who's the householder?'

'I am,' said Thomas. 'Come on in. We'll tell you everything
you need to know in a moment. But first, is the girl who
started the fire . . . yes, we saw her do it . . . Is she all right?'

'We'll be taking her to hospital in a moment,' said the
paramedic. 'Her hands are in a bad way but she was saved
from the worst by her helmet and her leathers. If you're
going to set a fire, then leather is the best protection you can
get. She's conscious but not making much sense at the
moment. Vowing death and destruction to all around. What's
her name?'

'We don't know,' said Thomas, whose air of authority was
quickly reducing an untidy situation to manageable. 'We believe
she works for Streetwise, the estate agency. If you look around
you'll probably find her motorbike somewhere close by. The
registration number should give you her details.'

Ellie realized this was the point at which authority was going
to require details. Names and addresses and statements. Who
was at the back of this and why? Well, she knew the answers
to pretty well all of it, but her mind was in such a jumble that
she wasn't sure she would make much sense when it came to
making a statement.

The policewoman said she'd summon reinforcements but
meanwhile no one was to leave.

Ellie invited everyone else to join her in the kitchen and
managed to put the kettle on and find some salve to put on
Jocelyn's cheek.

Even before the kettle had boiled, one of the firemen returned with news that the girl's machine had been located in what remained of the laurel bushes. The internet was consulted and the registration number gave them a name – Natalie Turnbull – and a local address. It was decided that one of the police would accompany the paramedics in the ambulance with the girl to hospital, with a view to questioning her about the arson when her burns had been treated.

The ambulance drove away, and Ellie recovered enough to assist Patsy in producing tea and cake.

At that point, a wild man banged through the conservatory, through the hall and into the kitchen panting. 'Fifi? You got her? I went home and those idiots were sitting watching television, but Fifi . . .! Have you got her? Did she come here? And, what the devil's going on out there?'

'Yes, of course,' said Thomas, handing the sleeping child over to Rafael. 'How's Susan?'

Rafael checked that Fifi still had all her arms and legs. 'She's a little Houdini, this one. They say they left her asleep and . . . Oh, yes. Susan's OK. And yes, we have a son. Looks just like me. I'll give that Coralie what for, letting Fifi escape . . .'

He disappeared the way he'd come, leaving most of the company blinking their surprise.

SEVENTEEN

Sunday evening, continued

It took time, of course. As the first round of milky, sugary tea was distributed, a detective inspector plus sidekick arrived to take statements. Thankfully this was Lesley Millard, who had been involved in the earlier incidents in this tangled affair so didn't need to be brought up to speed on them, although she was not too eager to reopen the cases which she knew the authorities considered to have been neatly closed.

One by one Lesley took statements from the group, telling

them they must only speak of what they personally had seen
or heard. Everything else was hearsay and not admissible in
court. If they tried to theorize, or speak of something someone
had told them, the shutters came down.

As Hugh and Thomas had already given statements on their
assaults by Archie, they need not repeat themselves.

Hugh used Thomas' printer to run off the photographs he'd
been taking of the destruction at Nancy's house, and of Natalie
firebombing Jocelyn's car. Good, solid evidence. Lesley accepted
that these incidents were clearly down to the girl biker, who
was now under police guard in hospital.

Lesley said that there was no evidence that the girl had firebombed Nancy's house and that, as the assembled company
had seen the girl setting fire to Jocelyn's car, she might be
questioned about the house fire but would only be charged with
that of the car.

Hugh and Jocelyn were given crime report numbers so that
they could claim on insurance for the loss of their cars.

Patsy produced one of the fliers alleging that the student
house was used as a brothel and said that several of their neighbours would testify that Natalie and her friend Archie had been
seen delivering the poison.

Lesley said that was hearsay. She said that if the neighbours
gave statements to the police, identifying the people who had
delivered the fliers then that charge might well be laid against
them as well. But that, as Lesley said, would be small fry as
compared to the charges of arson which would be laid against
the girl.

Ellie could see that Lesley would not even entertain the idea
that Avery Hallett, a local businessman, could have plotted such
a trail of destruction. Why would he do such a thing? What on
earth was his motive? Unless a link with Streetwise could be
proved?

Ellie's nerve failed her. She could not, no, she could not
mention Diana's name when she was not even sure that her
daughter was involved, or even if she were back in town. Ellie
did try to say that she felt the charity was under attack. She
muttered that it was all a matter of high finance and the small

print of legal agreements and could see Lesley was not going to take that seriously.

As a point of law, this was, of course, correct. There was no evidence, none. Lesley could not be interested in tying these crimes to a conspiracy aimed at the charity, or to get the police looking at who had inspired these two young people to embark on a trail of destruction.

Finally, Lesley departed.

Everyone else stayed, gathered around the kitchen table. There was a general feeling of dissatisfaction with the way things had turned out. They were still strung up but didn't know what to do about it. Hugh, who had lost belongings in his car, alternately made lists of what he must claim on his insurance and reassured himself that Nancy was happy to sit at his side.

Ellie suggested food and Patsy left Jocelyn's side to help her throw a meal together. Jocelyn said nothing, made no suggestions. He went out into the hall and made a couple of phone calls but didn't volunteer who they were to. He seemed content to do nothing but sit and watch Patsy as she flitted to and fro.

There was some talk about everything looking better in the morning, but no one was really convinced that it would be so.

Patsy and Ellie dished up spaghetti with mushroom sauce, followed by ice cream with Mars bar and condensed milk dribbled all over it. Nobody was bothering about diets that night.

Patsy sat next to Jocelyn, doing a Mother Hen act. Now and then he looked at Ellie in a considering, thoughtful way, but she decided she was too worn out to consider what this meant.

Into this scene of quiet, tired domesticity crashed Rafael, bearing a couple of bottles of wine and a grin from ear to ear. 'I'm celebrating! Coralie and her friend are staying the night to look after the babes and I'm looking for someone to join me in a toast to my son.'

With a jerk everyone sat up straighter. Introductions were made all around and a shade of enthusiasm came back to everyone's faces. Thomas looked out some glasses and Patsy polished them with a cloth.

Rafael was floating somewhere in the stratosphere, quite oblivious of their flat state. 'It was very quick. Got there just in time. Fine boy. Tom-Tom.' He shook his head, annoyed with himself. 'No, no. Not that. I mean, we haven't decided on a name yet . . . but yes, he's fine and Susan's fine, and she'll be back tomorrow with the baby. I said I'd get myself a wedding ring tomorrow to celebrate. Congratulate me! A son! He looks just like me.'

A wide grin, followed by a scowl. 'But what those two clowns next door thought they were doing, letting Fifi escape like that! I thought Coralie had more sense, but as for that boyfriend of hers . . .!'

Ellie tried diplomacy. 'Fifi came looking for you. She always knows when something's going on.'

That diverted Rafael, who dived for his smartphone. 'Yes, of course. I took some pictures. At the risk of boring you . . .'

He was going to show them anyway, wasn't he? And everyone was too polite to object.

Rafael grinned even more widely. 'The nurse said, "You can tell who his father is, can't you?" And it's true. He looks just like me. Look!'

He showed everyone his pictures, and everyone smiled and said the right thing. Rafael was going to be a doting father, wasn't he? He'd loved Fifi fiercely, but this was his boy, who looked like him.

Rafael's grin faded. 'What have I missed? All I could think of when I got back was whether the children were safe but . . . What's been going on? I tried to turn in and found the drive blocked and then there were all those fire engines and police. Whose were all those cars in the drive and why on earth did that woman set fire to them? Who was she?'

Thomas gathered all eyes to himself. 'Congratulations on the birth of your son, Rafael. As for the rest, the police have been dealing with the arsonist, and with the man who attacked me and Hugh. I believe Jocelyn and my wife are about to tidy up the loose ends.'

Jocelyn sighed deeply. He stood up. It took an effort, but he did it. He said, 'Yes, Mrs Quicke, we'd better deal with it now, tonight, don't you think?' He collected everyone's eyes. 'I expect you've all realized it by now, but there were not one but two targets in this matter. The charity was one, which was attacked through Streetwise and Walker & Price. I'm the other. My brother is hassling me to sign over an inheritance I received to him. And I am resisting.'

Ellie said, 'Ah. I did wonder. There was a family resemblance. Did Archie mistake you . . .'

'Possibly, though there's no proof. Piecing the story together after the event, I think that after Archie gave his allegiance to Streetwise, he had occasion to hear Avery sounding off about his brother refusing him his rights . . . Yes, Avery does say that. He really believes that the money ought to have been left to him and not to his stupid nerd of a brother. So when Archie spotted that a Hallett had advertised his birthday party on Facebook, he got tanked up and arrived with mischief in mind. Perhaps Archie set out merely to "have a word" with me about it. He saw Brandon, mistook him for me, launched himself at him . . . and Brandon was jostled or pushed over the balcony and died.

'I thought at first that Brandon's death was an unfortunate accident, but the very next morning I got a phone call from Avery who asked if I was ready to give him the money yet and then put the phone down. Now, I'm not saying . . . I'm trying not to believe that Archie meant to harm Brandon. I really do believe it was an accident, but Avery took advantage of it to try to frighten me. And set me thinking. Worrying. Not knowing what to think.

'My mother and aunt were in pieces over Brandon's death, my father said it was in my power to go home and look after them. Rightly or wrongly, I agreed. I tried to explain it to Patsy but without any proof . . . she was angry and in shock and she thought I was making it all up.'

Patsy said, 'You button it all up. You didn't tell me what was going on and I thought you were trying to finish with me. It hurt, but I couldn't beg you to stay. Every day I thought of ringing you, but . . . It was stupid of me.'

He held out his hand to her. She took it and held on to it. He said, 'Will you wait for me?'

'Of course.'

Jocelyn turned himself from lover to businessman. 'Mrs Quicke, my father has asked to speak to you. He's suggested we meet him at Avery's, and I've agreed to take you there.'

Ellie felt a hand clench around her heart. She didn't like the sound of this at all. Was he going to bulldoze her into giving up the Ladywood project?

Jocelyn was brisk. 'He's asked to see the photographs we've taken and any other written evidence you have. Shall I call a cab?' He picked up his jacket – which was no longer wearable but still had pockets – to search for his wallet and his keys.

Ellie said, 'I'll do that. I always use the same cab. The driver's Coralie's father and looks after me well.'

She looked down at herself. She looked a mess. An old white T-shirt over a grey skirt showing signs of children's activities. She took off her apron and ran her fingers back through her hair. Should she bother to find a lipstick? Probably not. If Jocelyn was prepared to go as he was, then she could do so, too.

Thomas said, 'You're both worn out, But yes, you're right. No matter how sweetly Archie and Natalie sing, unless you alter the balance of power, the police won't be able to convict either of the people who started all this. They'll pay good solicitors to defend them. They only have to say that yes, they were angry with the two of you, but had no intention, etc., etc., and they'll get away with a rap on the wrist. Dealing with family is always difficult but restitution of wrongs is required here.'

Jocelyn allowed Patsy to brush him down. He said, 'Plus, I've got to get Avery off my back or I'll never get Patsy to marry me.'

'Try to stop me,' said Patsy.

Thomas said, 'I'll have a few words with the Lord while you're away.'

Jocelyn looked at Hugh and Patsy. 'Will you stay here till we get back? I don't think there'll be any more trouble here tonight, but . . . just in case, I'd like to know you're safe.'

Nancy said, 'I haven't prayed for ages, but yes. Of course we'll stay, won't we, Hugh?'

Sunday, late evening

Sam, Ellie's favourite cab driver, had been free and said he'd drive her wherever she wanted to go. He was delighted that Ellie had called Coralie in to help, and how long did Ellie think she'd be tonight? Not that it mattered because he'd sit in his cab and watch something on his smartphone while he waited.

Which heartfelt words made Ellie feel a little better about the approaching interview.

Jocelyn gave his brother's address. 'He's had to downsize recently, but I understand he has company.'

Diana, of course. Ellie felt sick.

Jocelyn took her hand. 'Let's make a pact. If he starts on me, you come to my assistance, and vice versa.'

Elie did her best to smile. 'You should have brought Patsy along as bodyguard.'

'I have to do this myself. I think you know why.'

'I know several things about you, Dr Hallett, which you still have to disclose to Patsy. She's going to take the hide off you when she finds out what you did for her.'

He grinned. 'It was at a charity fashion show. Some silly girl got tipsy and fell into a flower bed. Her companions deserted her, Patsy helped the girl up and I saw . . . I saw what I'd been looking for all my life. We sent the girl home in a taxi so Patsy and I went for a quiet drink.'

Ellie said, 'Patsy told you the problems she and Mona had been having at their digs and you offered them rooms in a house which you didn't even have at that time. You got Walker & Price to set everything up so that the other students would think it was an ordinary rental.'

'I'd been offered a post in America which was very much in my line but I saw straight away that if I took a year out, I might have a chance with Patsy. I haven't wasted the time, either. The work I've done this year will be helpful whatever I do next.'

Ellie couldn't help smiling. Jocelyn really was something else. 'So, everything went well until you took Brandon on board and Avery turned up to check on you. Brandon filled Patsy's head with ideas that you were a womaniser, and you failed to defend yourself when Avery mocked you. Which meant that Patsy didn't know whether to take you seriously or not.'

'I've never been much good at defending myself. If they said I was stupid and clumsy and ugly, then that's how I felt.'

'You proved them wrong by taking out all those totties.'

'They weren't serious and neither was I.'

'Of course. You're much too sensible to marry someone like that.'

'It's worked, hasn't it? Patsy has begun to trust me. I risked telling her about my mother's illness and her need of my attendance on her. Patsy helped me decide what to do. I was beginning to hope when Avery came round asking me – no, ordering me! – to lend him money. He said he'd invested in a project that was going to restore his fortunes and I had to help him out for the sake of the family. And I refused.'

He shirted in his seat. 'You think I've been weak where they're concerned? You're right, of course. Both my father and I know our mother loves Avery more than either of us, and always will.'

Ellie was silent. She had wondered about the Hallett's marriage but hadn't realized how badly they were caught in the trap of loving someone who didn't love them.

Avery had a flat in a modern, luxury block. There was no parking available nearby so Sam took the taxi round the corner and found a space there. A top-of-the-range car, conservative and understated, drew up behind them, and a clone of Jocelyn got out. A quiet man in his sixties with hooded eyes, not much hair and an air of power well under control.

'Father,' said Jocelyn, acknowledging Councillor Hallett's presence. 'This is Mrs Quicke.'

Councillor Hallett inclined his head. 'Thank you for coming, Mrs Quicke. It was kind of you.'

Jocelyn rang one of the bells by the front door, and a disembodied voice said, 'What? Is that you, bro?' Followed by laughter.

The front door opened to let them into a square hall, subtly lit. Doors to the ground-floor flats led off to right and left. A lift door was directly in front of them.

A door on the right opened, letting them into a small foyer. Ellie glimpsed metallic wallpaper, a couple of probably priceless pencil sketches, and a full-length mirror which didn't flatter her appearance.

More doors. The right-hand one opened and there was Diana, in a gold-and-black kaftan, with a wine glass in her hand and an emerald on her ring finger. Again, no expense had been spared.

Ellie thought of Susan scratching around to pay for new shoes for Diana's children and stiffened her backbone.

Diana looked at the scarecrow pair and laughed. 'Avery, darling! Look who's here! Your father and your own dear brother come to give us their blessing. Come on in, Papa-in-law to be. Come in, Mother. You've come to deliver my personal invitation to the charity meeting tomorrow, haven't you? And, oh dear! Jocelyn! Avery dear, your brother's clearly been playing with fire!'

A tall man in designer wear casuals joined her in the doorway. Yes, he was a handsome creature, with smooth dark hair and a bold eye. There was a heavy gold watch on his wrist. Cashmere sweater over well-cut trousers. He was ever so slightly going to seed. A pound or two more on his waist and he'd have to buy a larger size in trousers. There were lines curving from mouth to chin, showing that his default expression was a sneer.

'Father, this is an unexpected pleasure. Ma's let you off the hook for the evening? Come on in. And Mrs Quicke. Well, well. I've heard a lot about you.'

He ran his eyes over her slightly bedraggled appearance. Ellie felt his scorn and wished she hadn't come.

Avery turned on his brother. 'Wipe your feet, little man. Been rolling around in the mud, again?'

Jocelyn said, 'Oh, grow up, Avery!'

Mr Hallett inhaled sharply but he made no comment on Avery's rudeness. He said, 'Thank you for letting us come at such short notice.'

Ellie wondered if Councillor Hallett was as clever as Jocelyn. She thought he probably was. So what was he up to?

It was Diana's turn to make fun of their visitors. 'Really,

Mother! Whatever are you wearing? I'm only grateful it's dark and the neighbours can't see you.'

Ellie thought, *How can I possibly fight my own daughter?*

Ah, but the Bible says that when you are weak, remember that God is with you. You need no other at your back. So please, Lord! Help!

Thomas was praying for her, back home. Possibly the others were, too.

Without being asked, Mr Hallett led the way into a large sitting room and settled himself into a comfortable chair.

Avery couldn't resist another jibe at his brother. 'Do you need your bottom wiped still? You know, Diana, he used to wet his pants even after he started going to school . . . and oh, I forgot, he's still in school, isn't he?'

Ellie felt Jocelyn's inward cringe. She looked around at the designer décor, and said, 'Well, this is a lot better than a prison cell.'

That wiped the smile off Diana's face. 'What on earth . . .? Mother, you're losing it, you really are. Not-so-early dementia. Senility strikes. I'm going to put it to the meeting tomorrow that you retire before you do something really stupid.'

Ellie said absolutely nothing. She wanted to but couldn't find the words. She let herself down into the nearest chair which was unfortunately far too large for her. She shifted forward to keep her feet on the floor, then shifted back and let her feet dangle.

Jocelyn looked around saying, 'Perhaps you'd better find some newspaper for me to sit on. I couldn't wait to change after the fire.'

'What fire?' Avery was amused, but not particularly concerned.

Ellie found herself burbling. 'Oh, I expect it'll be in the papers soon. I wonder if they'll put Jocelyn up for a George Cross medal? That's the highest you can get as a civilian, isn't it? He saved this girl's life. They say she won't die, but even if she does, we have it all on our phones so the award should go through all right.'

Avery guffawed. 'Little bro been fighting over a girl? I didn't think he was old enough to be admitted to nightclubs yet.'

'No nightclub,' said Jocelyn. 'It happened in Mrs Quicke's

driveway. My car, my laptop, my patience: gone. You haven't asked who was hurt? Possibly you don't know her, Avery? That would be the best defence you could make. That you've never set eyes on her. Except, that won't work as she's employed by Diana.'

Diana's face froze into a mask.

Jocelyn prompted, 'A girl called Natalie, who rides a motorbike?'

Avery frowned. 'Come on, Diana. There's a girl called Natalie who works for you, isn't there? Sassy little thing. Got something going for a man in another agency, hasn't she?'

Diana waved her hand. 'Oh, Natalie. She's never been satisfactory. I'm thinking of letting her go next month.' She seated herself on the arm of Avery's chair, making claim to her place in his life.

Jocelyn sat, gingerly, on the front of an upright chair. 'I'm glad you've remembered her at last. I assume your books will show how long you've known her. Father, you asked to see the evidence of what Avery and Diana have been up to. Mrs Quicke has it with her.'

That was Ellie's cue to lay out the photographs she'd brought with her and explain the circumstances in which they'd been taken: the wrecked frontage at the estate agency; the firebomb damaged at Nancy's; the assaults on Hugh and Thomas; the burning cars.

Councillor Hallett looked, and laid the photographs aside. 'What it amounts to is that the two junior employees of local estate agencies embarked on a series of misdemeanours, which escalated into crimes. Have you any evidence to link them to Avery and Diana?'

Avery wasn't disturbed. 'We're horrified! Naturally. We deny any knowledge. Completely.'

'Of course we do. The very idea!' Diana was amused.

Jocelyn said, 'Both youngsters are now in the hands of the police. The girl is in hospital with appalling burns to her hands. She misjudged firebombing my car. I saw her. So did others. She'll be charged with arson and maybe a number of other offences. The man assaulted Ellie's husband and a neighbour and is also in custody. They'll both talk.'

Diana shrugged. 'I told you; Natalie is one of my part-timers and I haven't been happy with her for some time. If she's been up to something, well, it's nothing to do with me. Nobody cares what lies she chooses to make up.'

Avery grinned. 'I get it. She's accusing Jocelyn of having tried something on with her! Is she actually crying "rape"? That's the trouble with you, Jocelyn, you've never been a good judge of women. Look at those tarts you've been squiring round town. They've only got eyes for money, my lad. Take it from me.'

Ellie's dander rose, good and proper. 'Avery, you don't know what you're talking about. Jocelyn's past girlfriends are all of one type; I grant you that. Yes, they liked going out with someone who knew how to treat them well, and I'm not totally happy about his using them for camouflage while he chased the girl he was really after—'

Jocelyn said, 'You saw through me, didn't you?'

'—but,' said Ellie, 'the girl he's going to marry is quite different.'

Avery laughed. 'What! That strapping great girl I met at his place? A miner's daughter, isn't she?'

'With brains and integrity,' said Ellie. 'She'll marry him for better or worse, for sickness or health, until death do them part. She'll last the course. She won't be suing for divorce in a couple of years' time. God willing, she'll give him children and teach them right from wrong, and she won't be afraid to argue with him if they have a difference of opinion. That's what I call a good match.'

Avery's eyes widened. Did he, perhaps, envy his brother for a moment? If so, it was only for a couple of seconds. He tossed back the rest of his glass of wine and said, 'Are you trying to say that congratulations are in order? What do you say, Father? Such a poor match won't please Mother, will it?'

'No, possibly not,' Jocelyn agreed. 'But Patsy will be kind to our mother, she'll listen to what Father says and she won't cheat on me.'

Mr Hallett said, 'Yes. I look forward to meeting her some time. Meanwhile, Mrs Quicke, let's sort out what's going to happen with the Ladywood project.'

EIGHTEEN

Sunday late evening, continued

I t was time for Ellie to take a hand in the game. She wriggled forward in her uncomfortable chair and put her feet on the floor. She said, 'Mr Hallett, I know you sit up with your wife every evening no matter what, so it wasn't you who attended the last council meeting, and it wasn't you who brought the Ladywood project to the attention of your fellows.'

Councillor Hallett folded his hands across his frontage. 'True. The first I heard of what was supposed to be my suggestion to compulsorily purchase the site was late on Friday evening when someone on the housing committee rang me to query it. The phone has hardly stopped ringing again all weekend. It's clear that someone has been taking my name in vain; one of the younger, newer women, only elected to the council this year. She's been learning the ropes, hardly ever spoken at meetings before.

'I finally ran her to ground and she said I'd asked her to raise the matter as I was unfortunately not able to attend the meeting in person. She thought it was a brilliant idea and just what the council should be doing; the community centre had long been promised, building it now would be a great vote catcher for the next election, and it would be one in the eye for the developers who were no doubt greedy millionaires who grind the faces of the poor. And so on. She's genuine in her beliefs and completely green about how to pay for them. The council has never had the money to develop the site and build a community centre, and even less to run it.'

Jocelyn played straight man. 'So how did she come to think you were behind the scheme?'

'A phone call. A man, who said he was relaying my wishes to her. He said he wanted her to have the opportunity to make her name in history. He flattered; she was easy meat. She has

no idea how the system works but she could see the headlines
making out she's the heroine of the hour.'

Avery and Diana were smiling. Avery said, 'But you didn't
contradict her.'

'No, I didn't, because she gave me your name. She was
quite open about it. She'd met you at some charity function
or other and, in her words, "You'd clicked!" She mentioned
the restaurants you'd taken her to and the outings you've
promised her.'

Mr Hallett switched his eyes to Diana. 'You understand that
Avery always has a mistress in waiting. He marries one and
makes a vacancy for another. I know he used every penny his
mother could scrape up to buy the estate agency and I hope
you got it put in your name, because otherwise you will probably go the same way as your predecessors.'

Diana's face was a study.

It was clear to Ellie that he *hadn't* put the agency in her
name.

Avery laughed, but with an undertone of unease. 'Don't take
any notice of him, Diana. We're solid, aren't we?'

Diana made herself smile. 'Of course we are.'

'And,' said Avery, 'you needn't worry about my father interfering with our plans for the Ladywood project. He may say
this and that but if he hasn't raised any objections so far, he
means to let it go through and you'll be able to move in to take
over the charity on Monday, as planned.'

'Now that,' said Mr Hallett, 'depends on what Mrs Quicke
decides to do.' He turned in his chair to focus on Ellie. 'You
must see that I can't come straight out and say that Avery asked
his new acquaintance to lie. The papers would be full of it. Her
career would suffer, Avery's name would be mud. The disgrace
would hit my wife hard. She only has a few days of life left to
her. I can't bear the thought of bringing such sorrow on her
now.

'You represent the charity. I've heard that what you say, goes.
I'm going to suggest a compromise which I think will be acceptable to all parties. The charity announces that they are turning
two of the houses on the site over to the council to act as a
community centre. You say that architects are already involved

to discuss how the buildings can best be adapted, and the council will soon be approached to approve an alteration to the existing planning permissions. My wife will die peacefully, and all will be well.'

Avery said, 'Do you know, that's brilliant! Totally. It satisfies everyone.'

'And lets you off the hook,' said Diana, her eyes narrowed.

Avery laughed. He brought her hand to his lips and kissed it. 'And you, my pet. And you.'

Mr Hallett said, 'Well, Mrs Quicke; what do you think?'

Ellie stared at him, and through him. She could see what he was doing, all right. She herself could feel the emotional appeal to keep his wife's last days free of scandal. And why not?

Well, for a start, if the charity set aside two houses for a community centre, they'd lose their profit for the whole project. The charity was not there to run at a loss. They had to build in a profit margin, or they'd not be able to continue making over old buildings for new lives.

What were the alternatives? An expensive appeal to law and hate mail if they were seen to be the baddies blocking a community centre which would do so much good.

There was an alternative; if the charity withdrew from the project they would have to accept a derisory price for the site. There would be an enormous hole in the accounts. Could she face the backlash if the charity lost so much money?

Avery said, 'Take your time, Mrs Quicke.' He was finding this all very amusing, wasn't he? He didn't think she'd fight it. She didn't think she could, either.

On the other hand . . . she knew what Thomas would say. She could hear him, in her inner ear. He'd said he'd do some praying while she was gone, and that was what she now had to listen to.

Two wrongs don't make a right. What they're suggesting is WRONG! Or rather, it's a sugar-coated pill. The sugar is that Mrs Hallett dies in peace and the project goes through but without making any kind of profit.

The pill is that if this new plan goes ahead, once the charity allows the council to alter the existing contracts, they would for ever be at the mercy of the council, who could decide this or that changes to their plans at will. She'd be handing over control of the project to people like Avery and Diana.

If she refused to go along with it, the charity was going to have to cut their losses and start again with another, smaller project. It was going to hurt, doing that . . . and it was going to hurt more than the charity; it would hurt the Halletts and the woman Avery had got lined up as his next possible mistress.

She sighed, deeply. And said, 'I understand your position, Mr Hallett, but I can't agree. It's a slippery slope, allowing something wrong to go through to save your wife a moment's pain. And it never works. Your plan looks good at first sight, but it would mean the difference between a reasonable profit for the charity and a big loss. So I can't accept that.

'If the council reneges on its permission for us to develop the site as planned, then we will have recourse to the law. That will be expensive and we can ill afford it, but then, neither can the council.'

Diana drew in her breath.

Avery lost his grin.

Jocelyn's eyes closed.

Mr Hallett's head jerked back. 'Don't be so hasty. You must think about this, consult your fellow trustees.'

Ellie shook her head. 'I have seen what happens when you compromise for the sake of those you love. To save your wife a moment of grief you used your influence to have your nephew's death ruled as accidental, even though later events indicate there were other influences at play. Putting the very best interpretation on what Avery and Diana have done, they have encouraged two misguided youngsters to commit criminal acts. You knew nothing of that but I do wonder if you put pressure on the police to downgrade the investigation into Mr Walker's death.'

His colour rose. 'I knew nothing of that until later, when Jocelyn told me what had been going on.'

'I do hope that's true. I appreciate the position you were in, but you don't give a diabetic sugar, however much they may crave it. It's tough love that's needed for your wife, not tea and sympathy.'

She hadn't known she had it in her to be so judgmental. It frightened her, a little.

All four of them stared at her as if they'd not seen her before. Correction: Jocelyn flashed one of his brightest signals to her. He approved what she'd said. That was heartening.

Councillor Hallett heaved himself out of his seat and found his smartphone. He tapped at it, frowned. Not happy. 'My wife! She's been worrying herself sick. Heard rumours, couldn't be pacified. I promised I'd ring her, tell her everything's settled. My battery's low. Avery, you have the same type of smartphone, don't you? May I . . .?'

'Sure.' Avery handed over his smartphone.

Diana glared at Ellie. 'You can't mean to drop me in it! Not even you! Your own daughter.'

'Yes, my own daughter, who abandoned her eldest son when she left her first husband. He's going to university soon, and you've always managed to wriggle out of supporting him in any way whatsoever. After various other adventures, you married a decent man and had two more children by him . . . whom you dumped on a neighbour's doorstep when he died. Perhaps you didn't know about all those children, Avery?'

'Why . . . I . . . Three children? You've got three children, Diana?'

Jocelyn got up, looking concerned. 'Mrs Quicke, are you all right? You look a bit . . . some fresh air, perhaps?'

Ellie wondered what on earth he was worrying about. She met his bright hazel eyes, and realized she'd been somewhat slow-witted.

Smartphones hold past texts and phone calls.

If there was anything on Avery's phone which would give the police information about what he knew about recent events, then the police needed to see it . . . But only if it weren't wiped straight away.

Councillor Hallett had swapped his smartphone for Avery's. Distraction was required.

Time for her to do her dithering old lady act. She put her hand to her head. 'Oh, dear. Yes, perhaps you are right. Can you help me out of this chair, which is very comfortable, of course, but . . .? I have some pills, somewhere. Oh, but did I bring my handbag? I might not have done so. Thank you, Jocelyn. I'm so sorry to be a nuisance, Diana. But perhaps a glass of water? Then, if I can find my jacket . . . Or, wait a minute, I didn't bring one, did I? Never mind the water, once I get out in the fresh air . . . Thank you, Jocelyn. You are being most helpful. If you could just hold the door open for me, Diana? I've got a taxi waiting outside.'

Jocelyn said, 'Do you use a walking stick, Mrs Quicke? Would one help?'

As if! She wasn't that ancient. Wicked boy! He was enjoying this, wasn't he?

She managed to get to the door but glanced back to see Mr Hallett laying a smartphone down on the table in the window, saying, 'Yes, Avery; this has all been most upsetting and we'd best leave you to it. I'll be in touch tomorrow. Sorry to have upset your evening at home, Diana. I have my car outside.'

The two Halletts 'helped' Ellie out of the flat and into the foyer. Jocelyn pushed open the outer door and they were finally in the night air. The street lighting was far from bright and they could see the stars in the sky above.

They stood there, recovering.

Jocelyn said, 'Nicely done, Mrs Quicke. Let's get round the corner where they can't find us, shall we?'

Councillor Hallett took Ellie's arm as they set off. 'I had a quick look at Avery's phone and found dozens of texts between him and Diana, commenting on what Natalie and Archie have been up to. I'll take the phone straight down to the police station now, before he discovers it's missing.'

'But—' said Jocelyn.

Councillor Hallett nodded. 'I know what you're going to say. The chain of evidence has been broken by the way I acquired the phone and nothing on it can be admissible in court. However, once the police have looked at it, they'll have good reason to demand to look at Diana's . . . and that should be enough to get them started.'

Clever stuff. And what's more – ouch! – it means Diana will be the primary target for the police in future AND NOT AVERY.

They came in sight of their cars.

Councillor Hallett said, 'I should say thank you, Mrs Quicke, for setting us right. So what are we going to do about the Ladywood project?'

She had no idea. None. Then, hesitantly, she said. 'I suppose you will want to thank the new council member for suggesting that the council team up with a charity with a view to setting up a much-needed community centre. You will say what a pity it is that she hadn't thought of it earlier, as it's too late now to change the plans for the Ladywood project, contracts have been signed, and so on and so forth. You will remind her the council don't have the money for an expensive court case.

'You could go on to suggest that finding another site for a community centre is such a good idea that you are going to recommend that the council start looking for another site straight away. Possibly you might hint that it could be funded by a grant from someone – not to be named precisely – who might endow said community centre rather than leave money to his family when he dies? That would give room for manoeuvre if either party decided the project was just too risky. But of course, that's all just an idea and you don't have to take it seriously.'

Ellie was astonished at herself. She was actually thinking like a business woman, instead of a housewife.

Jocelyn sneezed. At least, that's what it sounded like. It might have been a smothered laugh.

Councillor Hallett said nothing at all, rather loudly. Then he said, 'Well, it's true Jocelyn doesn't need my money and Avery has had all he's supposed to get and more. I could bear to consider that suggestion. Mrs Quicke, you are quite something.'

Jocelyn said, 'She is indeed. You must meet her husband, Thomas, too. A fine man. A man of principle. He said that restitution of wrong was needed here and he's right. Lives have been lost, businesses destroyed, careers, homes and cars wrecked. The insurance will pay for loss of property but not for the pain and suffering that has been caused. The police have both the youngsters and they will talk. In due course Diana and Avery will be charged with conspiracy.'

Ellie sighed. She had hoped . . . but no, it had to be.

Councillor Hallett also sighed. 'I know. I can't bail him out this time.'

Ellie thought, *This time? Avery's done it before? Of course he has! And Diana has cut corners, too, hasn't she? Oh dear, oh dear.*

It was no fun, tearing a family apart. Jocelyn lightened the mood. 'Looking on the bright side, Father, you have a pleasure in store. You must meet a little imp called Fifi. I'm desperately in love with her, but fear she considers me too old for her.'

Councillor Hallett put his hand on Jocelyn's shoulder. 'Bring that lass of yours round to meet your mother tomorrow, eh? And we'll keep the news about Avery from her as long as we can, shall we?'

Jocelyn nodded.

His father paused by his car with the fob in his hand. 'You'll take over the firm from me, won't you? Avery's had his chance and blown it. He's a reasonable salesman but doesn't understand what we do. I never thought he'd have the brains for the firm, anyway, but his mother . . .' He sighed. 'I know you've had other offers, Jocelyn, but . . . if you don't want to take it on, we'd better sell it.'

'I might,' said Jocelyn. 'I'll talk it over with Patsy.'

Ellie thought that taking over the family business was probably what he'd always wanted to do but hadn't known how to achieve. She thought Jocelyn could have made his name in Silicon Valley or anywhere else in the world if he hadn't come across a fiery Welsh girl in trouble, but that he'd succeed at whatever he decided to do.

Councillor Hallett got into his car and drove off.

Jocelyn helped Ellie into the back of Sam's taxi.

Sam said, 'Everything all right, missus?'

'Not really,' said Ellie, 'but about as good as can be hoped for.'

Tomorrow she must sort out the garden.